CHILDREN OF THE NEW WORLD

CHILDREN OF THE NEW WORLD

A NOVEL OF THE ALGERIAN WAR

...

ASSIA DJEBAR

Translated from the French by Marjolijn de Jager

The Feminist Press
at The City University of New York
New York

Published in 2005 by the Feminist Press at the City University of New York
The Graduate Center
365 Fifth Avenue
New York, NY 10016
www.feministpress.org

Library of Congress Cataloging-in-Publication Data

Djebar, Assia, 1936-
[Enfants du nouveau monde. English]
Children of the New World : a novel / by Assia Djebar ; translated from the French by Marjolijn de Jager.
　　p. cm.
ISBN-13: 978-1-55861-510-6 (pbk.)
ISBN-10: 1-55861-510-5 (pbk.)
ISBN-13: 978-1-55861-511-3 (cloth)
ISBN-10: 1-55861-511-3 (cloth)
I. De Jager, Marjolijn. II. Title.
PQ3989.2.D57E513　2005
843'.914--dc22

2005021564

This publication was made possible, in part, by public funds from the New York State Council on the Arts, a state agency, and the National Endowment for the Arts.

Text, composition, and cover design by Lisa Force.
Printed in Canada

12 11 10 09 08 07 06 05　　　5 4 3 2 1

Et pourtant de douleurs en courage en confiance
S'amassent des enfants nouveaux
Qui n'ont plus peur de rien pas même de nos maîtres
Tant l'avenir leur paraît beau

And yet, from sorrow new children amass
Who move on to courage and confidence
Who no longer fear anything not even our masters
For the future seems that beautiful to them

Paul Eluard, *Poèmes pour tous*

CONTENTS

TRANSLATOR'S NOTE

As the translator, I would like to express my great thanks to a number of important people. First of all, to Judith Miller goes my deepest gratitude for her very careful reading of the first version of the translation manuscript. Her insights into content and her feeling for the music of the novel helped immensely and her suggestions undoubtedly improved my text, as did reading the revised version out loud together: to her goes my most profound and warm thanks. Clarisse Zimra's personal knowledge of culture, time, and place as reflected in the novel contributed vastly to helping me understand specific details, as did her close reading and linguistic observations, for which my most sincere appreciation. Finally, my loving thanks to my "first reader" who knows no French but has an unfailing ear for fine English, David Vita, my husband and dearest friend.

Marjolijn de Jager
Stamford, Connecticut
October 2005

CHARACTERS IN ORDER OF APPEARANCE

Cherifa, 29, Youssef's wife, Ali's sister

Amna, Hakim's wife, Cherifa's friend and neighbor

Youssef, local political leader, Cherifa's husband

Lila, 24, Ali's wife, Bachir's cousin

Concierge, superintendent of Lila's apartment building, European origin

Ali, 26 or 27, medical student, Lila's husband, Cherifa's brother (in the resistance in the mountains)

Bachir, 17, secondary-school student, Si Abderahmane's son

Si Abderahmane, a baker in town, Bachir's father

Suzanne, 24, Omar's wife, Lila's friend

Hakim, police inspector, Amna's husband

Salima, 31, female teacher at a girls' school, Mahmoud's distant cousin

Mahmoud, political leader (in the resistance in the mountains)

Touma, a young woman, early 20s, Tawfik's sister

Jean, about 55, European origin, chief of police

Martinez, 38, European origin, police captain

Omar, lawyer (has left for France), Suzanne's husband, Mahmoud's former political comrade

Bob, French Algerian, 19, in love with Touma

Saidi, former manager of the Baghdad Café

Khaled, 35 to 40, lawyer (settled in Algiers)

Hassiba, young girl, 16 (crosses the city)

Rachid Selha, 45, Lila's father (left for France many years before)

Tawfik, 16 or 17, Touma's brother

1 ••• CHERIFA

In the old Arab quarter at the foot of the mountain the whitewashed houses all look alike. Before the city grew larger, this was the only place where affluent families would come to find a bit of cool air, near the brooks and orchards at the end of the spring. Each home is at the end of a cul de sac, where, after wandering through a maze of silent little alleyways, one must stop. All that can be heard is some vague whispering suddenly interrupted by the shrill cries of children, whom the mothers are trying to keep at home, but to no avail. The military guard can show up at any moment. Then there is barely enough time to gather the children and muffle their voices behind closed doors. Once the soldiers have gone, the mothers, each with her own brood, settle down again at the back of their room, on the tile floor or on a mattress. There they stay for hours on end, and through the door, with its raised curtains opening wide onto the courtyard and fountains, they quietly watch the spectacle the guard had announced is about to begin: the mountain under fire.

The days of intense fighting pass quickly inside the homes that people still think of as unseeing but that now gape at the war, which is masked as a gigantic game etched out in space. The planes are soaring and diving black spots that leave white trails, ephemeral arabesques that seem to be drawn by chance, like a mysterious but lethal script. "Oh, God!" a woman cries out when one of them nose-dives into the flames and the bullets that they can picture in their mind, but then it shoots up out of the smoke running along the ground ("Death, the damned thing has brought death in its wake!"). There it is again, spiraling way up in the sky; then nearby artillery fire ruptures the air, so close that the walls shake.

This spectacle can last for an entire day. A whole day in which the women neglect their household chores and, with their children clinging to their skirts or pants, grow bold enough to pass comments in excited voices from one room to the next. In every house, which generally contains four or five families, one family per room, there is always one woman—young, old, it makes no difference—who conducts the choir in its impassioned verse lines of exclamations, sighs, or groans punctuated by silences, when the mountain bleeds and smokes. "This time, they won't get them!" "With so many planes stacked up like that in one area, they must be bombing a *douar*—a village!" "Look, we're getting back at them!" (Cheers!) "Yes, did you see that, you saw that, didn't you, they just took down a plane! A plane, did you see that!" (One of them throws caution to the winds and goes out into the courtyard, dancing with joy.) "A plane shot down by our fighters! They really can hit their target!" The others stay in place, petrified; it's a significant moment. One of the children pulls loose and moves to the doorway: "A second one down!" he exclaims, mistaking the dive-bombing of another plane for a crash. More artillery fire. And the terrified child covers his ears and blinks his eyes with each new barrage. The silence in the house hangs in the air for a moment, for the women are afraid that a bomb fragment might fall on the terrace. It has happened many times before; the last time, it killed old Lla Aicha who was sitting crouched in the courtyard by the door of her room, a place she hadn't left during the daytime for years. She wouldn't even give in to the appeals for caution, because she had decided that, however great the excitement or danger outside, this was where she would end her waning years. The shell had fallen. She bowed her head a little more, shuddered, shuddered again, and that was all. When the neighbors came to help her up, several hours later, they shrieked when they discovered a dead body in her place.

When these spectacles occur, which is regularly once or twice a month, only the women are at home, because their husbands have already left for work, unless there is a surprise attack, as was the case the previous month when the mountain fighters boldly came down and stormed the center of the town. The night was just falling and the counterattack didn't come until the following dawn. Outside in the street, in the marketplace, or in the small shops of the old commercial center, when an area is cordoned off in conjunction with the military to check identity cards and intimidate in other ways, the men stay where they are, unless they're hauled off by the army, which happens just about everywhere.

In the coolness of their room, the women sometimes don't move; they grow tense momentarily, eyes wide, staring into space, hearts pounding like those of the children, as each imagines her husband up against a wall in the sun at high noon, no doubt shaking with a fear that he must make every effort to conceal. But the wife recognizes it at night, when everything is over, when the mountain once again assumes its arrogant nakedness, when the men are finally free to circulate through the streets and get home by curfew. Wordlessly, they watch the wounded moaning on their stretchers in the back of military trucks, scenes that the army unsuccessfully tries to hide from the eyes of the population—later in the day, when death retreats, having licked the blood off the overhanging russet slopes, and when the day ends its course through a cloudless sky. The fear the men share is a brief surface tremor, beneath which—and during dinner when they come together every member of the family senses it without needing any explanation—lies the rock of certainty composed of fierce awareness of the current times, solidarity with "those on the mountain," and hope for victory after the bloodshed. What springs up, too, is hate and a desire for revenge, but very little of it, especially if the head of the family is dispassionate as he recounts his day, with the disdainful calm that the men of this town instinctively have when they've come through almost every stage of a life they had expected to be without surprises: working hard to eke out a living, marriage, children, and then around fifty, finally, a kinder life, less rigid in striving for humility, kneeling in prayer, and being immersed in the meditation that follows. Still, along this poverty-edged path that manages to level everything the soul comes up with—ambition, bitterness, exhaustion, all the old lacerations—as they approach serenity at last, what remains is the icy feeling, more tenacious than time itself, of always knowing there is an enemy. An enemy whose presence they despise far more than they despise its excesses, its never-ending intrusions, its free will, even its familiarity that likes to see itself as paternalistic, and its informal manner of address that is supposed to be protective. It is a faceless, eyeless presence, as anonymous as they, its victims, who attempt to refute it as they bend over their work at the back of the shop.

"Yes, it's almost easy to forget," a man thinks when he comes home at night and looks at his wife, whom the other one, the omnipotent master outside, will never know. They call her sequestered, but, while he speaks without addressing her directly, as tradition prescribes, the husband thinks of her as freed. And that, he decides, is why she is his wife and not merely a body he embraces in the dark without speaking, without caressing, without daring to watch time flow by and his life slip away, in all the vulnerable nudity of her shape, a body that gives itself without trembling because it does not dialogue with a gaze. She is not merely a companion worn out too early, one whose breasts were soon engorged from successive pregnancies or prematurely withered; she is not merely a weary glance when she can finally stretch out on the bed at night, often a very high, gleaming, copper four-poster that one reaches by narrow steps, as one does a throne, on which she lies reassured by feeling the man's thigh next to hers. And below them, underneath the bed behind curtains are her children, and all she has to do is stretch out her arm to touch the cradle suspended from the base of the bed and holding the last-born infant. She sighs; it's been a hard day. The husband beside her turns over, not forgetting the *chahâda*, the prayer that helps him face sleep, his heart empty with that peaceful emptiness that faith brings, pure and simple as light. And here he is, in that last moment when the creaking of the cradle still reaches his ears, the whispering of the children below him, the deep sigh of his wife falling asleep, her heavy form awash in sleep as though in the current of a river with no return. Here he is, inexplicably set free. Alone.

What does it matter now, the fear that had held him captive throughout the day as he stood in that chain of men also standing erect with their hands behind their necks, their eyes blinded by the sun, when an officer approached and picked out one of those suspected of being a suspect; behind him, a soldier stops, his face hard with hatred ("Three of our men died today in this rotten war," he thinks, "three more, this very morning"); he, too, feels like killing them, these trembling old men, ludicrous figures, killing them right on the spot at high noon. The man doesn't return his gaze; he concentrates on forgetting his fear by daydreaming with open eyes, despite the brilliant light, about the theater of fire that unfolds as a majestic ballet above the city ("Another search," he thinks, "there goes another village they'll destroy"). He also thinks of his wife, in her corner at home, for whom there is nothing left to do but watch—watch, as they all do. And his children: the oldest is growing up fast, thirteen years old now; two more years, maybe three, and then the mountain will beckon him; it will be his turn to play a role in the spectacle of those burned-out valleys. "God! As I stand here before you, is not a man, a child, with weapons in hand more worthy than this body I'm forced to hold up? Standing here?"

Pointing his submachine gun, the soldier nudges his belly: "Stand up straight! Straight!" And the man, whose vision is blurred with exhaustion, repeats to himself in a final effort, "Stand up! Stand up!" His legs begin to sway, his knees buckle. "Stand up, you dog! Son of a bitch!" the soldier shouts, having adopted the insults and passion of this country. "You dog!" he says more softly, to himself, to the other.

The man thinks, light-headed now: "Soon the little one . . . in two or maybe three more years . . . " His knees give way; the earth receives his body, a broken puppet. The guard doesn't look down. On the ground the man is delirious, now free: "That's it, it's finished! Three more years for the little one . . . and she at the back of the room, she watches, she sees everything . . . before, she never saw anything . . . It's finished."

The soldier does not look down. He shouts, "This rotten war!" and the mountain in front of him, intermittently streaked with flashes of light and whitish plumes of smoke, turns into the face of the hidden enemy. A bar that stretches from horizon to horizon. No, he doesn't lower his eyes. He lowers his weapon. The man at his feet. Oh, to force his weapon into the body on the ground, that vanquished body of this rotten war. He's tired. It's a tiring business always having to watch over these exhausted shadows with their arms eternally raised. ("Almost-old men; the young ones are all over there on the mountain, hiding out so they can swoop down on us by surprise and slaughter us.") These old ones are afraid; he knows full well that fear alone keeps everything else concealed. He looks down; the man is lying in the dirt, bent in three, at the knees and the head. "A dead dog," he thinks, "dead as a dog!"

"What's wrong with him?"

"No idea," the soldier answers, startled. "Maybe he fainted."

The officer stops.

"It's hot as hell today," he says and moves on, looking at the sky.

The soldier salutes, raises his head, raises his weapon, and continues his guard duty.

"Rotten war!" he mutters again as his eyes follow the retreating back of the officer, a coldhearted man who came, asked a question in passing, and then left.

•••

When around nine in the morning on that particular day the spectacle starts up again, Cherifa is busy hosing down the courtyard to cool off the house. As soon as she notices the first sign of smoke on the mountain—and she doesn't need to go up on the terrace to see it—she alerts Amna, her neighbor. For she has no children of her own to call back inside; "Not yet," she sighs. From her room, Amna is already calling out sharply to her twins. Cherifa pours a final bucket of water on the tile floor, then hurries off to the kitchen to prepare the food. The basket that Youssef, her husband, had brought back from the market before leaving waits in a corner. Absentminded and sad that Youssef will not be home for the midday meal, she goes through her usual motions. A moment later she has settled down at the back of the room, like Amna, the door open wide onto the horizon.

It's been two weeks since the death of Lla Aicha, her mother-in-law and, other than her brother and Youssef, her only relative. It is surely because she has no children and lacks a family network to envelop her that she feels so fragile. She dreams, and from the void that death has left in her house, her eyes follow the first planes that come into view.

Lla Aicha, she was so old. As the bewildered Cherifa had looked on, Amna and the women next door had shaken her, she who hadn't budged in years, but her body was already stiff. In spite of the turmoil of the days that followed—an attack right in the heart of the town, two raids, and arbitrary mass arrests—the next morning in the Arab quarter they were obliged to observe the funeral rites as best they could: platters of couscous to be given to the poor, even though during those days beggars no longer appeared at the front doors of their various homes. Youssef had to carry two huge baskets of provisions across town and deliver them to a widow they knew near the river. The neighbor women, of whom Amna was the most energetic, and those who came via the terraces of the few nearby houses had washed the body, chanted the dirges and organized the wake, which lasted barely an hour, as the day dwindled away before curfew. A wake without litanies, without weeping.

Through the open door the pounding reports of the artillery fire were still reaching them, followed by the patrols that could be heard passing through the alleyways late into the evening. The atmosphere was such that, instead of speaking with respectful emotion, as is ordinarily the case, of the qualities of the dead woman, of her life, the children she had birthed, her share of adversities, the women around the dead body were silent, fascinated by the spectacle's final rockets, each one trying to suppress the fear of not seeing her man come home before nightfall. Every now and then a voice would be heard:

"It's been three days this time! Three whole days, oh, almighty God!"

Then another:

"My husband told me yesterday that he'd run into an old farmer at the market who had escaped from one of those wretched *douars*. He'd gone to bed in his own house, a farm with wheat reserves, his two cows, his donkey, and other possessions. When he got up the soldiers were there. An hour later he had nothing: everything was in flames. My husband told me this man was talking about his disasters as if they had happened to someone else."

"Time doesn't count anymore! Sometimes I wonder if the end will ever come. I hesitate, I have my doubts . . . " (a sigh) "but everything is in God's hands."

"The end," someone whispers, and then recites verses from the Koran to ward off bad luck. "That will be a marvelous awakening, a deliverance."

Cherifa listens. Every now and then she looks over at the dead woman, her body already cold, submerged beneath the sheets. Cherifa feels no pain. Since she came into this house five years ago, it has seemed as if her mother-in-law had always been dead. Right after Cherifa's wedding, when as a new wife she took over the household under the watchful eye of Youssef, who never left her side, Lla Aicha chose to turn into stone, right there on the threshold, and Cherifa hadn't understood it or dared to say anything.

She rises. The women at the wake follow her with their eyes as she lights candles and incense, solemn and mysterious in the silence of her motions throughout the room. Then she drapes a spotless piece of linen over the huge mirror that faces the entryway. The scent invades the room, chasing away the odors of the war they can all imagine: its gunpowder, its cries, its drying blood. While one of the chanters continues dropping vague phrases into the lake of oblivion that settles in around the corpse, they all watch Cherifa's silhouette approaching and all have the same thought, without any jealousy but with the calm that unquestionable truths contain: "Cherifa is still the most beautiful."

It is true. At twenty-nine, she holds on to her reputation as the town's most beautiful woman. Her complexion is flawless; her hair, a black river, falls down to her waist; her wide eyes, with their somewhat unhurried look that does not waver, settle on other people, forget them, dream, wander off—her eyes could enrapture—and above all, her figure, with a bearing that would provoke comments from the old women at celebrations when they watched her come in, traditional Arab metaphors, improvised in a murmur that would get lost in the din ("A gazelle running across the sand," "A heavenly angel disguised as a thoroughbred horse," "A quail quivering with modesty on a branch," and so on). In short, her shape was such that Cherifa would have appeared heavy had she been publicly visible to all eyes in a short skirt. In her life as a Muslim woman, wearing loose-fitting clothes and used to sitting on the tile floor for hours on end (tailor fashion on a mattress, squatting while performing the slightest tasks, and barefoot), she maintained a peaceable elegance.

At these earlier celebrations, even the young girls would salute Cherifa's nobility and her charm composed of a distant reserve. Yes, even they, the young girls beginning to be emancipated, buying magazines and reading novels that they kept hidden under their pillow—the youngest of them could hope never to wear the veil or be locked up inside the home but, on the contrary, continue school and then, one day, perhaps dare to go out to work (two or three of them had already liberated themselves this way)—all these adolescents, slightly vain and boisterous, because their luck in having grown up at a time when the customs were coming apart seemed to them a personal victory. (Politeness prevented Cherifa from smiling; she remained silent, stifling on these patios heavy with the persistent evening fragrance of jasmine and the mingling perfumes of the city's middle-class ladies, present only to show off and nibble honey cakes and sweets.)

She knew that at these gatherings she was the queen. She admitted to herself that it pleased her. Her first husband—a wholesale merchant in olive oil and food staples who was scorned for his all-too-rapid success, his previous, inevitably shady dealings, and his present compromises with the local authorities—enjoyed one of the best positions in Arab society. Throughout her long days, Cherifa was able to make sumptuous gowns from the multicolored silks that he himself chose and brought to her and that were often large yardages of the only pattern he had liked. This crass extravagance irritated Cherifa. She said nothing, barely thanking him, but then with feverish pleasure her fingers would spend hours cutting, sewing, and trying on. What marvelous recreation, but recreation that was a translucent pause in a lackluster life.

Nothing worse, she told herself as she sat down again beside the corpse, while the light of the candles began to grow longer and trembled along the walls in the gray ending of the day. Nothing worse than being forced to live with a man whom everything inside her had instinctively rejected. She had never really known why, for the three years of her marriage, she had made such an effort not to ever change her refusal by a fraction—a refusal she said came from God so as not to have to justify it—faced with this man who begged for her love night after night before taking her, always as if she were a cold statue. Nonetheless, he knew full well that the possession of a glorious body that kept itself so unapproachable—those aloof eyes in which even defiance was not to be read although they never stopped staring at him as he took his pleasure—was worse than rape.

After three years of marriage Cherifa still had no children, and quite comfortable with the idea that she wouldn't have any with this man, she found that the divorce was actually easy. Before, he had suddenly clung in a moment's flash to the hope of holding on to her through a pregnancy, which was after all a necessity in their world. He had begun to want a child, in a wild frenzy that would stab at him while he checked the books each evening, obsessed as he was with the fear that his employees, his servants, or his assistant—a nephew whom he had adopted and then trained—would steal from him. To have a child with her!—his child, from his demanding flesh—to be able to discover her again, discover her (he would be moved after an attack of helpless rage), to reach her.

He would become almost sentimental, no doubt as a result of all the years of struggle during which he had stolen from, sneered at, and cheated his fellow citizens, including the Europeans he knew—his lawyer, the bank manager, the smallish Spanish settler from whom he bought the olive harvest every year. Because he had made it big, he now wanted to breathe easy, without vulgarity, by God, to enjoy the prestige he had won, the burning envy of the others: merchants, ordinary workers, the only Arab teacher at the secondary school, who used to come to the store to play dominos two or three times a week. While he played, he silently tried to figure out how much the other, the ignorant upstart, could possibly be making. He himself was earning ten, twenty, a hundred times more than this man with all his diplomas, the respect of those close to him and of his French colleagues, principal and superintendent included. "Our intellectual," the oil merchant used to call him in a burst of sarcastic laughter that could be perceived as affectionate.

"A child by you!" he would implore.

"No!" Cherifa hesitated. "No, I will not go for treatment."

"You will go for treatment and that's an order."

"No! God has not given me any children. I don't want any!"

"You'll go for treatment," the oil merchant repeated that particular morning, his face ashen. He couldn't get over it—yet at the same time, it was so comforting to see she had finally exposed herself, at last! That her contemptuous silence was broken, at last!—he couldn't get over seeing the refusal and the glare in her brown eyes, usually veiled by the lashes that were too thick, but through which at that very moment a dark glimmer passed. He would smash her rebellion. He would. He had decided. The child was of little consequence to him; in a rush of weakness he felt like telling her that, but how could he make this confession to her, standing so straight before him, liberating herself, she who . . . That morning Cherifa was wearing an ivory-colored negligee he had given her many months before, one that had cost him a great deal. Until now, she had never bothered to wear it in his presence (how marvelously it clung to her, baring her throat, her neck, her arms!). It was the first time he had seen her so incensed, superb, in this house that looked so modest from the outside but inside had a patio of marble that continued deep into the garden, then the orchard, over which many other rooms had a view. It was a house of faded luxury that he had bought from the town's former mufti (one of the once middle-class families who were now poverty-stricken).

Instead of offering a confession, or displaying rage—or why not violence (yes, beat her up; bellow at her and beat her; she was his wife, wasn't she?)—he began to admire her in the silence that had come between them in this conflict he would never have imagined, that no husband could ever have expected from any wife.

"I don't want any children," Cherifa repeated softly, perhaps frightened by her own outburst, in a tone she would have seen as reprehensible insolence before. "I don't want any . . . " She seemed to hesitate, raised her head, which had been slightly bowed before, and with one of those unfettered animal motions that he loved, shook her long hair, whose movement ran like a wave down to her lower back. She was going to turn around, leave.

But a harsh desire for her suddenly assailed him and he was panting, right there in the bright light, in the middle of the courtyard and all its marble. He moved toward her. He touched her. Cherifa didn't understand. Then, in his arms, she heard the confusion of the

man whose lips were running over her neck and throat. What a foolish idea to have put on that particular gown this morning, showing so
much of herself! When he was gone, she, alone in the house, felt so
carefree! She had listened to the hoarse voice of the man mumbling
gibberish. He, her husband? He, who was more of a stranger than a
stranger to her. She refused. Those caresses, that accelerated breath;
no, she said, no! Her entire being, her whole body, was saying no to
that blinded intimacy he was trying to stir up within her with words
that he meant to be tender but that she found insulting. No!

She extricates herself. Part of her negligee tears. It had seemed to
her that the man's face as it remained there suspended, and his arms,
and his breath, had all been ripped out of her.

"No!" she screams; she turns her back on him, flees, crosses the
patio, moves around the pools, the fountain, while he, haggard and
slowly coming out of his ardor, no longer sees the figure of the
woman running, her hair bouncing and swinging on her back, until
she reaches one of the back rooms that in her hours of solitude is
hers alone.

Cherifa remembers; she locked the door and, leaning her back
against that barrier, began to sob. Quietly at first, then heaving so
deeply that it tore her apart; gradually she was delivered from her
incomprehensible turmoil. "No, no," she kept repeating, not knowing why. Still standing braced against the door, through her mind's
sudden need for explanation she confronted what she had just
begun to feel.

She had known from the beginning that she didn't love this man.
She had also known how to erase from her spirit any memory of
their furtive nocturnal contacts—her "duty as a wife," as they say.
During the day none of it remained, not even the inevitable boredom that was so common in most of the women she knew, whose
blooming and self-discovery she saw only when they reached the
illuminated regions of the dawn of motherhood. Or, for some of
them, it lay in the possessive vanity that seized them to be mistress of
a house, which was often nothing more than just a room. And all of

them then disappeared into the flow of time, to be swallowed up by the man they had to respect or fear, or even value, without ever wondering whether he might join them once, just once, inside that dark part of their being that would be the depth of their belly, their soul, and their heart, all in one. No, a discovery of that nature would run the risk of opening some wound, some anxiety, a problem whose ambiguity, they believed, was reserved for "other women," an expression that encompassed both women of easy virtue and foreign women whose morals, whose ostensible freedom, obviously made them members of another race. This reasoning was a form of precaution rather than a condemnation.

Thus Cherifa, who until now had not considered herself to be different, unless it was in the haughty but instinctive pride of her bearing, questioned herself; and that effort came as a surprise to her. What had she experienced just then, in the arms of that man? Her refusal—she no longer added the words "sent by God"—but by herself! Had this burst forth from the man's desire, brutally hurtled at her in the sun without the excuse of conjugal nights? From her disgust? As she searched for an answer, she struggled against some form of complacent ignorance that could have turned her into a puritan one day, just like the other women in her world, but the questions kept rushing at her so pointedly that she almost felt awed, without quite understanding why. It was a feeling of having faced an enemy at last, if only for an instant, and of having been able to stand up to it, to be.

The room was dark. The sun filtering in through the shutters threw its light on the fine fabrics scattered across the room. Cherifa had been busy sewing an outfit when she was forced to go and open the door to the master of the house, who, for some inexplicable reason, had come home in the middle of the day. She returned to her habitual quarters, where it was quiet, where the floor was littered with her silks while, lit by the rays of the light, dust particles played with their prints. Slowly she regained her calm, but also discovered a buried decision inside herself that sought to be unearthed. She couldn't go on this way; she knew that going back to her sewing and other such frivolities would prevent her from completing the arc she herself had inscribed somewhere up in the air, an arc not yet finished. Something had been revealed. But what—that flash of lightning, what was it? She needed to give form to her refusal. "No," she repeated and was surprised to find that it was not a cry anymore, it was just a word.

That was the moment (while she opened the shutters, rearranged the pieces of fabric, thread, thimble, scissors, left the door ajar, undressed, and changed clothes) when a violent insight told her she no longer had a place in this house. "I have to leave"; and she realized fiercely that to go on living there would mean living a lie. She felt the energy that had taken her to this point as an awakening as well. Yes, all her life until that moment had been nothing but a long period of lethargy, certainly not devoid of voluptuousness—which gave her the aura of being not quite present, illuminating her during celebrations on patios when the eyes of other guests would confront her apparent coldness. The old ladies interpreted this as virtuous modesty and the younger ones as mystery.

Not yet knowing what she was going to do, she saw immediately she was ready to obey the lightning inside her—she sensed her own tenacity now; nonchalance and indifference were gone—and a sense of elation pervaded her at the urgency of this departure.

"I have to leave!" she whispered.

She then had to suffer her husband's cries of rage and fury; he beat her and, in a final sign of cowardice, pretended to be resigned, a turnaround he refused to translate as an admission of helplessness. After an interval of several days—even at night she stayed in her room at the back of the house, thereby enjoying the small pleasures of defiance—he came in one night, his face inscrutable and his voice hard, to announce that he was repudiating her, since she hadn't been able to bear him any children. His businesslike expression was a mask that allowed him to save face.

He had uttered his sentence very deliberately in the final hope of being able to convince her otherwise; very deliberately, in that dry impersonal tone that always succeeded with his subordinates. He had waited, then raised his eyes with a final spark of hope because she had no resources whatsoever, no parents, and a brother who was much too young to take charge of her; because she wouldn't have the courage to leave this way, abandon the marble courtyard, the large empty rooms in which she loved to dance by herself in the semidark of dusk, where he had once caught her by surprise. Yes, she would beg, weep, implore; he still had this hope; he looked at her. Cherifa was facing him; her eyes were not lowered; a simple movement of her head shook back a lock of dark hair; her mouth opened slowly only to trace a mercilessly gentle smile, the smile of triumph.

2   ...   LILA

How long had she been living on the top floor of this empty building that stood by the side of the road? Lila couldn't say. She didn't question it; why count the days? It might have been before dawn today or yesterday at daybreak or perhaps three or four days ago that she was slinking around and had entered this freshly painted sunny place, as if mere chance had driven her in this direction. She had followed a hurried little man, the concierge. The elevator? No, she wouldn't take the elevator. Yes, she wanted to see everything, go through everything at the same pace; she had all the time in the world. (What did time mean since Ali's departure? A black ocean sprawling before her with nothing moving across it, not a sail in sight, no open view, nowhere to go.) The little man in front of her rushes, explains:

"Two apartments on each floor. I would suggest a southern exposure. Sun all day long. It's a new building, completed last year for civil servant families. A special architect from France. Yes, it's still empty. Well . . . with what's happening today some people don't want to risk living here. It's far, you know. The neighborhood as well. Are you alone?"

"I'm alone," Lila says to herself. "I'll be living alone. What's the difference?"

"Pardon me, little lady, but what I was telling you was just meant as advice. You should carefully choose a *fatma* to work for you."

"One *fatma* always chooses another *fatma* with care!"

She was accustomed to responding in this vein; her lack of aggression, with just a hint of cold irony, always puzzled those who, because of her bearing, her clothes, and her complexion, took her for a European and therefore in all good faith played on this form of solidarity. The concierge takes the answer as a snobbish foreign quirk; but he, too, has his doubts and dares not pursue it any further. He will see her name later, unless, he thinks, she is one of those, unfortunately too many, French women who come from France with the sole purpose of marrying an Arab.

Lila had spent the whole morning there. She had seen every one of the apartments on all six floors. She had inspected everything: the whiteness of the walls, the way the water heater worked in the shower room, the view from the windows over the town and then over the river; the concierge didn't recommend the latter. "Why?" She asked the question nonchalantly and as he answered, the little man thought: "Yes, she really has to be a foreigner, because she doesn't avert her eyes from the plot of wasteland and the wretched shacks piled up there where the shantytown begins behind the hill. Or she really is a *fatma*, as she said; why not? No, she has nothing of the hussy. Even when those people want to look like us, something of their origin always remains. A *fatma* never has green eyes!" he concluded, to reassure himself.

She said, "Why?" and stayed to contemplate the river, and sure enough, he could tell she was hardly paying any attention to her own question. She began to go through the whole place again, empty hallways, steep stairs, at the same calm pace, as if she were far away, wandering, uncertain, with that same look, a shimmering gaze she would quickly train on others before she turned it back inward to her dreams and their smoky whorls.

A strange young woman, the concierge thought again. He made an effort to hide his growing, nasty mistrust of her beneath a garrulous flow of words, providing her with information to which she wasn't listening; he knew it and was hurt. A strange young woman, suddenly emerging from nowhere without any luggage, as if—good Lord!—our town no longer was an embattled place but a resort for solitary tourists attracted by rest and exile. Why here? There were plenty of hotels in the center of town where she could have stayed. Her desire to live here alone, in an empty building on the edge of town, was truly very odd. For she was moving in.

"I'll take this apartment," she decided. It was the last one she had seen, on the top floor, and was the very one he had advised her against, even though the view over the river was very beautiful, were it not for those deplorable gray shacks, "that squalid district," as he had added. She was scornful of the details he had offered and in the face of her disdain the little man, still out of breath, felt like refusing, claiming that nothing was for rent. Still, he told her that she could move in whenever she wanted, yes, that very day, why not; that the rent was due in advance on a monthly basis; that under normal circumstances there was a deposit to be paid and forms to be signed but he would exempt her from this. She was his first tenant; it was the least he could do.

Lila let him talk. She was beginning to feel weary. On the threshold of each apartment she had asked herself, "Could I live here?" and then the whiteness of the walls or the small size of a room would already make her feel the oppression that would surely grab her if she were imprisoned there. She stood in front of a window contemplating the town, her back to the concierge—"My town," she sighed—and before this panorama that was both new and familiar, an expanded strip of land at the foot of the burned-out slopes of the mountain, she finally felt a bit of her former peace, of her childhood and of her recent days of happiness. It was the first time that she saw her town like this, laid bare in an immense circle, white in the center but with the verdant spots of a few orchards at its perimeter, the remains of a cool, shaded past now swallowed up by modernity on one end and glaring misery on the other. Her gaze continued to wander: that speck was the kiosque, a colonial-style bandstand on the square with its ancient palm tree; next to it, the old Arab quarter, the market; and behind that . . .

She moved away from the window and with a dry tremor in her voice: "No, I don't want this view." "How about the river?" She'd take a look at it. "And the humidity?" "I'm not afraid of humidity." Then, as if she really were concerned, she added: "The upper floors would have less of that, wouldn't they?" The concierge offered his opinion, servile in his indefatigable patience in which Lila saw proof that these apartments had not been looked at in a very long time. She followed him up the stairs to the next floor. Before she crossed another threshold, the same question arose inside her, and she felt her very soul being engulfed, slowly drifting away: "Could I live here? Could I do it? Alone." Another glance at the walls, another stop in front of the picture window. The concierge was breathing hard as he raised the blinds, whose smooth functioning was hindered by the paint that had dried between the hinges. She watched him struggle, knew his efforts were pointless because she might just as well have grumbled to him at the beginning, "Give me the most desolate, the coldest place." She said nothing, watching, dreaming. Every now and then she asked a question just so she'd appear as if she were actually hesitating before making her choice; but her thoughts were drifting elsewhere: "How to live alone in this place? How to live alone?" Again she turned to the little man.

He was fat and he perspired profusely, though he did not seem exhausted at all. Still alert. His eyes furtive. And when, overcome by a confusion she had trouble masking, she faced him, his gaze moved swiftly away from her. His voice, that of a small yapping dog, stopped for a moment when he panted with fatigue or anticipation, then poured out a stream of words in an accent Lila couldn't place. With a shrug of her shoulders that revealed a wounded grace, she turned around and continued on her quest through the dark hallways, rooms never lived in where it suddenly seemed to her that she might keep on wandering for the rest of her life, keep on wandering, a figure lost in oblivion's snares. A figure that takes a few steps, stops, a supple branch leaning from a window, turns around so that her slender shadow saunters on the immaculate walls again; sometimes softened by the light as it slips through the blinds that the little man was still trying to raise.

Her whole life, here. From now on, time, the future, the waiting would flow on like this. She repeated these abstract words and they became salutary. She knew no bitterness. Is this not how one glimpses the hallways of death, with the sadness of a smile? But what good were questions? She wanted just one thing, the same thing that earlier had made her stop in front of the building whose facade ill concealed the landscape that lies exposed behind it and that she now has at her feet beneath the window: a meager river—the wadi—whose sole trickle in the too-wide, pebbly bed seems to snub the first shacks of the shanty-town. The early morning desire that had urged her to approach the concierge, listen to his explanations, allow herself to be dragged along on this visit of such bitter absurdity now invaded her again. Oh, to sit down in an empty house, lie down on a mattress or the cool tiles as in the opaque hours of a lengthy siesta, and lose herself at a wide-open window in contemplating the silence of the motionless blue sky, to forget, stop living, barely even shiver as in the drowsiness of a slow morning. The head is heavy then, but at the very depth of the void of the submerged consciousness, attentiveness reveals itself, a muffled willingness attempting to summon wakefulness from the bottomless pillars of one's being. Then the body comes undone, breaks its moorings, gets lost, in spite of the ripe morning and the heat.

Yes, she wanted to stop somewhere, in a haven that would offer a familiar, serene face right away; to stop, sleep, forget, in the solitude of these intact rooms, suspended at the summit of abandoned places, forget especially herself, she, alone, left even more alone by Ali's departure.

• • •

They had conceived of their love as a headstrong tête-à-tête, a confrontation whose fascination had immediately conquered her. Distracted at first and as if protected, she conveyed through her eyes and the smile of her natural naïveté an excessive enthusiasm that always became a bit overwrought. In the early moments of their love affair, she discovered such an intensity in herself, both pure and gluttonous, for rushing forward into life that for a long time she thought this still-timid frenzy emerged out of their very love, a secret power she couldn't identify, or out of Ali's passion. With his principles and well-defined morality, with his militant nationalism, and in spite of their shared exhilaration, Ali opposed the unarmed fervor and youthful unawareness she herself so badly understood. His rigorous will expected to make an ideal woman out of the wild young girl, entrapped in her wealth of devotion.

And so Lila began to surrender to amorous passivity; she yielded to Ali's ambition more with radiant pleasure than with gratitude, not noticing that by wanting to mold her he would also limit her. Then, too, came the inevitable downward slope of a barely acknowledged duel between two equally fierce personalities, its drama, and its scenes and turmoil. Distanced now, Lila measured that first exaltation: a struggle she had lived through in wonderment even in her exhaustion. Their aspirations and dreams, woven together, had quickly made a place for war and its pursuit, for the chains that bound them to each other more and more, yet with an inflexibility they hated.

Ali persisted in wanting to shape Lila—the now so rebellious Lila—in projecting her as closely as possible onto the absolute form he had in mind. To this end he used a method—perseverance—a tactic that with greater tenderness or perceptiveness she would have found touching in its very blindness. But she had not yet detected Ali's inconceivable innocence; he was too virile, too authoritative; what struck her were only his arrogance and the madness of his demands, which had become the very essence of his passion. Their conflicts increased but they didn't succeed in shaking Ali's conviction that one day the end would be reached in the road he had chosen for her and for himself. Often after a storm—and, in the heart of the fog, how gratitude blazed as clear as a sky!—Lila let herself be persuaded that their perfect bliss, the miraculous fusion of their souls and frenzies, would spurt up like a geyser.

Alone now, or abandoned rather, she questioned herself and had her doubts. Was she, too, not responsible for their rifts, and not just Ali alone? She had taken so much pleasure in them. She remembered: how many times in the course of their quarrels had she not been surprised by enjoying the feeling of tragedy that floated above their never-ending noise: pleas, reproaches, bitter curses, sparring matches that were ludicrous in their eloquence and rage. Their love thus rose up as a monster with two heads that tried to devour each other. An incident would inflame Ali's jealousy and Lila's insolence again. And again the illusion would work on Lila. She believed, with a twinge in her heart and at the same time with cruel inner detachment, that her entire life, "her destiny," as she put it with youthful emphasis, depended on that exact moment—on the power she had to convince Ali when he accused her (of what? it didn't matter) or to control her own rebelliousness, a revolt that had shaken her at first until she could only live in the eye of the storm.

Ali was less unstable than she; or perhaps he suffered more deeply from the friction, which for her was turning into a pretext for excitement, nothing but a game she ended up needing. Ali did not play; he resisted. He was trapped inside his unhappiness; he would gather up all his hostile forces, a barrier with which he opposed her, his eyes dark—"His brow!" she sighed, the brow she so loved, as if it were the only thing of this male body that remained present to her. It was an enemy she wanted to caress in spite of their argument, or just furtively brush with her hand, knowing with sensual intuition that once the gesture was made their apparently irrevocable divorce would vanish; that she would be back in the usual world, the one in which she lived with Ali, fused with him day and night, not leaving him, nourished by his presence. "His brow!" she whispered, but her hand hung in the air, its turn to be paralyzed now, by a spell that bound not merely their feelings but also their attitudes. Habits had lost their effectiveness too.

Time: she remembered that as well. But what was the use of remembering it: now time was always the same, a sagging stretch, like a little girl's jump rope dragging in the dust. She no longer said, "Tomorrow," "Soon," "In a bit," those commonplace marks that carry us forward without letting us forget the road—a road trodden with such tiny steps that it produces the sensation of an expanded present, one we think we possess, of a future without any danger, one we believe we're always on the verge of enjoying, the illusion of a future, the illusion of its enjoyment.

Hereafter Lila saw herself as an unraveled object, handed over to the despair of living motionlessly. Forever? The question made no sense. Absolute indifference took over, while during the earlier ups and downs a force would push her to take Ali back again, in spite of the torment, in spite of the hate. Now she felt nothing but resignation. Had she aged? No. Was she tired, weary? Perhaps. But what ailed her was absence. Ali present, an astounding miracle! Even at this moment, when she thought she was in definite exile, he would have provoked alarm in her as great as that of an animal when it smells danger and confronts it. Lila stared at the man she loved, his face, his eyes, his body, his shadow. She smelled him, inhaled him, despite what emanated from him, something cruel that arose as much from resentment as from a terrifying logic. Suddenly she wondered: "Maybe that's it, it's the instinct of man, of his destructive energy that mistrusts itself, defies itself, that seeks to liberate itself from the female, from her, the female with her tenacious womb, her humbling devotion, maybe . . ." She knew nothing any longer other than that she had really struggled stubbornly and for a long time.

Merciless, Ali listed his grievances, thinking himself the accuser. Hypocritically, gently, patiently, using slowly learned skills, she had tried to liberate him from these imaginary chains, from the ghastly mechanism that made him into an enemy. He whose narrowed eyes smiled when they caressed, which turned her strength into abandon and made her warmth into such a vulnerable need for tenderness, he whom she finally saw at the end of the tunnel of misery, to whom she gave herself. Gave herself with a flash of pride in her eyes because she had succeeded, because she knew she would always have to succeed.

She surrendered, she gave herself up, as she received the fragrances that filled her soul, irrigated her, a confident soil, open soil, suddenly magnified, alive, puerile, carefree, crazy, happy, solemn, strangely blossoming with an earthy voluptuousness that surprised even Ali.

Now Ali was no longer there. She repeated the phrase a thousand times, staring at it in the emptiness of her mind. Then one day she asked herself whether the determination she once put into conquering him anew and at the same time—she thought with supreme self-assurance—into saving him was not what had disappeared first of all, in turn provoking the disappearance of Ali, of happiness, and of the always uncertain miracle.

After all, do we ever clearly know what our image is in the other, what echo, once sounded and then returned, creates the desert between us?

• • •

The day after old Lla Aicha died, they had come late in the morning to take her body away, the ceremony was short; some prayers were said, and then the first to leave the house were four men with the coffin on their shoulders, actually a wide board of polished wood on which lay the body, wrapped in white linen. Youssef followed with his head so low that Cherifa, in the next room behind the raised curtain, from where she could see the procession as it left, couldn't tell at that moment how intense his sorrow was. She regretted it, prepared as she was since the beginning of her second marriage—"Happy," she sighed—to watch for every emotion on her husband's face, which in a movement of spontaneous mimicry she then instantly took on. It filled her with a vague joy to feel an identical intensity so immediately. "His mirror," she said to herself, "I'm nothing other than his mirror anymore!"

A few neighbors accompanied Youssef, with the exception of Amna's husband, of course. He was a police officer, and since the beginning of the war, a policeman more than anyone else in this world had to take a stand. Previously, his Arab brothers spied on him, waited for him, or, like Youssef, ignored him. Cherifa was thinking about all that and about the circumstances that now established wastelands between the men in the same house. She thought of Amna, too, her only friend. Overwhelmed with emotion, she turned to her; standing by the door with her children clutching at her skirt, Amna was weeping bitterly. Having lived with Lla Aicha for twenty years, Amna had been more attached to the dead woman than Cherifa had been and had not stopped talking about her since early that morning.

"If you had known her before, you would know what a fine woman she was! Always the first one up, directing everything with an iron hand like a man, and never tired. At thirty she was alone with four children to raise, protecting what little she had from the vultures that come crowding around defenseless widows, and she herself went to see the lawyer while closely following the court case. Oh, ten of our men together couldn't equal her!" Amna's tears poured forth; then she picked up her litany again. "No, you didn't know her in her good years! You had barely crossed the threshold of this house when she began to go downhill, poor thing! One would have thought she was waiting for you, for you, to whom she gave her only son—oh, very much the favorite one—in order to say, 'My work is done.' No really, I'm telling you, you didn't know her!" Amna continued weeping and then said simply, "May God be my witness, today I am losing a true mother!"

Patiently, Cherifa consoled her, found the words that should be said when someone so dear is gone. But Amna needed to go to the very depths of her grief and experience untamed relief. She moaned, took out a huge handkerchief and sneezed into it. Her two frightened tots, still clinging to their mother's clothes, began to cry out, heaving in chorus.

Cherifa had a routine for situations like this. She stopped paying attention to Amna, turned to the little ones, took them away from their mother, and sat each of them down on one of her knees. Then she gave each a piece of cake and told them a story, making faces and big eyes, and ending with a song, and soon the children—twins who seen separately had no particular appeal but were charmingly irresistible as a pair—smiled at their "sister" Cherifa, as they called her in Arabic. They asked for another story, more sweets, more faces. Although tiring of their unflagging attention, she didn't stop, and pulsing with an extraordinary and vivid delight like sap in springtime, she forced herself to keep in mind that this was a day of mourning, so she would not passionately seize them, cover them with kisses, laugh and chirp with them, caress and embrace them, and find happiness in this wild exuberance primed by unfulfilled motherhood—childlessness without bitterness, nonetheless.

How powerful the taste of happiness is, and yet how sweet as well! She would discover this incessantly in her second marriage, to Youssef, a bit reserved in front of others, but whose hesitant tenderness and pursuit of her, which he performed with scrupulous attention, she loved. So much so that, just as with the children, she would begin to shiver with blind exuberance in an irrational desire to drag him off to . . . to where she didn't even know, unaccustomed as she still was to the dialogue of their mutual fascination.

Having cried herself out, Amna stood up and wiped her eyes and briefly observed Cherifa's face, together with those of Hassan and Hossein, her twins.

"What a wonderful mother you'd be!" she said. "May God now fill your home, after having destroyed it! May he shower the seed of life on you!"

Cherifa raised her head.

"May God hear you!" she answered gratefully.

• • •

Outside, the procession moves along slowly. It has to cross the old quarter and reach the center before it can take the detour that leads to the road out of town, which runs along the river to the cemetery. That day at this hour the city is calm, with no greater police presence than usual. On any day following a massive operation and its upheaval, inertia moves into the streets; it seems as if no one dares look up at the mountain, visible from every point, as if everyone wants to savor a pause before the next alarm, the next panic.

Youssef leads the way, right behind the body. Behind him are only five or six men, who from time to time replace the bearers up front. They are all neighbors and relatives, but not real friends, Youssef's friends having already left town a few years earlier. As for the relatives, only his brothers-in-law are there. While Aicha was alive, it was Youssef who had to marry off his three sisters to ensure their security; now he is freed from any further obligation. His youngest sister, Zineb, had caused him quite a bit of concern. Since she had been able to attend school, learn French, and go on to secondary school until the age of sixteen, she had trouble accepting being closeted like the others and one day being married off to someone she didn't know; it was normal for there to have been some struggle. No, there was no point in lying to himself, Youssef thought, it had been much more serious than that. He knows but wants to forget, for he feels responsible—responsible for the unhappiness of a young woman who wouldn't stop crying on her wedding day and throughout the months that followed. Zineb had dared to answer back to her brother (was she really shameless, as the others claimed?)—"Her own brother!" the gossips would exclaim—when he questioned her in a worried voice.

"What do you hold against him?"

Rebellion in her tone, she answered, "Nothing, I just can't stand him," and then, more gently, to herself, "He isn't handsome, he isn't ugly, but I don't want him to come near me, I don't want him touching me!"

Youssef could only lower his eyes, turn his head away, and crush the remorse in his heart. "Am I really responsible?" he asked himself. "Have I really ruined the life of this sister whom I love?" He then left.

No, it was not shameless of her to have said it, yell it out so she wouldn't suffocate. Then when Cherifa told him about herself and her first husband, in that absent voice she would take on and with those hard eyes that made him ache, he understood his sister and remembered. In the deep waters of his wife's eyes he thought he saw the image of so many drowning women whose destiny had been taken away forever and who tried to fight back. Cherifa would talk, tell her story; in the end he would say: "I know . . ." and think of Zineb, but by then she had finally grown accustomed to her husband, who "came near her," and to her growing children. Were it not for that shadow that darkened her features (even at twenty-three, when only a few years earlier she had been so pretty and plump, so dazzling), one might say her household was without any problems, like so many others. One day you think you're choking; then, sooner or later, you're resigned.

As the procession is about to reach the center, it passes the Palais d'Orient, a café known as Moorish, like all the others in this street, because the clientele is strictly Arab. A police officer at a nearby inter-section watches. ("All these pointless ceremonies; these days, they should forbid any large gatherings at all, even for their dead.") Two or three groups of men rise on the terrace of the café. Silently they join the procession. One of them had recognized Youssef. The others don't know him; he is just a modest carpenter with a very small shop near the market. Moving at the same slow pace, they follow the cortege and find an ancient gentleness in this necessary, reverential silence that accompanies the body of an old woman who died the night before (the whole town had heard the news: a shell exploded, its frag-ments falling in a courtyard that was too exposed; one more victim. Thank God, she hadn't suffered!). Nostalgia overtakes them. "Where are the days," one of them thinks, "when we were wholly involved in these ceremonies with the calm gratification of our unchanging ways, so much so that when it was over—whether we had attended a wed-ding, a baptism, or a death—we were strengthened and comforted by our numbers, our world with its rituals, its past, and its customs. But what are those really, the past, customs?"

They're in front of the next Arab café—there are two or three more before they reach the square—(and now there is a policeman watching the procession: "Maybe one of them is a terrorist . . . how can you know before they come closer? . . . No"). Other patrons rise to join the procession as well, mostly elderly men. Before long, they'll go home and simply say, "Si Youssef's old mother died. We accompanied her to her last abode." One of them is a young man. "How old is he?" the man next to him wonders, "Strange, but I've never seen him before."

"Excuse me, son, but who is your family?"

"I'm the son of Si Abderahmane, the baker."

"Oh, Si Abderahmane's son. How can that be? So big already? How old are you now? I knew you when you were just a little boy . . ."

The adolescent blushes. "Seventeen."

"Are you the one—speak softly, I must speak more softly; the men in front of us are turning around, but I want to know, we see so few young people these days—are you the one in Algiers, who was sent off to a secondary school in the capital, obviously a very brilliant student?"

"Yes, I'm in boarding school there. I arrived yesterday to see my parents."

"May God keep you safe for them! We, too, are very proud of you!"

The boy looks down. He knows no one here. As soon as the troubles and suppressions began, his father sent him away as a precaution. He's his only son; he's determined the boy will be a doctor. In ten years (he planned the timetable), he can set him up in an office in the center of town. He will be the second Arab doctor here. The first one is old; by that time he will have retired. Then he, Si Abderahmane, will be able to close his bakery. He will be "the father of the doctor." He will wear the white *gandoura* every day of the week, not just on Fridays. He'll take walks; in the afternoon, he'll play dominos for hours. As they play, one of his old friends will say, "Well now, it seems that your son operated on so and so!" And he, the father, will modestly go on playing as he mutters, "You know what Bachir is like! He doesn't like to speak about his work at home."

At the center of the procession, Bachir is intimidated. It is the first time he has participated as an adult in a funeral. Suddenly he's afraid that once they arrive at the graveside there will be some ritual he doesn't know. "Why am I here?" he wonders. He feels no emotion; neither the solemn religious ceremony nor the atmosphere of collective silence affects him—that long silence that keeps moving forward.

The procession leaves the city, enters the highway, passes by a freshly painted building that rents the sky with its gloomy bulk as it stands there. "Why did I follow these people?" Bachir wonders again. He has been wandering around the streets since morning, not able to find anything of his old universe ("And yet," he says to himself, "a year, it's barely a year"), not the sounds in the center, not the activities of the craftsmen close to the Arab market. Furtive glances; some turn around as he goes by because they don't or hardly recognize him. "Is it possible he has grown this much since last year?" He is searching for—for what?—a custom he can recognize again, a face that looks familiar; he is rigid and unhappy in his solitude, so different from how he is at school, where in his math class he is the only Arab, where he doesn't speak, straining with the effort of being the best, for he has long since accepted that through his academic success he is to satisfy his father's fierce pride. Si Abderahmane's eyes crease with pleasure; he wipes his powerful arms on his stained apron, and standing in the door of his shop as if he were making a proclamation to the whole town, he repeats, "My son is the best of his class!" Bachir is at a loss. Isn't this his town anymore? Then, as he had stopped on the terrace of the Arab café, thinking, "Perhaps I'd better go back to school tonight, work tomorrow, even if it's Sunday, work . . ." the long procession had come by. He'd watched it. He'd looked at the policeman in front of him and had stood up. Near him, at the same moment, others had left their table and they, too, mixed in with the flow that moves on, and as usually happens with a crowd that feels alive, no one can say who was the first to take the initiative.

The cortege has passed the large lonely building. Bachir is still questioning himself, although he is generally averse to such attempts at self-analysis. Until now, his one and only passion has been mathematics. He is amazed that the image of the policeman stays etched in his mind. "That's it," he thinks, "I caught him by surprise in his fear, his hatred . . . I stood up without giving it any thought. What warmth were they radiating, those men moving along so quietly?" As he follows, his eyes on the distance and not noticing that the man beside him is studying him ("So, this is the young man whose academic achievements are so highly praised! When our country is independent, he could be a scholar some day. For we, too, will have a wealth of doctors, technicians, teachers . . ."), the young man tries to resolve the problem: what was the feeling he had that made him join this crowd, he who has never liked crowds?

"These are my people," he says quietly to himself. And again he realizes clearly: "I have no friends, I've never had any friends, but I have people like me. This crowd, these men, are my people."

At the head of the procession, Youssef slows down and then stops in front of the cemetery gate. The men who are his mother's pallbearers wait. He steps forward and opens the swinging doors just a crack. His gaze lingers on the place. "Just like a garden," he thinks as his eyes slide across the white stones and the grass growing on the tombs, "a real garden." He opens the gate wide and takes the place of one of the bearers. With the weight of the body and the board on one shoulder, he is the first to enter. Behind him the men have begun to chant the prayer for the dead, a gentle hymn, a murmur, while the others, now in large numbers, spread out in the cemetery scattered with flowers, then regroup before the grave, open and black.

Bachir has stayed at the gate. He does not go in. He, too, contemplates the stones and the ceremony beyond that is coming to an end, the old woman's body lifted by her son—a slow gesture of love, a gesture of peace beneath the sky. For a moment Youssef, his arms tense, stops, then he bends over toward the earth, toward the hole.

•••

Lila is sitting on the bed facing the window. Except for the bed, a mattress, and a box spring she bought, together with the absolute necessities, the room is bare. She had never owned a single piece of furniture of her own, not even in her bliss, she had never wanted to own anything, no house, no cumbersome pieces of furniture, because she had never felt poor and she despised wealth. Still, on the day she arrived, she herself had to supervise the move: standing motionless, she had waited until the movers were completely done—two young boys in rags looking somber, whom the concierge had called from the neighboring hovels. They worked as they cast sidelong glances at the young woman standing there, frozen in place, a mute statue, and since she seemed indifferent, they were devouring the place with their eyes. At last they'd entered the building they had watched going up for such a long time as they sat in the dirt in front of their hovel. Then once it was finished, it remained empty and closed like a tombstone thrust up vertically. They had left then and closed the door, and amid the disorder of suitcases thrown around haphazardly Lila suddenly felt like crying.

She had opened a suitcase by chance, spread out the familiar objects: two or three books, not many—she didn't like to read, but once she made the effort, which was as arduous as that of growing accustomed to new people, she would become attached to the book, would spend months tirelessly reading and rereading it, randomly in any direction or starting in the middle and thus continue, like a child, as if the novel were becoming a freshly created labyrinth that she never wanted to do without. Somewhat faded photographs of her father, not a single one of her dead child because, clenching her teeth, she had ripped them all up to take revenge on fate; finally the pictures of Ali, which she barely took out and then with aching heart tossed back into the suitcase.

She knew them all too well; they were traces of happiness, all of them, images of Ali that she herself had taken in a thousand different poses at a time when the days streamed by fluidly, phosphorescent sprays in a nocturnal sky. She had a flirtatious way of going into raptures over Ali's beauty, his straight brow, the long arch of his thick eyebrows just like—she would tell him with impertinent tenderness—those that some women paint on, his smile, his angry pout; all this became a pretext for Lila to cry out in emphatic wonder. "You are as handsome as a god, as a faun, as . . ." she would sigh half in jest. In his irritation with so much noise and fuss, he still managed to be touched at times by her admiration and would laugh when she threw herself on his chest and kissed him. She did so without any expertise, the way a child would act with a fabulous toy of which he doesn't tire. Ali would escape from her and scold, "You're making me waste my time," wanting to get back to work, to review for one of his exams. She'd stop dead in her tracks, stop her feigned coaxing, rankled, offended, cold, or at least trying to be. He'd sit down at his desk, turn his back, and put on his glasses (she hated him that way and he knew it). She'd make one last effort to take him away from his books. "So, why don't you do some work too!" he would advise with seeming severity. Only she'd moan in a shocked voice, "I'm pregnant and you want me to work!" He would smile, stirred by the seriousness of her exaggerated ways, and yet he didn't really understand why she became so absorbed in this well-organized indolence. Since her marriage she liked to be available this way to experience every little moment of their love; like this, always a string ready to vibrate, to speak, above all to listen in her innermost self to the echoes of the smallest sensations, rapt as if lying in wait, and secretive as well when she was the recipient of pleasure, which was the only gift she accepted voicelessly, and in a state of such utter turmoil that it deeply moved Ali. Sometimes it seemed to him that it was this ignorance, this awkwardness in the early stages of learning about love and her senses, that she tried to mask and escape from in her explosions of childishness, laughter, and theatrics.

"Charming," yes, that was what she called herself to provoke Ali; and she was. But also noisy, self-absorbed, egocentric even, Ali thought as he kept his back turned to her, focusing his will on the preparation for his internship in medicine—though what was the use? He wouldn't make it anyway, he had no "mentor." She was ego-centric, but her very unawareness of it made it charming, and she didn't understand why Ali didn't spend days on end at her feet, ask-ing her what the sensations of pregnancy were (just three months now). She would have described them in impassioned detail, would have invented them if need be. Or at the very least, he could have dreamed with her; she loved dreaming, planning, making up stories.

The many games did not in any way connote the burgeoning of her approaching motherhood. She had a manner of standing before the mirror with a comb in her hair and asking loudly, "Ali, do you think I'll love this child?" Then there were her occasional sighs—she had decided not to go out as long as she was pregnant, not in the least alarmed by the five or six months of imprisonment to which she was deliberately sentencing herself. "Didn't I just barely escape being a sequestered woman?" she said to justify her fantasy. "My God!"—and she'd arch her back, turning over contemptuously when Ali examined her. She asked, "When will I get my slender waist back?" Ali didn't answer. He was less and less inclined to enter into her childish diversions lately. Perhaps she sensed it and couldn't find any method other than to keep on with her thespian antics that he had once found so beguiling. They exhausted him now. He had to go out: an appointment in town, a contact to be made, a meeting to set up, ordinary duties in a working life that he didn't disclose to her. "I'm going out," he would announce as he put on his jacket. Suddenly locked into a sulk, a silence, a peculiar smirk directed at him, and with a visible effort not to show her curiosity she would repeat, "You're going out?" He would leave. He loathed explana-tions. He would return more relaxed, he would come back to Lila with renewed indulgence to make her forget his absence. ("Why not tell her?" he would wonder to himself indignantly. "After all, she does know there's a war, a struggle going on; it's not just about the two of us . . .") But upon his return he would let himself be taken in again by her laughter and loudness. He would be captivated by her in the happiness that she knew how to create so spontaneously and that she was frittering away.

They spent marvelous evenings. Stretched out on the bed side by side in the half-dark with the window open, the sounds from the student hostel reaching them as if from distant places suspended somewhere in the shadow of blue skies, they would chat. When night came, she especially liked to adopt that tone in which she excelled, to engage in the vibrant philosophical explorations that might seem so uselessly abstract. But Ali appreciated the fervent effort her intelligence forced her to make, when the night had undone all her masks, to justify her wasted hours, her unproductive days; "My diversion," she said, and then more softly, "My voluptuousness." He listened attentively, interrupting her with a word here and there. Their dialogue continued long into the night.

She had a singular ability to take some distance, to "review their situation" as she put it, never having doubted that their love was like an imminent harvest, and thereby, in her evening voice scored by deep tension, to awaken all that their shared life had been. Their first encounter when she was still a high school student and he barely any older, their three-year engagement, their student marriage that had seemed strange to their circle, in which a union could only be conceived of in stability and order, starting with a man's employment. To her everything made sense. In the end, her speeches became a monologue from which Ali did not feel excluded, for in their relationship he discovered that a course, a flow, was being mapped out. He was particularly indebted to her for that.

Had she been gone or dead, he would have understood that the bond between them was what she knew best. Others, her women friends whom she had so egotistically neglected since her marriage, might blame her for her indifference, "her lack of reality": in the passionate student discussions that year she had never been heard to speak, to define a political position or to lapse more easily into some general diatribe. Seeing her in public like that, closed, cold, one could not have surmised her flights of fancy, her distractions, her enthusiasms. As for Ali, he could have held against her the forced silence he kept concerning his political involvement; it was a very grim silence for him, since he had thrown himself so ardently into their love because it had provided him with an exceptionally free dialogue. Still, he sensed that if anyone was to belong one day to the new times emerging that he, for one, impatiently awaited, it was perhaps Lila. With that same lucidity he saw her use to find the truth of their love, only she would be able to restore the thread that would be fatally broken, and was already breaking, between the period of submission and silence and the approaching one that had set the mountains ablaze and run across the land and whose eruption of blood but also of hope pierced the illusory opacity of the towns. "Only Lila," he said, and listened to her talking of the future, of the child she was having, of the love she needed, of death. She often mentioned death, too often. It was an obsession with her. Her mother had died when she was barely ten years old and the memory, which surely explained her being haunted by the thought of any rupture, would still pierce her night in a heartrending cry.

"I remember," she whispered, "I'm running down the street. A street in my town" (Ali's town, too). "A narrow street in the old quarter where children are rushing around with the little cars they've made themselves, just a board on four wheels. I'm running! I ran out, out of our old white house up the hill, not far from the barracks. I'm running. I'm crying, I'm crying as I run. I'm crying: 'My mother is dead! Dead!' and I remember the faces of the storekeepers in their shops, the grocer, the baker, the fritter vendor, the herbalist, every one of those faces questioning me, perhaps crying out with me. I'm shrieking, 'Mama is dead! Dead!'"

She interrupted her story, heaving and gasping. Then she repeated, her eyes staring wide into the past, clouded by that funereal day: "Death, other people's death," she moaned, "I always sense it beforehand." Ali calmed her down, for in her pregnant state this kind of emotional upheaval was really harmful. She patted her belly. "He's here," she said in a wholly different voice as if the child would come and protect her. "He's here," and she smiled at Ali with a brave smile to apologize for her fears.

• • •

Lila got up from the bed, where she'd been sitting for a very long time. Had she forgotten the present: two, three hours had gone by, she wasn't sure. She went over to the window, where she hadn't bothered to hang any curtains. She never lowered the blinds, not even at night, when she didn't budge, lying on her bed, absorbed in her contemplation of the milky sky growing gradually darker. And as had happened once or twice since her arrival, she also observed the mountain, given over to the war pounding away at it. She watched the spectacle without excessive interest, waiting for the moment that the shell would fall, and then saying to herself—a phrase that fell from her mouth without any discernible shock in her soul—"Perhaps Ali is up there! Fighting! He's alive . . . alive!" and to her eyes the mountain became a maternal power, weighty like a woman in the contractions of labor whose generous and fertile body was protecting Ali.

She opened the window, leaned out. She noticed a part of the road that curved at this spot. Her gaze lingered on a line of men. She didn't understand at first, but as the procession slowly disappeared, she thought, "a funeral," and felt no sadness. She had forgotten that the Muslim cemetery was somewhere in this direction.

Earlier, when she was a child, she used to go there with the women. On holidays they would bring brioches and painted hard-boiled eggs that they would eat seated on the tombs. In the spring she picked wildflowers there amid the white veils of the women sitting closely together in little groups, busily chatting for hours on end in the sun, a soft twittering that was supposed to comfort the sleep of the dead. She had not gone back there; she had never wanted to see her mother's grave, its dust. No!

Lila leans out again, follows the shadows as they move away in the distance. "Death," she begins. She thinks of another death, stops, tenses up, then leaves the window. She stands for a moment, a trembling silhouette in the middle of the bare room. Soon it will be noon; the sun is harsh. The river outside is dried up. Bravely, so as to accept it, she says again, "My son, that is how they must have taken him away that day. A line of men. Four carrying the board, or maybe just two, a child weighs so little."

Lila sits down again; she forgets her loneliness, and the present, and the silence.

•••

Ali had never understood her excessive grief, she continued to think somewhat resentfully. A baby of scarcely six months; he hadn't really been interested in him, which apparently was normal: a father doesn't become attached to the child until the age that it begins to babble, crawl, and live other than as a blob of miraculously formed flesh, intent only on its feedings, its naps, or the games its flailing little fists play above its head, making mysterious arabesques.

He had died. Became sick and died on the same day and on that same day was put into the ground. It happened in the capital city, in the student housing where they lived: death's intrusion onto the island that Lila had created for herself. Not one of the familial traditions had eased the severing: no faces of relatives, no old women with their serene look coming to wash the body, none of the things that bring acceptance. A death via a pharmacy, it seemed to her. Doctors in white coats, coldhearted nurses, and she being restrained while the child was taken from her. ("But he isn't dead! You're lying," she screamed, "You're lying!") Women she didn't know consoling her. ("Where is my grandmother, where are my aunts and all the other women in the old houses at home to be with me, to keep me company in this grief-filled delusion?") Then there was Ali, his eyes above her: how long had he been watching her? She had stayed in bed a long time. Sick for several weeks, nightmares in which her mother came back, a gentle shadow, her child, Ali. Ali above her; in a firm voice: "Be brave!" Imploring her: "Be brave," and saying it over and over again. Inside her, refusal prevailed, a stone.

This interruption came to an end. Through his presence, Ali had managed bit by bit to draw Lila out of the hole in which she had burrowed. He rarely left her side and then only when she fell asleep after he had made her take a sleeping pill. When she woke up, she found him at her bedside, watchful. He had taken advantage of her sleep to attend to some of his activities, to his other life. She knew this. And now he knew that she knew. They wouldn't speak about it. Ali was present: that was all that mattered to her. In spite of a year and a half of war, that certainly was miraculous. She found miracles normal. She thought it was her right.

Assassination attempts and arrests in the capital had increased recently. A new era set in: when outside, people caught themselves walking faster but being careful not to show it. In the bright light of day the city streets were becoming like tunnels; a stranger in the crowd began to look like the enemy. Fear infiltrated everything. Despite a few remaining interludes of normal life, the war was weaving its strands treacherously: some feared the strands of traps and death, but others? Others also trembled but dared to feel hope when they occasionally perceived something like a breath of the future.

Despite the new atmosphere during that academic year, Ali, like most of his fellow students, appeared to be immersed solely in his studies. Lila now accepted that a second life might be interlaced with theirs. She wasn't afraid. She felt like telling him, "But of course, it's only natural." It seemed to her that as soon as she gained her strength back, as soon as the memory of this nightmare was gone, and with the child—who in the shadow of her sleep continued flailing his lovely little fists above the cradle in whimsical spirals— and its frail ghost buried, denied, dislocated, she, like Ali, could be open to the new world that would no longer belong to the others alone. She would say to him, "We have done everything together. I'm coming with you. What are you doing? I'll do it with you."

The months went by. She didn't speak. And yet she was recovering. But she felt different. Along the way, her resources of laughter and girlishness, the pointless, noisy outbursts of her youth had gotten lost in a shaft of nothingness. She was calm now. Most often silent. Not at all sad, although a concerned Ali would sometimes shake her: "What's the matter? What are you thinking about? Speak up! You're usually so talkative!" She'd talk but only in that serious, somewhat defeated tone, whose new resonance was surprising.

In spite of the mayhem outside—the mass arrests, the alerts, the many uniforms, the glimpsed face of a fearful man in a startled crowd who shows his identity card and who is afraid, in spite of his wrinkles—Ali and Lila had developed a liking for taking long walks in the streets. They walked aimlessly, always straight ahead and at an even pace. Ali no longer attended his courses; it didn't occur to Lila to be at all surprised, although she knew his studious habits. Since her pregnancy, the birth of her child, and then his death—all of which had happened in a single spurt, as it were, a clean break—she had dropped her studies. She kept postponing the date to pick up her courses again. Philosophy! What good could that do her now? Worse, she now had a horror of entering that branch of knowledge, whose discipline she had so passionately loved before. "I like to understand," she used to say with naive seriousness. No, from here on in, all that was left behind, as if with a shrug of the shoulders and without turning around, she had dropped it like an old coat, unconcerned about its destiny or its price, since it was no longer any use to her.

Apparently, Ali let himself be won over by this idleness. She asked him no questions. She never allowed herself to question him on anything other than their relationship; the reserve she had learned to practice might even have looked like indifference. Besides, he said nothing anyway; without any explanation, he would be gone for whole mornings. When he returned he would just look at her: "Are you ready?" She had lunch opposite him, conversing about anything and nothing, about one of the books she had reread ("Pavese . . ." she would begin and then go off on the flow of the novel as if on a journey). He would listen, sometimes not very well. She would stop. He'd apologize. She would start up again.

In the afternoon, they went for walks again. No matter where. In the wide streets where no laughter could be heard anymore, there they were, a roving couple resembling each other, guided by some dark force. Lila drew a druglike enchantment from this chance wandering, as if she were on the threshold of a fruitless subterfuge. At night, before falling asleep, she would sometimes think, "This isn't going to last." She'd dismiss her fear, feel her foreboding of yet another separation, but of what kind? She'd wrap herself around Ali, envelop his body the whole night long; she slept badly like this but was reassured. Afterward, even in her dreams, anxiety that Ali might suddenly vanish would overtake her; she'd wake up moaning. Ali would turn on the light, see her cheeks wet with tears. She'd smile at him and go back to sleep. In the morning he would leave again—it became easier for him, because Lila, incurably lethargic, languid, stayed in bed late, reading or sometimes watching the other students going off to class from the window, as if from the top of a world that no longer concerned her. "They're studying," she said to herself, "they're learning!" Cold dawn shadows, they moved off in small groups before her eyes.

Without any true determination, she turned to Ali, to his absence. "I must talk to him! If he has to leave, I want to leave. I want to participate." She did not talk to him. As the days went by, she was watchful of that other life eating away at Ali's mornings, sometimes even his afternoons, a life that was becoming ever more invasive, a slowly approaching sea. In his presence, she began to act like a jealous wife imagining a rival. She scrutinized his slightest distractions, a frown, a silence. What was she afraid of? What was she fleeing from? To herself she said with great precaution, "What if Ali were to leave?" Where could he possibly go? To prison, and why not? Into the resistance, and why not? Three of his closest friends had already disappeared; she had heard this by chance without Ali's having told her. No. He couldn't leave. He shouldn't leave.

So many questions, refusals, cries. They clutched at her morning drowsiness. At night she told herself anew, "This cannot go on." It became harder and harder for her to drive away those crazy-making words. She'd curve herself around Ali's body again, a deceptive recourse, to hold on to the illusion of always remaining rooted like this, always.

Had someone knocked at the door? Lila shook off her daydreams and stood up. Who could it be at this hour? Who wanted to see her here at the top of this cold building? She left the room, went to the door, and opened it.

"Suzanne . . ." she said to the visitor under her breath.

3   •••   SALIMA

Having hosed down the courtyard and abandoning in the kitchen the meal to be prepared, Cherifa sat down in her room with the twins beside her as the spectacle began, as if it were an enormous circus watched by a female audience of the old quarter. That same morning, Hakim, the policeman, came home at a most unusual time: not quite ten o'clock.

Cherifa barely had time to lower the curtain to her room and keep Hassan and Hossein from going to their father, who seemed to be in a rush. From where she sat, she heard the sound of the parked jeep, its motor still running. Cherifa could well imagine how all the women of the neighboring houses must be trembling while their men, outside, have to remain where they are, most of them lying low in their shops, others coming to a stop in the street, still others . . . Hakim, in uniform, however, has the authority to come and go without fear. Probably one of the old women has already started muttering verses of the Koran through her missing teeth, because she dares not think about what a man in uniform might see, hear, or do in these violent times.

Cherifa herself is not thinking about anything. She doesn't judge. She could almost feel sorry for Hakim. He's not really to blame for having chosen this profession ten years ago. Four children and a wife to feed; and then there is an old mother, unmarried sisters, and a young brother in a different house, even more dilapidated and humid than this one. Cherifa doesn't want to judge. Neither does Youssef, she knows that. She has never heard him criticize Hakim, he simply doesn't talk about him and no longer addresses him. This has developed wordlessly between the two men; and wordlessly they let their wives live together, as one lends the other a dress, a veil, or else some sugar, some coffee, or a cup of oil.

Outside, the motor is turned off. The jeep does not start up again. "It's waiting," Cherifa says to herself. "Hakim will soon leave, he probably forgot something." She notices the sound of voices, murmuring. She keeps the children close by her side. Every now and then Hakim's voice rises but she can't make out any words. Perhaps he is arguing with his wife. Hakim is a gloomy man with a taciturn personality, but he's not a violent husband. Amna has never complained; when she does sigh, it is from the exhaustion of her difficult pregnancies, and often because of financial worries as well—she has never grown accustomed to Hakim's habit of sharing his salary at the beginning of every month, half of it going to the other house, to his mother, sisters, and brother. Amna always grumbling (not to her husband, which she wouldn't dare, but she has to let off steam to Cherifa): "As his own family, shouldn't his children come first? I'm not even speaking for myself. His brother is twenty-four years old, he's a man now! Why doesn't he work too? Why doesn't he take care of the rest of the family?" She knows her protestations are pointless. Hakim made his decision and will tread the same path for a long time to come if need be, so that his brother can continue his studies in France. ("Over there," he likes to proclaim, "there is no racism; at the university everyone is the same. Professors don't think, 'That fellow over there, what's his name? Ahmed . . . I'll remember that.' Everyone is equal in that country.") Hakim himself will go on with his lousy job (and he repeats, "Lousy job") for as long as it takes.

Cherifa thinks, "As soon as he's gone I can raise the curtain again and go back to watching the show. It's a vast operation today. Please, God, let it be calm in the city. I've never seen as many planes as today and they started early, too." Had Youssef still been home, she would have begged him to stay, she would have found some pretext to keep him there: "It seems that now they're coming right inside our homes, entering and frisking us! They have a woman with them who speaks Arabic, like us. Please stay, I'm afraid." But she wouldn't really have said anything. She wouldn't really have been afraid and couldn't have acted as if she were afraid, not even to keep Youssef close.

Hakim briskly crosses the courtyard and goes out. He hadn't even bothered to cough as he usually does, a cough to alert Cherifa to cover up, should she be in the courtyard. The front door slams shut. Cherifa hears the jeep pull away, then silence. Is Amna coming over—she stays in her room, not budging; there must have been a scene. "Be really good now," Cherifa whispers to the children. She raises the curtain, hesitates, and then, moved not by curiosity but by compassion (yes, Hakim's voice had risen and burst out with reproaches, yes), she leaves her room and heads for Amna's, and stops in the doorway.

It is a very large, dark room. At the back in the semidarkness a four-poster takes on a majestic air. On the other side is a varnished wooden armoire; there are mattresses and cushions on the tiled floor, as is the custom. Cherifa looks around. Amna is sitting on the floor in front of her. Her body heavy, stiff; her distended legs stretched out before her; her ruddy face with its full cheeks; her wide eyes with their tearful expression. The woman sits there, mute. When Hakim so abruptly came in, she was nursing her last-born child. Her swollen breast hangs out of her lace bodice; the baby in its swaddling clothes lies beside her. Then he begins to moan, faintly and steadily. Amna with her breast exposed turns her eyes to him but doesn't see him.

"Where is she?" Cherifa wonders. "Your baby!" she whispers. Filled with a tenderness that springs up so spontaneously she can't control it, she takes a step as if to bend down, then stops. "Your baby!" she mumbles again, though in surprise. This time, Amna looks up, gasps—suddenly with that voice, that voice!—"Oh, my

God! My God!" Cherifa straightens up, waits. Perhaps things are more serious than she thought. "Oh, my God." Amna is breathing as if death had touched her. Had Hakim uttered any irrevocable words, had he repudiated her? Amna meets Cherifa's eyes, stares at her, and looking crazed, says:

"My sister! My little sister! Ask God to protect me!"

The child on the floor is screaming now. "He's hungry," Cherifa says gently. Blindly, Amna stretches out her arms and the child is passed from one woman to the other. At that moment Cherifa feels herself melting with compassion, and because hers is a simple soul, because she has rarely been so close to another woman (her beauty and her former rank used to set her apart), because in that soft forsaken voice ("Oh, my sister!") she perceives such deep distress, her eyes fill with loving tears.

Amna puts the child on her lap, gives him the breast that the voracious mouth immediately bites into. She feels the milk pour out, a thread pulling at her, taking her far away, outside herself. "Come back," she thinks, "come back here!" and slowly, with difficulty, she comes back to herself and then snaps out of it. Cherifa is here. Cherifa? She doesn't look at her now but says, "Sit down, do sit." Cherifa sits down on the mattress, waits in silence. She had said something just before. Amna forgot what she'd said, but not the affectionate tone. Cherifa is her sister; she called her, "Oh, my sister!"

Amna lets the baby finish nursing, then calmly goes through the usual gestures. She closes her blouse, her breast back in place, and lays the satisfied baby down in front of her. Cherifa is still there; perhaps she's watching the spectacle outside again. Amna begins; her tone is hard and in it Cherifa notices a new crispness. But she doesn't give any heed to the words at first, so that Amna has to repeat them; it is now she who must catch Cherifa's attention. She repeats:

"Youssef didn't come home last night, did he?"

Cherifa doesn't answer.

"Did he?" Amna says again in a voice that trembles briefly with a note of annoyance, then more reassuringly:

"Don't be afraid to tell me! You think I don't know? You think I haven't noticed, for a long time now, that when my husband has night duty at the police station, Youssef doesn't spend the night here but comes in just before dawn and then, like every other morning, gets cleaned up in the courtyard, gets ready for the day, and has breakfast. Don't say anything; don't be afraid. You are my sister, after all, aren't you?"

Cherifa listens.

"You are, you're like a true sister to me."

"Amna . . ."

"Don't be afraid; I'm telling it as I see it. Have I ever spoken against my own heart? Have you ever caught me saying things that contradict what's in my heart? You are my sister. Men have their own concerns, their own worries. Sometimes they devour each other like starving jackals. But I promise you—we've been living together for five years now and there's never been anything between us, not the slightest little incident, you don't think that's by chance, do you?—when a woman like you is dear to my heart, then I treat her the same way I would a blood sister, as if we'd drunk the same mother's milk. I swear to you, on the head of this little one whose eyes have barely opened to life."

Cherifa tries to respond.

"Oh, Amna, thank you for that!"

"Don't thank me. I have to say this to you today, but why, why do we need words?"

Amna's head comes closer, with a probing look. No, it was not terseness that made her voice tremble a moment ago but willpower, a newly found willpower in the heavyset woman with the tired body.

"Listen!" she speaks hurriedly. "Listen, I know Youssef wasn't home last night. But listen carefully to this and tell him when he comes home: my husband—because he's my husband, such is my lot, alas, and today for the first time I question God!—my husband went out of his way to come here and interrogate me. He didn't tell me why, but I'm sure it's his superiors who want to know, curse them. He said, 'Was Youssef here last night at the usual time, from sunset to early this morning?' He asked the same thing several times over. He knows I don't lie. I've never lied to him. I'm not one of those hypocritical women who take pleasure in hiding all sorts of things from their master. He knows that with me he can come home at any hour of the day or night, that in the home I run everything is open. No, I've never lied to him, as God is my witness."

"What did you say?" Cherifa interrupts, as she waits, rising, wanting to leap up and run across the city to look for Youssef, find him, warn him: "You're in danger, in real danger!"

Amna smiles, "What I said to him was, 'Youssef was here, as always, beside his wife.' Yes, I lied to him. May God forgive me. I lied to him and I'm not sorry that I did."

• • •

The jeep has left. Hakim sits next to the driver. A strident siren precedes them through the alleyways. That is how the inspector goes through his native quarter.

He thinks of Amna, of the tone of her voice when she answered, of her eyes, in which he read a certain dread that had irritated him. He had long ago become used to her silent presence, a wan person who listens to orders, bends her head, goes away, a faithful echo. Hakim considers it normal that his household runs without any problems, flat, a blank slate. This time, however, when faced with Amna's surprise, which in turn had surprised him, he had felt like crying out, "What's the matter with you?" In fact, he said it: "What's the matter with you? I asked you a question about Youssef. I need to know!"

Amna stares at him, still in the grasp of the same dread. "Was it really dread," Hakim wonders, "or could it have been contempt?" But he puts that idea out of his mind. Since, by virtue of her passivity, the woman has become a part of him—a lifeless part—he is tempted to read in her eyes what for a long time now he has not dared recognize in himself. He questions her again, but in spite of his growing irritation takes care to lower his voice because he senses the presence of the other woman, Cherifa, who is undoubtedly spying on them from across the courtyard with its basin.

"Woman, tell me what you know! I order you to do so. Did Youssef spend the night at home? Did you hear him come in at the usual time? No later?"

"Yes, he came in as usual." (Amna raises her head and holds his gaze.) "I even heard him cough in the middle of the night. This morning . . ."

Hakim got up, with a quick look at the baby she had put down in front of her. "Why did she stop nursing?" he wonders suspiciously, watching sharply. "Ordinarily she's so calm. Why is she staying there, one breast out? Her eyes shining. She's never answered in that tone before like . . . like the people I interrogate and who then challenge me." He wipes his forehead with his hand. He feels feverish. He tries to calm down, "What's happening to me? Here I am, playing the cop with my wife, my own wife! Lousy job . . ."

Amna doesn't even think of picking her baby up or nursing him again. She waits. Perhaps there will be another question. She stays where she is, doesn't move, quietly mastering herself, "He is my husband, oh God! The father of my children, the father of Hassan, Hossein, my eldest daughter, and the newborn who lies here, vulnerable, before my eyes! Lord, this is the man you gave me!"

Hakim had launched into a speech. Now he doesn't exactly remember it anymore, as he absentmindedly looks at the shops, where some semblance of activity seems to prevail in spite of the military operations nearby. The police station to which he returns is at the other end of town. Streets file by, hazy shapes slipping into his doubts, his imaginings.

"What did I tell her? Why so many words, so many sentences directed at her?" He feels somewhat uneasy. It's the first time he's ever wanted to justify himself to Amna. Humiliating and meaningless chatter! Even if she weren't listening to him—and her complete lack of reaction surely proved that—she still must have noticed the mad, disjointed tone of his speech. He suddenly remembers that he had spoken of their children (to crown it all, he hadn't said "my children" or, as when he explodes, "your children," but "our children," "ours!"). She hadn't offered any answer; she kept her head lowered, as though—once the first question about Youssef had been asked, the question he tried so clumsily to drown out and destroy with his chatter—for her he'd left their room forever.

Hakim didn't talk about his work at home. When he came in at night he might say, "I saw so and so, the baker Si Abderahmane, or the teacher, or the oil merchant. He told me his son is coming. It seems he's remarried," and so on, as he sat at the low table to eat his dinner opposite Amna, who didn't need to keep feeding the conversation. Hakim had enjoyed lending consistency to his brief moments outside the police station, harboring the illusion that his days were filled solely with encounters with compatriots, with exchanges whose banality established a deep connection between his brothers in the faith and Hakim himself, although he knew he was the "highly placed" Arab police officer. For more than a year—actually, he couldn't really place the precise moment when it had begun—he hadn't uttered these words any more. Gradually, the dinner conversation across from his wife—a ritual—had abated. "I saw so and so," he would begin, but that person had greeted him very hastily and rushed by; there was nothing to say about him. In the end, it seemed he no longer ran into anybody. More or less during the same period, he had decided to buy a car, a secondhand Citroën, and it had cost him dearly because that same month he had needed to pay doctor's bills for one of his sisters. If he no longer saw anyone in town—he himself didn't hear anything of interest anymore, about weddings or deaths, only heard rumors about other people's daily life through stooges—it was because he went to work by car, or so he told himself and sometimes professed the same to Amna.

"Inspector, is this where we turn?" the driver questions. Hakim hesitates.

"No, go left," he abruptly answers.

The jeep enters the long street of the old business center: carpet shops, leather and copper stores; it's what remains of a traditional district where more recently new businesses have been established, selling bicycles, radios, new furniture. At the end is the rustic-looking Arab market where the farmers come to sell their eggs, goat cheese, freshly killed or live poultry. This morning the usual liveliness seems frozen.

The jeep is going slowly. Passing patrols stand aside and salute; there won't be any searches today. Hakim looks straight ahead. "What's come over me?" he wonders. "Where are we going?" But he knows the road. He knows that Youssef has his store, a small place with a large window, at the end of the street on the left corner near the pharmacy. Suddenly he wants to confront him.

"That's my job, after all, isn't it? Am I not the inspector? I'll go in and start by saying, 'A question for you, Si Youssef . . . and may peace be with you.' Just like that, amicably, with the first words in Arabic, like people who respect each other. Because, in spite of our coolness, we're neighbors too, after all, and maybe even relatives— old Aicha, Youssef's mother, liked to remind me that our families are from the same tribe on the other side of the mountain. Then I'll ask my question and he'll respond. He'll really have to." The jeep is about to reach the other end of the street; the pharmacy is already visible. "Yes, Youssef will be obliged to break his offensive silence."

Hakim braces himself. Every time he thinks of Youssef the wound opens anew—living in the same house on the other side of the courtyard, sensing the man who lives there and refuses to speak to him, who turns his head when he meets him, or is careful to go out at different hours to avoid meeting him altogether. Every day this past year, for Hakim, Youssef has represented the entire city and through him all those townspeople (even those who continue to greet him, while the most cowardly still stop and chat with him) who want to remind him he is no longer their brother. Never again will he be valued the way he once was, given such consideration, even if it was just a formality; and formality still counts a great deal for the impoverished middle class. From now on, neither compromise nor courtesy. Hakim belongs to the other side; object, valet, or ally of the enemy, it matters little. Youssef lets him know it with his silence and it is for this that Hakim hates him.

In the back of his shop, Youssef raises his head; through the window he sees the jeep approaching from afar. His eyes are good, he recognizes Hakim. "Where's he going?" he wonders. He, too, remembers. Last year, about fifteen months ago now, the same jeep approached slowly like this and then stopped in front of the bakery. A few minutes later, Hakim hauled off Si Abderahmane, a man whom everybody knew, who was made to follow, staggering, his white apron still on over his loose traditional pants.

The whole town worried for three days: "Has Si Abderahmane come home yet?" His wife, in tears, came to implore Hakim at home, but Hakim stayed out of sight. Then Si Abderahmane was dumped back at his house and immediately the rumor spread, "More than thirty hours of constant torture." The bakery stayed closed for a month. That same day Youssef spoke to his mother and to Cherifa—to move, he wanted to move; to feel comfortable, be with his own people. Not have the other one's presence next door, not be obliged to avoid him all the time. "Move," he repeated to Cherifa who was already handing him her jewelry, two heavy bracelets, some clasps, and a necklace of *louis d'or coins*. "Here, this will help to pay for another place to live." Yet a few days later he changed his mind, "We're staying! This neighborhood is beneficial to me." From that time on he began to watch Hakim's schedule. He took advantage of his nocturnal absences to attend to his new activities. He gave the jewelry back to Cherifa, saying, "Take good care of these. One day, if I'm caught, they may be of use to you."

The jeep passes in front of Youssef's shop. From behind his window Youssef signals to his assistant not to go out. Hakim sees him. "He's seen me," he thinks. Hakim puts his hand on the driver's arm, thinking, "He should stop! I'll go into Youssef's store, I'll interrogate him and take him away. Once down there I won't let the specialists do the 'work' without keeping an eye on them. Surely we'll get better results than we did with the baker. Surely . . ."

At the corner of the street the driver turns his head, questioning Hakim. "Inspector . . ." Hakim is still looking straight ahead, at nothing.

"Keep going, straight!" he says. Then frenetically he repeats to himself, "Amna didn't lie to me. Amna never lies. Amna . . ."

• • •

The police station is at the other end of town and in the same complex as the brand-new prison. It's an eight-story building whose construction began the year before the war, as if the authorities had foreseen that the time would come when the existing prisons would no longer be sufficient, every one of them soon full of suspects and already doomed; too full.

The town's prison is painted light gray and stands opposite the high school for girls—mostly daughters of settlers from the wealthy neighboring plain who, throughout an entire academic year, had been able to watch the walls of the new prison gradually rise. Taking up position behind their large cross-barred gates, they would watch the approach of some young suitor. They would've had all the time in the world to imagine what kind of "boarding school" there soon would be across the street, surely different from theirs, but very similar in color, and one that would contain a section for women and the rest for men. Naturally, that wasn't at all what they thought about. Instead, they'd pat down their skirts, arch their backs, stand on tiptoe in their shiny pumps or casually undo their pink uniform pinafores, and then, exquisitely weightless silhouettes, sigh through the black bars. "My God, next year we won't be able to see a thing!" "He'll be coming from such a distance and I won't even be able to signal to him; that's really bad luck!" And another, "What do we say to the supervisor when she wants to chase us away from here? How do we look unyielding and then exclaim, 'Look here, mademoiselle, I have to wait for my correspondent! See, mademoiselle, that little

man there with the glasses, the one coming here now!'" And they'd
be so amused as they said all this, they'd titter with such impudence
when they imagined Mademoiselle's discomfiture, followed by her
assured pronouncement that, since next year there was to be a prison
there, next year could never come soon enough. No, really never.

Three years later, where would they be? The oldest ones already
or on the verge of being married. Forever gone from their mind
these walls, which for a whole year had been growing upward to the
sky; forgotten, too, their wait behind the bars of the school. They
could now be imagined on family farms, still exquisite silhouettes,
standing in the doorway of their expensive homes hidden behind
cypresses, amid wheat fields and vineyards, still sighing, "Why this
damned war, why the unrest that keeps me from going out, riding
my horse, playing tennis?" Then, they fall silent in the presence of
the young husband whom they find too self-satisfied in his territori-
al guardsman outfit and who, perhaps, annoys them.

Salima is now in one of the cells of this prison. She doesn't know
what time or day it is. This morning they let her rest, at last. They
even brought her a bed. It's been so long since she's been able to lie
down. A bed! What a miracle after constantly sitting on a chair or
standing up for the ten days of interrogation, or eleven, or twenty;
she doesn't know anymore. On the cot, she stretches out her body,
her back; the pain in her lower back won't stop. Not to move anymore, never to move! She would so much like to sleep, but she can't.
She's cold.

"What season is it?" She searches. "Is springtime gone? Let's see;
the day they came for me I'd bought a bouquet of white carnations.
I had six carnations in my hand as I was going home. Yes, I remember now, it was a Saturday; a Saturday, of course, because it was the
afternoon of outdoor activities with my students. My students," she
thinks in her half-drowsy state as she summons just enough strength
to worry about them. "Did they at least find a substitute? Now
there's real professional conscientiousness. So my reputation among
my colleagues wasn't a fabrication," she reflects with some irony. She

shivers. High up on the wall the skylight has opened. How to close it, she wonders. She looks at the little chain that hangs way down; she doesn't understand. Her attention drifts. "Where are the six white carnations I was holding when they came for me?" It wasn't her habit to buy flowers. That day was the first time she had ever done so. She smiles. For the first time, out of sheer delight, she had spent money; how much had it been, five hundred francs, not more? Really no more than that? Suddenly she feels a regretful indulgence for herself in spite of the stabbing pain in her back: twelve years a teacher and still scrimping on such meager expenses. "It's a habit, from having been poor as a girl; one day when I'm no longer responsible for my mother or my nephews, I'll become positively stingy because I'll be so used to pinching pennies and I'll be alone. No, I'll never be able to spend money pointlessly; no, I'll never spend a dime on cosmetics, just on those carnations . . ."

The door of the cell creaks partially open: a man. Without coming in he whispers, "Do you need anything?" Salima recognizes him, remembers, doesn't respond. He comes in. "You're shivering?" He looks at the window, goes over and pulls the chain, then comes close to the bed. "Still trembling, my sister?" His Arabic is coarse. Salima opens her mouth to answer and realizes she has no voice left. She smiles; thinks it must be more of a grimace as she feels the pain at the corners of her lips. Her throat is dry but she isn't thirsty. The man is still looking at her. "Are you thirsty?" She shakes her head, no. He doesn't move, looks around. "I can't bring you a blanket now, it's daytime. I'm on duty this evening. I'll be back!"

He's so old, Salima thinks. Gray hair, a short, almost white beard, drooping shoulders, and wearing the pants of a vagrant. She has seen him before her like this, three or four times. She didn't have a bed then; how many nights did she sit up that way between interrogations? The only thing left in her memory of the recent past is the ghastly reality of the chair, the hallways, the empty offices they made her go through in the middle of the night on the way back to her cell, where she would then be left, forgotten, for an entire day. Or sometimes it would be just to doze off for a few minutes, only to wander back again through what seemed to her like a labyrinth, at the end of which she had to really fight, as she stood for hours on end. Usually the guard came at night. The first time he had told her his name, Taleb. He'd come in the same way he did now; it may have been the second night she spent on the chair without being able to sleep, because she hadn't yet mastered the awkwardness of that position.

"I'm one of the guards!" he had said as he came in. "My name is Taleb. I'm bringing you a blanket. I'll take it back before morning. They shouldn't see me." Then before he left he came closer and muttered with oddly garrulous emotion: "Oh, my sister, my sister!" and she, turning her stiff, numb head in his direction, told herself sadly, "How beautiful our language is, so simple and lyrical in its very plainness!" "My sister, I thank you for not talking. Don't tell them anything. Hold on!"

"Hold on!" In her half-sleep, her eyes closed, she tried to forget everything except those words. He came back several times after that. The same lament, the same plea. He expressed it with contained passion; one day he wasn't able to speak, he sputtered as he came closer and closer to her, and repeated, "I'm one of the guards. My name is Taleb! My sister, oh, my sister!" and he was trembling like an orphan.

Once she asked him for the date; he didn't know what to say. He couldn't read. But the next time he came, he slipped her a bit of paper on which someone had written in a childish hand "24 May 1956." She had been absorbed by the one word that smiled at her throughout the night, "May, May . . ." and softly told herself, "May, it's springtime everywhere outside." She thought of the end of school, figured out how much time remained; then everything in her aching head became scrambled. As she handed him back the paper, Taleb said it was her tenth night there. How many days had passed since then? She no longer tries to find the answer. She is spent. Because she has no voice, she doesn't want to make the effort anymore. Why place herself somewhere in that black river of time?

The day will come when she'll be thrown back out on the embankment. She'll rest. That will be the end. She'll be able to sleep; sleep.

Taleb has leaned down, looked at her with his staring eyes. "Oh, my sister, my sister! I thank you. You didn't talk. You . . ." Salima suddenly feels sorry for him. Perhaps he's gone mad. She closes her eyes. Taleb turns on his heels; he doesn't know how to be of use and at the same time he's afraid of being caught; anxiety clutches him. He lingers. It is morning; today he's on duty until noon. Salima seems to have fallen asleep. He blesses her gently. He weeps. He goes to the door, leaves.

"I should have tried to thank him," Salima says to herself; her limbs are numb and her head is heavy. "I want so much to sleep!" She doesn't sleep. The carnations come back to her, a clear memory. She had chosen white ones, out of sentimentality, she admits with shame. White like the dress she would have worn had she married. That sunny day when they arrested her, she had felt so lighthearted; ever since morning, since the time she had found the note she'd been waiting for in her letterbox: "Don't forget to buy a bouquet of flowers." These were the words they had agreed upon, the ones she herself had suggested to Mahmoud before he left. "With that I can calm your wife," she'd explained. And in that deep voice she loved, as she could now admit to herself, Mahmoud came back: "Why a bouquet of flowers?"

She had to explain: "I don't know. It just came into my head," then confessed, "I've never bought any flowers for myself. I've always wanted to but never did. The expense bothered me. Our people, we're just not used to doing things like that, you know that. Flowers, books, and a thousand other things, they all seem pointless to us. When we have some extra money, we show our sudden wealth by stuffing ourselves. Sometimes in some homes—so much food! As if they can't get enough of satisfying their hunger."

She was feeling bitter. But Mahmoud was still listening patiently—a brotherly patience, she had no silly illusions, it was the same patience he had for everything he did. "To forget your belly you need money, and you need a whole lot more of it if you want to forget money itself." So they had decided she would buy flowers on the day that he'd let her know he was safe. Then she would immediately let his wife know.

She'd reread the note several times. Her heart was pounding. She rushed out so she wouldn't be late for her class; the principal would have been all too happy to fault her for something. She leapt into a taxi. Another expense! But the sun in the streets was gentle, and the town, known in the region for its roses, smelled like one single enormous spray.

It seemed she had done so many things that day! The taxi stopped in the Arab quarter, not far from Mahmoud's house. Her meeting with his wife, a first cousin of hers, took place in the bedroom. Mahmoud was also a close relative, so working with him wasn't a problem for her at the beginning, because the family bonds protected her. She had begun to feel free and find her natural self again; her austere simplicity would suddenly be broken by a burst of gaiety while with strangers; in spite of her financial independence and her years of experience, she never could rid herself of the somewhat gaunt rigidity that made her look lifeless and ugly, and she knew it.

Mahmoud's wife thanked and kissed her. Salima had to refuse any coffee, pastries, and a thousand other little things that would delay her ("Wait, I'll put some perfume on you. You can't refuse! It's a very happy day for me." "No, please, I'll be late. Thank you, though. No, I can't take anything with me, no cakes, thank you.") She'd left, slightly unnerved. Even more so right afterward when, in front of the taxi, a dark-haired young girl with bright eyes had called out to her.

"Hello! Don't you recognize me?"

"I'm sorry! I rarely come to this area."

"Neither do I," she said. "I don't live here anymore." And since Salima stood there questioningly, she continued, "I'm Touma. Let's see, it's four years now, four years already, my God! You used to come and see us at my mother's house."

"Touma! Of course. How is your mother?"

"How would I know?" she answered and burst out laughing.

"I apologize but I'm in a hurry. Touma . . ."

She'd then forgotten all this, even the girl's shrill burst of laughter in the sun (did she really know her, she couldn't remember). She'd engrossed herself in teaching her courses with cheerful ebullience. She loved her work. When she came home at night, it happened often enough that she felt like screaming, out of solitude ("What do I really have in my life? Why am I not like the rest? Like the others: married, with children who'd preserve the lineage?"). Her features would harden, she'd be somewhere else, no longer even trying to hide her pensiveness from her mother, who was chirping away, from the nephews and nieces around her clamoring for advice, problems to be solved, homework to be corrected. Sometimes she would rise and quickly say "I have work to do!" She'd go to her room, a tiny room in the old house, where for the past two years she'd been able to work alone, light the lamp, open the grubby notebooks of her students, and surrounded by the smell of ink and crumpled paper, the many details of preparing for class—manias she was beginning to cultivate, harshly calling them "my old spinster's habits"—she'd forget everything else.

This is how she forged a world for herself that she knew to be artificial but that connected her to the earlier years of studying, teaching, reading, making the effort: for instance, she perused every pedagogical journal, ordered them from France, and stayed informed about new methods. In the moments of relaxed conversation that ended their meetings in Algiers, where she would go every Thursday, she'd say to Mahmoud, "One day, after our independence, we'll be needing these methods!" He'd answer, offer statistics, and ask for specific details about her readings, which she gave him, and admiring her constant openness to the slightest problems, he would immediately consider them in the light of the future they foresaw.

Lying on the bed without a blanket, but no longer cold, Salima thinks of the elated sweetness she'd managed to conceal that inhabited her during the time she worked with Mahmoud. Mindful, she noticed everything about him, his caution, his swift decision-making, but his warmth as well, and the somewhat bitter ardor he sometimes let shine through in her presence. He valued her. He felt a protective attachment to her that wasn't justified by family relationship alone; it had the same affectionate quality he showed toward his wife, his sisters, and perhaps his children. Outside this bond, he was possessed only by an abstract and overarching passion—which was in no way as emphatic as one usually would expect in a political leader—when he spoke of the future.

It was that controlled enthusiasm that she loved in him. No, she couldn't ascribe her attachment to Mahmoud to her own emotional void. Of course, it was hard for her not to feel smothered at times when the sensation of slipping into the darkness seized her, when she saw herself forever pursuing the same monotonous path. (But if not for him, what else would she have been if not a passive and useless object?) She shifts on her bed, tries to escape from the strain of her thoughts. Yet how precious these reflections, these memories, seem to her! For she is certain of one thing. It wasn't her spinster's sadness, that slight mustiness at the bottom of her heart, that grew confused when she was with Mahmoud. (How many times had his name come up in the interrogations! His photos, endless details, so the police really did know everything about him! But it was too late!) She repeats the precious word, *future*, that sky blue opening as it appeared in Mahmoud's speeches and in his hasty, impatient monologues. A stranger might consider them naive, but she was convinced that the heart of the revolution really lay there, in that almost sad exhilaration. The future . . . that fundamental word connected her to Mahmoud.

Then calm invaded her. She loved the truth, especially finding it alone after explorations such as these, groping around for a long time because her thinking was slow and burdened with scruples. "I'm not in love with him," she concluded. "I'm attached to him. That's not the same thing."

She finally fell asleep, on a bed, for the first time, after two weeks of interrogation.

•••

Shortly thereafter, they come to wake Salima. They tell her nothing. "It's starting again," she thinks. She gets up. Two men in front of her. She doesn't look at them, struggles against a dizzy spell. She goes out behind them. Through the long hallway again. How many times has she been through here? She remembers that at some point she was interrogated two or three times on the same day; now she says to herself, "They wanted to catch me through fatigue," as if the thought could help her emerge from her first haze.

How long has she slept? Certainly not very long. She glances through the wide windows of a hallway. Across the street she notices the gray facade of the girls' boarding school. "My old school," she thinks, "and here I am, right across the street." Suddenly it seems to her that it was only yesterday; yesterday, endless hours of courses in which she felt alone, bracing herself for the effort. "I have to pass the entrance exam for the teachers' college," "I have to stay up to write this composition tonight, but where?" Often she was the only one to catch the whispering of some unprincipled girls behind her. "They're so stuck-up," she'd say to herself, concentrating with a frown. Her teacher facing her, a mature city type who at times avoided her, sliding her gaze up and down over her long braids ("Moorish style," a young beauty, coming to class in high heels at age fourteen, once mocked behind her back), over her too-dark complexion ("Perhaps she's got black blood, too," she'd hear as she passed by). And then Salima would tense up again, having chosen once and for all to persevere, to continue in spite of everything—the contempt of these foreign girls, the indifference of her own people—in spite of so many other obstacles. Her present rigidity, and more specifically her air of severe rectitude, was what was left of her opinionated, adolescent silence, at a time when the dominant impression was one of choking, but with clenched teeth.

Was that period really only yesterday? It was fifteen or sixteen years ago. At the time she was the only Muslim girl in town to continue her studies. Her father died when she was at the age to be cloistered like the others; a bit of luck, in short. But her mother and all the rest of them remained the responsibility of an uncle who was hardly well off. Did she really have to learn humility? She saw herself again at age fifteen, deciding, swearing, since she was the oldest, that she would "behave like a man." She'd confront any difficulty so she could take care of the rest of her family as soon as possible.

What she remembers of that time is not just the willpower that sculpted her—no, that disfigured her by forcing her to become independent in spite of herself, while like so many others she would otherwise have become effaced and sweet—but a sense of pride. The first time she felt that pride was when she left high school, her diploma secured, and then again later, under similar circumstances. She'd always been gripped by the conceit of believing herself to be the delegate of her people to another world.

After all, yes, she'd proved herself to be faithful to her oath: she'd behaved like "a man." It's the same brave, tough stand she now takes—she thinks of the coincidence—in this building across from the other one. Pride ("You and your pride!" the commissioner had said during one of the interrogations; it comes back to her now) is her best weapon in the end. A somewhat anonymous pride, she realizes, that doesn't come from the depths of her own being (for if she had listened to her secret self, it was undoubtedly just a calm and passive water that would have flowed, surged up in her, would have swallowed her, who knows), but from other people: from her widowed mother, drained from the many tasks she once accepted doing in the homes of the bourgeoisie; from her imprisoned brother, sentenced six years ago and transported someplace in France; from all the silenced women she used to know. It was an armor given her by the whole town (she still believed in this idea, even though she sensed its naïveté), and though it ground her down, depleted her, it was also a very precious burden! And it was good this way.

"I'm just a link in the chain," a phrase she uttered to Mahmoud one day, the day of his departure. She repeated it when they made her go into the office she recognized all too well—it even seemed to her as if it were a familiar place from her childhood; her eyes dazzled by the light of the lamp deliberately directed at her, she'd spent so many interminable hours here that they seemed to be displayed across her entire memory.

The chief of police—a sharp face with desiccated features, a long nose, an air of defeated refinement—still behind his wide desk as if he'd never moved, with the same persistent stolidity he had put on to besiege her with questions, for hours and hours on end, never seeming to grow tired. His same questions. Then different ones. Then he'd talk ("You see, we know everything"). The tone of his voice didn't change.

In the beginning he seemed to try to vary his repertoire to shake her up. But very quickly he had to limit himself to a haughty attitude that he intended to be frightening in its coldness, a formal propriety that was his by nature. He left the other roles to his aides: vulgar familiarity (and Salima ready to come right back: "I ask you not to address me so informally!"), seductive intimacy ("Mahmoud is just my cousin!"), threats ("I'm not afraid. Why don't you just torture me?"). Then the police chief would freeze up. As if he suddenly felt it no longer concerned him, as if he were assessing the true value of the absence of limits to which his yes-men would go. When he resumed, alone with her, she stiffened with even greater effort, and he knew it, perhaps flattered, before he went on with the interrogation in that affected tone of excessive worldliness he claimed as his own.

Toward the end, however, around the tenth day, he had dropped that tone. He seemed tired; with scathing irascibility, he began to toss out his questions, the same ones, his attempts at persuasion along with photographs ("I don't know any of these people! I don't know who's in charge of the network in town! No! I won't say anything! I don't know anything!"). "You and your pride!" he had suddenly cried out, in a lackluster voice. He was weakening.

Then they had pushed her outside. They would move on to a second round, she told herself; she was sure of it. And that is when the brutality would commence. Why not? She was expecting it. They had left her alone then, not in her cell but in a hallway. She looked at the sky—suddenly happy, given over to a feeling of plenitude that had unfolded within her, which seemed to prepare her for that location in her soul where she could strive to deal with torture. Whispering sounds reached her through the half-open door of an office. Then the voice of the chief, Jean, exploded.

"I'm sorry!" he yelled. So he, too, could yell. "I won't do it to women. No! Not in my building. Not here!"

More whispering. Again, she and the chief before her. He had looked up at her. She understood. For the first time (in ten days she had become familiar with his mask) she saw him pale, with clenched teeth; an imperceptible shiver he tried to suppress ran across his face. "A vanquished face," she thought. Suddenly she'd felt like saying something. Had he touched her? "He does have principles," she said to herself. She stared at him. On the other side of the wide desk, under the white light that separated them from its pool and that he had no intention of turning off, Jean had thought that Salima had a new look in her eyes.

"I thank you, sir!" she'd announced without a smile.

"That damned way I always have of being sentimental," she thinks now, sitting down on the same chair, facing the same desk. She regrets the words. They seem improper to her, as if they had taken on the significance of a confession. These words linked her to this man, if only for a second, and that brief intimacy, provoked by her clumsiness, irritates her.

Jean, the chief, looks her up and down. Accustomed as he was to examining her in the white circle of the lamp above her, he finds her to be different. "She's not attractive," he thinks, but his gaze lingers on Salima's stubborn forehead, on her overly large eyes. "She's the stronger one," he thinks again and that grim idea will never leave him.

"We're done interrogating you, mademoiselle. Therefore . . ." He continues in a cold voice, as if forced to say an early good-bye in someone's living room. All the same, he adds some details, some further comments: everything was properly done, she won't need to lodge any complaints. He is reading the indictment against her out of pure kindness, for it is what the judge should do.

Salima listens without answering. Jean continues with the same patience: She will see her lawyer today.

"My lawyer?" she exclaims. And says to herself, "One of their lawyers."

"He's been asking to be in touch with you for a long time now. We didn't think it wise . . ."

He stops; the door opens. They are calling for the chief. He controls a rush of irritation. There's a lot of work; he wishes it were possible for him to finish his task with every suspect to the very end, continue to the very end with the same punishing game, this subterfuge, with the other person or with himself. "You won't need to lodge any complaints." It's not often that he speaks these words to a headstrong woman, but rather to men, whose faces are usually still swollen, and that's not the worst of it. Brought in by his deputies, they sometimes appear to be whole but are devoid of any substance. He knows this to be true. He continues his fool's game.

"Just a moment, I'm not done here!"

"They need you, Chief," Captain Martinez, his deputy, answers. "Excuse me," Jean says mechanically as he turns to Salima and, she thinks, barely suppresses a small bow, swept up in spite of himself in that bit of ludicrous courtesy.

The door stays open. She waits. She looks around. The chief does not return. "They've forgotten about me," she thinks and sighs. She wants to get back to the bed as quickly as possible, sleep as long as possible! She gets up. Never sit on a chair again! Her back still hurts. She takes a few steps forward under the sudden impression that she is free, that she's merely stopped by this office for a visit. The door is ajar. She goes to it, stops. She gives a start.

Stunned, then horrified. Like ice. She goes back to her chair and slowly sits down. "Too late!" and she sees Touma's face again. "The young girl I met that morning, who approached me . . ." Touma, in the next room, hadn't seen her. She was chatting, laughing; her mouth open to the man, no doubt Captain Martinez. Touma . . . What's she doing here? Salima remembers some of the things said during the interrogation:

"You've been seen more than once in the capital, on a Thursday."

"You've been seen more than once at the house of Mahmoud's family." ("He's a relative of mine," "His wife is my cousin," she answered doggedly.) "You've been . . ." Salima is still sitting. She feels faint. Cold.

But her common sense gets the better of her: "What's wrong with you? That girl, she's not your sister . . . and even if she were, the only comrades these days are those who share the struggle. These days . . ." She talks to herself, and consoles herself, so to speak, as she discovers, even greater than her disturbing surprise, a new and ignorant part of her heart: all she has experienced in life is exertion, hesitation, quest, but never ("No, never!" a fervent voice inside her repeats), never betrayal.

• • •

"What time is it?" Hakim asks the driver curtly, while the jeep heads for the police station after its long detour through the center of town.

"Eleven o'clock, sir."

"It's very hot this morning. The sirocco will be here in the next few days."

"Yes, sir."

Hakim looks at the new prison in the distance, the offices of the chief, of his colleagues, and of his own, on the second floor. He wants to get back there. Quickly write up his report and then close the door and be left alone. He won't go home at noon. Amna won't be waiting for him; she's used to it.

In front of the high school he thinks of his daughter. She began there this year. He registered her as a boarder. Every Sunday he goes to pick her up and bring her home, feeling happy and proud.

"Should I stop here or go to the garage?" the driver asks.

"Stop."

Hakim jumps out. Stepping lively, he enters the station. "My report," he thinks, "my report." He can already hear himself addressing Jean, the chief, in his own neutral voice.

"The previously mentioned Youssef was home last night. I am sure of it."

"Then there's just one left on the list of suspects?" He'll complete his report with a few remarks, a few suggestions. Perhaps he'll add, "I know the man personally," and will draw a detailed portrait of him to show how intelligent he is. And his boss, who respects him, he knows, will say once again, "Keep going . . . I trust you."

"Excuse me, Inspector." A young, sardonic voice. Touma stands before him, having bumped into him on the stairs.

"That one again!" he thinks with disgruntlement. He doesn't like her. He doesn't trust her. "Girls, whores, acting like informants, we know what that's worth . . ." He grumbles a hello and passes by. But behind his back, arrogantly, is Touma's voice: "What about our little business, Inspector?" She bursts out laughing, a happy, sustained laughter, whose youthfulness scatters through the gray hallways, which normally resound with the echo of individuals swallowed up—far off inside the prison, from the world of interrogated suspects. Touma's laughter rises to the ceiling as she continues down the stairs on her high heels.

"Whore!" Hakim insults her in Arabic. "Dirty whore!"

Outside, bored with waiting, the driver takes pleasure in watching the figure of the girl who teeters for a moment at the top of the steps that lead to the front entrance and then, in spite of the heat, starts out on a casual walk toward town.

"Suzanne, it's you, of course."

Lila lets her friend in. Suzanne immediately notices the bare walls, the sparse furniture.

"It's almost cold here."

Lila doesn't answer.

"What possessed you to come and live here? All by yourself. You're alone, aren't you?"

Lila still doesn't say anything. Smiles. She had forgotten that she sent Suzanne a letter the day she moved. She had been seized by a desire to write, to convince herself that Ali had really left, that she was indeed alone and that in her solitude she wouldn't be able to adjust to the capital city, which was too large. She needed the familiar scenery of her youth. She had written and sent the note, then gone back up to the sepulchre of her room.

Suzanne checks it out, wandering around the apartment, exclaims, asks questions. Happy, Lila follows her.

"That letter, it took me a while to find your address, you know. I'd already torn up the envelope."

Lila turns her head away. A letter. It was more like a cry. For many long years she's made it a habit to ponder her relationship with Suzanne this way. Egotistically, she conceives of friendship as she does love—as a mirror meant to return her own image, more real than it is in the void of loneliness. Protective as well.

There are so many memories that attach Lila to Suzanne, from childhood and high school on. It just so happened that for six years they didn't see and hardly spoke to each other. Then, in the end, it took just one exchange to reconnect. Since that time, each absorbed in her own private affairs and in spite of the separation, in spite of life, or its semblance, a constancy has linked them and brings them back together, one on one, quite alike. Lila needs the stability; she is grateful to Suzanne as for an inexhaustible offering.

With every incident in her love life, when Ali seemed to be vanishing and with him all connections, when he was becoming the other, the enemy, the stranger, Lila would flap her wings, lurching pitifully. A call to Suzanne. A visit. A note, a phone call. All Lila wanted was Suzanne's presence, Suzanne's attention, Suzanne's silence, so she could then better listen to herself. She'd complain about Ali, his inquisitive jealousy, his impossible mulishness—but soon her reproaches would be replaced by self-criticism, for she liked to condemn herself, and lucidly, too, when she hoped for indulgence in return. Other people's indulgence, Suzanne's, and sadly—why not—Ali's. "He judges me, and I don't want to be judged," she complained with the face of a spoiled child. Her grief was already beginning to fade. Suzanne smiled, consoled her, without ever entering into her maze.

Lila would often phone once Suzanne had come to live in town, where her husband, Omar, was a lawyer.

"Suzanne?" Lila's voice in the distance sounded plaintive. "I'm calling . . ." And Suzanne, motherly as she caressed her daughter Nadia's curls:

"What's wrong?"

"Nothing. I'm down. I wanted . . . I wanted to hear your voice!" Suzanne listened patiently, then remembered she had forgotten the milk on the stove or the iron on the table: "Wait a second."

"Yes." Lila obliged. A minute later Suzanne came back and ("so openly good, truly good, just like Ali," Lila thought, half consoled) gently inquired: "How's Ali?"

"Fine, fine," Lila stammered. ("I'm not really going to describe the scene we had over the phone.")

"I'm hanging up now. See you soon! Hugs."

Suzanne would laugh. When Omar came home later, she enjoyed telling him about their conversation—Lila's small voice far away, Lila submerged in the capital, in her entanglements, her delayed adolescent hesitancies, and finally the self-examination she shouldered so clumsily but with such passion. Omar didn't understand. "Just childish!" he decided, with a severity that Suzanne found unfair. He had a tendency to be absolute and cutting about others and she couldn't tolerate it very well. She persisted in trying to explain Lila and not only out of friendship but also because she wanted to penetrate this man's deep-seated strength that had once attracted her—but that she now took for a wall.

"You're so rigid," she said to him calmly and coolly, because she was falling out of love with him and sensed it ever more inescapably. "You're inflexible. You're sectarian."

Omar who couldn't tolerate such reproaches, would get up and leave. Never any scenes for them; at most some elucidation. The desert between them was already laid out and prevented any entanglements, any wrenching.

In the empty room that her arrival fills, Suzanne does her best to forget her own anxiety and continues her conversation with the newfound Lila.

"I'll make you some coffee."

"No, I'll do it. It will be better and it gives me a chance to wait on you." As she answers, Suzanne vaguely thinks, "Our old words and habits are still so soothing." She goes to the kitchen and in passing gives a quick caress to Lila, who affectionately repeats, "It's so good to see you again," and to herself, "My days have been so empty. So long and so empty!"

From the kitchen Suzanne asks, "How long have you been living here?"

"A week, maybe two. I don't really remember," Lila mutters; she's dreaming. Suzanne has opened the door to a forgotten rhythm.

"What do you pay a month for this prison?"

Lila answers without even moving ("Yes, Suzanne brought peace and harmony with her . . ."), inhales the smell of the coffee. Suzanne comes back in, a tray in her hand, prepares the table, serves Lila and then herself.

"And I bet you don't even go out . . ."

"No. Why should I? Where would I go?" Lila sighs. Suzanne chides her, begins a very serious sermon in which she mentions Lila's sluggishness, Lila's nonchalance, her weakness, her cowardice.

"Cowardly? You really think so?" Lila worries, and Suzanne bursts out laughing, abandoning her zealous mock authority.

"No, look, let's really talk: what are your plans?"

"My plans . . ."

"You're going to have to go to work because you really don't want to stay here. You should find a teaching job for the next school year, right?"

"Yes, I should, of course, in principle." Her same indecisive answers; suddenly, with tears in her eyes, Lila bursts out:

"I don't know . . . I haven't thought of anything without . . ."

Suzanne strikes.

"Without Ali?"

Then Lila cries.

"Good God!" Suzanne thinks. "A breakdown; here's the defeat, and here's the child inside her, for all to see. Laid bare her unquenched thirst for some presence to protect or shackle her." Lila weeps with what is now a certain solace. She takes out her handkerchief, blows her nose, cries again; her tears won't stop. She attempts a smile through her sobs—a grimace. She apologizes. It's been so long since she's heard anyone speak out loud about Ali, it seems to her; she, too, had wanted to pronounce his name. She couldn't. She tries to smile, blows her nose again, but still can't stop whimpering.

"Please excuse me, always those tear ducts of mine, you know!"

(She laughs through her tears.) "It's no joke to cry so easily. At the movies, for instance, I always make a fool of myself." Suzanne gets up. Lila: "No! No! I'll calm down. Pour me another coffee, all right? Yes, it's good . . . you make it so well!" She calms down, tries to understand.

"What I've noticed is that when I'm alone, when I don't want to see anybody, reality vanishes, dissipates. Where my son is concerned" (she stops, doesn't say his name, cannot do it), "someone would barely utter his name in my presence and I'd break down in tears. Still, I'm not really all that sensitive!"

"But your husband is alive," Suzanne exclaims, "very much alive!"

Lila starts to cry again. "Here I go again, my God! I'm going to get tired of these tears. I assure you . . ."

Near her, Suzanne takes a handkerchief, wipes Lila's cheeks and forehead.

"I assure you," Lila protests with a pale smile, but tears still streaming, "I'm not suffering all that much now."

"Cry your heart out once and for all; just let go. It'll do you good, you'll see!"

Lila puts her head on Suzanne's lap. "This feels so good," she says to herself, lying on the bed like that, and through her tears she delights in smelling the persistent aroma of the coffee and Suzanne's usual perfume next to her and tasting her own tears all at the same time. "It feels so good to let yourself go like this, close in the care of someone who's willing to be there for you! It feels so good to give in to sleep, so sweet to let all the unremembered knots inside loosen up, to . . ."

Suzanne watches her friend doze off. She is weary. She, too, wishes she could bathe in tears, let herself be submerged like Lila in half-true puerility; find herself stripped of the past and its shadows! She envies the strength in her friend that can suddenly put her back on an even keel after she seemed so exhausted and lost in the soul's thousand windstorms (so laughable and meager, after all,

Suzanne decided). Ah! she wishes she, too, could seem overcome for a while, like Lila, who had the willpower to lock herself up in this gloomy place, blinded and paralyzed for a moment before waking up again. (Suzanne knows her so well: all this is just a pause she unconsciously wrought for herself to catch her breath, and then she'll notice that only her self-centeredness, her nonchalance, had delayed her on her way.) Arch her back, and then, while others were thinking she was stifling—as she once was in her happiness, then in her motherhood, and now in her solitude ("Lila, so completely not made to be alone, to live alone . . .")—she would be reborn. She would be vibrant. Suddenly her words, her silence, everything would light up in her. And this raw youthfulness caused people to forgive her the rest.

Lila characterized Suzanne as "strong." ("You're an adult," she liked to say. "A real woman, the way I'd like to be. Really serious, keeping your calm. That's real maturity, isn't it? Self-control. Yes. I envy you . . ." and Lila would again start her sometimes-so-tiring game, "I'm really a sad case! And since nobody wants to pity me, not even Ali, who's always criticizing me, who loves me so he can criticize me, I'll just pity myself!" and she'd keep on simpering.) Suzanne watches her sleeping friend. She can't rid herself of her own fatigue. She feels bitter and hard.

Alone, as well. She hadn't told Lila, what was the use? True solitude was just that: not being able to talk about it. How could she divulge it the way she'd done with the others the past few weeks: "Omar is in France." And then the response was, "Of course, he's in danger here, they would end up arresting him." Some poor women would come right to her house. "Si Omar is gone? What do we do now? They've caught my son! I have no news of him. What do I do now? Si Omar is the only Arab lawyer in town." They'd leave. New ones would come. Suzanne would close the door and take care of Nadia (she was two now and becoming so lovely), trying with difficulty to erase the resentment that had been building up for so long ("How long!" her heart would sigh) against Omar. Why did she see his departure as flight, something she had felt from the very start? Moreover, she had told him so.

"We had an argument." She, too, could blame herself; but Lila sleeps and Suzanne would have kept silent anyway. Whatever she feels, whatever she does, she won't be able to burst into tears, let herself go; whatever the presence beside her, she will continue to be mired in her loneliness.

Omar wanted Suzanne and Nadia to leave with him. "No," Suzanne had replied. And Omar knew it would always be no. "Our place, for all of us, is here! This is not a time to leave. No." She had repeated it, oh, very calmly; she didn't have enough violence in her to give her decisions any appearance of bravado.

Omar had left at dawn. They had talked all through the night. She, still distant, and he with a note of vehemence in his words, startled at something she'd say, too cutting, as was his wont, but a second later containing himself, confronted with his wife's eyes, where lately he feared he saw anger.

"I want to know what happened between you and Mahmoud," Suzanne stubbornly insisted. She felt that was the key: Mahmoud, Omar's political comrade, his former study mate, more than a brother to him. But Omar dodged the question.

"Nothing," he said, "nothing important!" Then he lost his temper. "I'm not at Mahmoud's beck and call!"

Suzanne kept staring at him, mumbled:

"I want to understand! Why are you leaving? You're in danger, but no more so now than a few months ago. If so, I'd be the first to suggest that you leave town!" Then with a last bit of hope: "At least here you're defending other people! You're helping the victims, if not the fighters and the revolution. Defending one out of ten, twenty, a hundred; I've no illusions, but it's still something, isn't it?"

Omar was annoyed with her logic; it was accurate: he was fleeing. Or actually, no, in his desire to reinforce the certainty of his decision he corrected himself, he was holding to his position. He had defended it to Mahmoud; he would defend it to others, elsewhere.

"I want to understand," Suzanne almost implored, then, softer, "I'm staying; I won't leave, I won't."

Omar, still filled with the desire to take her, bring her along (she, his lighthouse, his tree, his sword held out before him for the future), answered sharply:

"Stay if you must."

"Don't worry." Still in her nightgown, Suzanne stood up, tucked in their daughter, came back to him, "I'll stay here even if it takes ten years. If I leave you one day" (she had spoken without looking at him, but very calmly), "I won't divorce you until it's all over, when the end has come, when the country is free."

He left the next morning. "I'll write you. I'll send you my address in France," was all he said. A kiss on Suzanne's forehead as if he were going to work, as if he were coming home for lunch at noon. Nadia was still sleeping, and it seemed that in Omar's leaving the little one his expression was more pained. At the last moment, Suzanne was afraid she'd weaken.

"Do you really want to stay?" (Was this an appeal? His tone was so light!)

She nodded affirmatively, without a word, then had the strength to smile: at her past, her youth, her old battles (against her parents, with whom she'd broken when she married, against so many other prejudices), and especially at her dying love. But so many things were disappearing, she thought, as she went to wake up her daughter, who would need to be calmed during the next few days when she wanted her father.

• • •

"I'd like to explain to you," Lila had retorted, "that ever since I've been here, in this empty house, I've been looking for . . ." She was justifying herself.

"I'm not trying to excuse myself, I'm searching, that's all . . . and . . ." She begins again more softly (at the same time, she gets up, brusquely opens the shutters, as if all of life will suddenly come in through the open window, like a trembling bird with broken wings): "I'm angry with him! That's wrong of me, I know. It comes, no doubt, from some inadequacy inside myself, something deeply rooted I can't quite identify. No doubt!" She stops, turns her back to the deep blue sky. "He left, you see, he chose to leave! I couldn't help myself but thought right away, and have been thinking ever since, 'What about me?'" (She's furious). "At ten in the morning he tells me he's leaving at noon! Two hours later! I let him talk, then yelled, 'And what about me?'" She screams now, "What about me?"

Listening, knowing that Lila is only addressing Ali now, addressing the desertion of that day at ten in the morning, Suzanne repeats in a whisper: "He's gone!"

"He didn't forgive me for what I said. The next two hours were spent arguing. Not even, more like a conversation between deaf people. 'You have the gall to think only of yourself when right now the world around you . . .'" (she makes an exasperated gesture). "The speech of a true radical, and to me, me, his own wife! I didn't answer; I listened to him calling me every name in the book: self-centered, indifferent, bourgeois, conservative . . . on and on."

Suzanne laughs; Lila almost does: having just barely avowed her anger and resentment out loud, she realizes that they've vanished completely. She stops, looks at Suzanne. "I'm boring you, I'm sorry." And answering this bit of coquettishness, Suzanne says, "Oh, please, that's what I'm here for." She really believes it. At that moment, thinking herself at an impasse, Lila needs her. "But is she really lovesick?" Suzanne wonders.

"Yes," Lila continues, "in the end it was all just a pretext. We'd been living side by side for such a long time, no longer immersed in one another, hostile even. I let it all come apart! What was the use of saying to him, 'Let me go with you! Let me participate in what you're doing!' as he was leaving? There was no place for me in his activities; I'd neglected to find a place there for myself. He'd come up with this adventure on his own, like a stage where he needed to test himself again, but alone, without daring to say to himself, 'Free from her.' Perhaps I was a burden to him?"

Suzanne starts to protest, but it isn't worth it. She should let Lila search, unravel by herself all the cords that are presently keeping her immobilized and from which she's been trying to free herself for the past hour in the bright light of day. As she came in, Suzanne had mentioned the funeral she had come across at the front door and Lila had answered, "To depart like that in the sun, how lucky!"

"I let him leave me without protesting! You can't go back very far in time in two hours, and darkness came between us at the very moment that we should have cleared it away. I didn't want to say anything" (she grumbles); "he already saw me awaiting his return with the patience of a submissive wife. He gave his orders: come to this town and stay with his sister (I haven't set foot in her house yet), find a teaching position. He was in such a hurry to leave me with his conscience clear, but first he had to put me up somewhere! And I who cry so easily, I said good-bye to him with dry eyes. I thought I hated him! Well, there you have it," she finishes.

Silence. Suzanne doesn't move. She gives Lila another cup of coffee, reheated while her friend was waking up. She smokes another cigarette. "That's it!" Lila says again. She snaps out of it, sits down on the floor, feels relieved.

"Why don't you come and live with me?"

"With you?"

"I'm alone with my daughter. Omar isn't there. Yes . . . he's in France."

Lila hesitates.

"No, I don't want to be in your way. No . . . I'll see."

"You're not going to stay here all summer like this in this spooky apartment."

"You don't think so?" Her voice is like that of a sick person waking up from a long coma. Lila doesn't know how to conceal her uncertainty. She gets up, closes the window. What else is there to do?

"I'll come and see you," she promises, thinking that this way she'll have time to come slowly out of the oasis. For she will have to pick up her life again, won't she, with careful steps. She'll have to . . .

Suzanne has started to talk again. About others. About the town, people who are growing accustomed to the war. Then: "You remember Salima?"

"Of course."

"She was arrested the day before yesterday. Her mother came looking for Omar. I recognized her. I made it my business to call a lawyer in the city. Yesterday he tried to get some news of her by phone. So far nothing yet. He'll come to our town as soon as he's able to get in touch with her."

Salima arrested? How long has it been since Lila has seen her? They used to meet from time to time, because of some distant family relationship, at the home of friends. In spite of a mutual interest, they had remained distant. Lila regretted it: Salima, all tense and shy, and Lila, a very obvious veil of inattention over her face, smiling so spontaneously that it stunned people ("I'd like so much for you to come and see me at my house, since you often come to Algiers!") but she'd forget to give her address. At that point Salima would think, "She seems sincere," but then warily, "No, it's just out of social decency, and I'm being taken in by it!"

"I should go and see her mother," Lila decides. Suzanne is caught by surprise, and is about to ask why. Then she answers:

"She's a relative of yours, isn't she?"

"Yes, by marriage. Every family here is more or less related."

"Oh!" Suzanne delves no further. She has never understood Lila's preoccupation with holding on to family ties. She had seen that same gregarious affection for the ancestral tribe in Omar, in Mahmoud himself. She had wanted to make fun of it once, but had encountered such offended surprise in the two men that she'd suddenly felt isolated in this community, which before, from the outside, had seemed so simplistic, because all she could see was its faults. Since then, she tells herself without any irritability, she has learned about its internal laws as well as its dirt.

"Yes, you really should see her!" she says, "She must be very anxious. As for material worries, I'll take care of that. I should meet with Salima's principal, her superintendent, that could be useful."

Suzanne is so thoughtful. Lila admires her. As she sees her to the door, she tries to think of what to say, thank her, tell her that it was a good thing to have come to see her this morning, that she's suddenly opened everything up and erased the shadows, that friendship brings fresh air and all else dies away. She'd like to say . . . She smiles. "I will come! I promise," she says, and closes the door again.

• • •

Amna hasn't budged. The door is still open. The sun, now almost at its zenith, hits the room from all sides. Satisfied, the baby dozes on the broad lap of his mother. Amna is breathing hard, eyes straight ahead, lost in the obscured underbrush of her soul. Cherifa has gone out. She didn't hear her leave. She is alone.

Across from her on the mountain, whose dark, blue-tinged peaks she can see from where she sits, the spectacle goes on. Planes still sketch uninterrupted arcs in the sky; one can imagine homes burning; all this accompanied by an undertone of curses from the other women in neighboring houses, open, like hers—rooms, courtyards, and silence—to the distant drama. But Amna isn't watching; she barely flinches when a burst of gunfire deafens the area with its nearby roar.

Hassan and Hossein have come in slowly, on tiptoe, one behind the other. They don't understand; their eyes have that shocked look characteristic of children who are more used to unchanging habits than to anything else. Why did Cherifa send them away? She usually keeps them so close, even lets them fall asleep in her room before she brings the entwined little bodies back to their mother for the night. They're bewildered. Cherifa had been restless. "Your mother! Your mother!" Standing in the door, she called them; equally lost in contemplating the planes in the sky, they got up, crossed the courtyard, as Cherifa supervised them from her place and whispered:

"Your mother is waiting for you."

Now, here they are. Amna doesn't raise her eyes, doesn't look at them. "Come now, sit down!" she says in a voice that troubles them. Hassan starts crying spitefully, and then his brother does the same. Their mother's voice, elsewhere, as if she is immersed in some battle from which she cannot extricate herself, starts up a lullaby that rocks her own soul to sleep, with the perplexed children before her. "Come, Hassan, Hossein!" She repeats their names, dwelling on the consonants. They approach and sit down. Amna's hands look for them: "Come close, closer to me!"

They drag their feet a bit on the tiles. Each one, beside a motherly knee, looks at his sleeping brother, a drop of milk still hanging on his lips. In the middle of the group Amna once again becomes a tree, spreading out all its branches. There won't be anything else; why this fear, this anxiety drumming away? There won't be any more blasts of wind.

More gunfire. Hassan begins to cry. He's not afraid. He's bored. Amna looks at him. "You'll wake up your brother!" she says, but doesn't really reprimand him.

Hassan stops; his mouth is open, his eyes follow a fly buzzing around him, then the flight of those insects on the horizon, whose humming one could almost hear in the questioning hollows of the silence that weighs ever more heavily on them. Amna sighs, a deep sigh into which she dives, from which she then emerges, still sorrowful.

"My little ones," she moans, raising her arms in a single movement and placing her hands, still a little swollen and red from last night's laundry, on the heads of the twins. "My little ones!" the now recognizable voice repeats and on their heads the children rediscover the weight of the protection they need. Amna puts her hands back on her knees; an ample but peaceful Madonna, she once again lifts her eyes to the suffering mountain.

With the children gone, Cherifa has lowered the curtains over her door. Now she paces the room. "What to do, what to do?" she says and wrings her hands, trembling with helplessness in the half-dark. "I have to do something, I have to . . ." She checks the time. "A quarter to eleven! Eleven! I have to do something!"

She sits down, stretches her willpower to make her mind go blank; to catch the decision by surprise: she wants to act. A strange desire overtakes and worries her, to do something, something daring whose luminosity will astound Youssef. What she's looking for, and doesn't yet dare see herself, is not so much to save Youssef (it seems to her that Youssef won't need anybody, that he'll be able to handle any danger alone) as to find a new way to reach him. The usual paths of their mutual trust, the sensitivity they agree upon, have been exhausted—a smile, a halting phrase hanging in the air that already finds its echo in the other. She straightens up again, wants to be as clear as on the day when, panting, after her flight, leaning against the door to her room, she had tried to grasp what she needed to do next. "I have to act," she says cautiously, invaded by a vague fear.

For a happy wife, living inside a house she never leaves, as tradition has prescribed, how for the first time to decide to *act*? How to act? It's a foreign word for someone imprisoned in custom (and to experience that custom as an instinct, as if every woman in her family, in the neighboring homes, in all the previous generations, had bequeathed it to her in the form of imperative wisdom). The custom of having that behavior be intended only for a man, the husband, the father, or the brother, of being able to glimpse the thousand incidents in life only through the shelter of his authority, through the mirror of his judgment. It is a new word toward which fate is pushing her ("fate, really?") and suddenly she sees it emerge, rich in promises and results: "Me, act? Me?" Perhaps that's what Cherifa is telling herself; perhaps she takes herself for a person at ease with the semidarkness, accidentally thrown into the sun and then overcome by the intuition that she cannot be satisfied with the light that blinds her but must also create a new step, a new approach—a different way of seeing, being seen; of existing.

"I must warn Youssef! Hakim is going to come back; maybe he'll discover that his wife was lying. Maybe they won't need any proof to arrest him. Maybe . . ." But Cherifa no longer needs to dwell on words. She has made her decision. Motionless, she still trembles: an arrow about to be launched.

She rises, opens her armoire, takes out several white silk veils and chooses the oldest among them. The wide mirror stands across the entrance, immense. Just this morning she had removed the white sheet that had covered it since Lla Aicha's death as a sign of mourning. She wraps herself in front of it, leaving only her eyes visible. She scrutinizes herself, fears for a moment that her hesitation or audacity can be seen in her eyes: it is the first time she has gone out alone, and alone into the heart of the town.

Amna, her children around her, is too absorbed to see Cherifa pass. But she does hear the front door close: she's not going to look. What does it all matter to her, the street, the house, Cherifa? Amna is looking only for peace; just peace.

•••

The old Arab quarter is connected to the center of the city by a street heavily congested in the morning with vegetable stalls and carts. When by late morning and in the afternoon the Moorish cafés that line both sides of the street have their tables and chairs out on the sidewalk, one has to wend one's way through two thick rows of either noisy or dozing café-goers. They play cards, dominos, checkers; or else they dream alone in front of the only cup of Turkish coffee they can afford—another day in their blank time of perpetual unemployment. Nevertheless, when a women happens to pass by, more often than not a girl from a poor neighborhood on her way to a cleaning job, all of them turn their heads to the road with the same watchful curiosity. With the same practiced glance at her veil, her gait, her ankles, her eyes, they recognize the walking woman.

Middle-class women actually never frequent the streets in the center of town. When a woman must go out—only to go to the baths or for special ceremonies, parties, or days of mourning—the escorting spouse walks in front of her and guides her by a roundabout route to the appointed place. When he has to take her to the other side of town where an area of private homes surrounded by gardens is located behind the new prison, he has her make a very wide detour along the river to avoid the center.

Cherifa walks the long street for the first time. Her slow, lightly balanced tread is going to attract the gaze of the men on the terraces, who are playing, talking, or drinking tea or coffee. Cherifa's heart beats in haste and shame and she stares at the end of the street as if it were her salvation. She wishes she could walk serenely and indifferently, as she used to on holidays, but her veil is no protection for her. She walks straight, her step is regular; already eyes are looking up at her, imagining her as a languid figure, wandering around in the sun. They notice her slim ankles, her shoes that have not been worn down—these aren't old-women's slippers—her silk veil that differs from what the river girls wear. Last, they see her rigidity, the staring eyes that make no contact; these, too, every one of the onlookers notices.

At the Palais d'Orient, the largest of the Moorish cafés, which Cherifa now approaches, the Chicou brothers sit at the table closest to the street. They start their daily game of checkers. As on every other morning, before they get settled at the Palais d'Orient which serves no alcohol, they first stopped at the Spanish bistro, well known because it's one of the few bars where workers of all ethnic backgrounds mix. The early shot is enough to bring them to a state of serene and slightly flushed euphoria, the first stage of their day, which will end with the evening's liberating intoxication, watched by their usual public: the puritanical bourgeois, who'll take a seat later on when their workday is over, and the drowsy unemployed, who yearn for distraction. The show will begin before their eyes.

"The Chicou brothers!" one of the patrons announces. "Our official drunks," another continues ironically, and each of them watches for the first signs of their noble fury. "They're not brothers, they're brothers-in-law," someone at the next table explains to an unfamiliar new arrival who is surprised by the ritual. "They argue like this in public every night, then they fight until they're exhausted, whereupon they need to be carried off to the back room. When they get up again, they embrace, they kiss, and at night they go home, their arms still around each other, swearing eternal friendship." The stranger shrugs his shoulders. "Poor bastards, just like so many others!" "No, no," the speaker protests, "they're our poets!" and perhaps that is precisely the only beauty they know, the beauty of mad intoxication.

Cherifa approaches, her eyes straight ahead; she senses danger. The crowd is huge. She wants to cross the street, move over to the other sidewalk. A cart blocks her way. She keeps going in her slow gait so as not to attract any further attention.

One of the Chicou brothers raises his head. He is known as the "real Chicou" to set him apart from his brother-in-law, who was not a born Chicou, not of this family whose arrogance is equaled only by its wretchedness and innumerable members. This one is from the "mountains," they say; his father came down some twenty years ago, barefoot, looking fierce, to work in the town's slaughterhouse.

Cherifa passes by. "I want her to look at me!" the real Chicou says to himself with querulous sadness. "If only she'd look at me!" his heart echoes, as if, through the first alcoholic stages, the shadow of the veiled woman passing so majestically had come to quiet his ranting. "If only she'd look at me!" he groans and stops playing.

"What's your problem, you son of a whore? Do I have to beg you?" the brother-in-law scolds, four or five hours ahead of himself with his first curse. He confronts his partner, whose image gradually begins to move away but whom he will make the effort to reach through insults that are soon to be exchanged with cheerful fervor. "Son of a whore, or actually, whore's brother!" he begins again, an additional four or five hours ahead of the second step they ordinarily take together, going after each other with these abominations whose obscenity swells and radiates like a new sun in the heart of the white town.

"I want her to look at me!" the real Chicou murmurs once again, and his lament pierces him, because the woman whose veil almost brushed the table, is now gone. "Gone, gone, without giving you a single glance, you son of a bitch, infernal drunk, you dirty drunken boor." Without even following the figure any longer, the figure that has vanished from his dreams and desires, he turns the words over in his head, lost, in a daze, in the street whose brouhaha and Arabic wailing on the radio are growing into sirens of solitude inside him.

"Dirty race of drunks!" he yells and suddenly pulls his chair back.

"Whore's brother!" now responds the brother-in-law, who with meticulous persistence has just begun to go into a trance; nevertheless, he himself even seems baffled by the different wavelength that has entered their usual dialogue. "Whore's brother, you whose sister prostitutes herself night after night in my bed! Just last night, oh, people!"

From the next tables the habitual customers are wondering about the Chicous: what's come over them today to be trotting out their lines at this hour? It's almost noon. The real Chicou stands now.

"Don't you dare to claim that my sister, the dew of my blood, of my father's and all my forefathers' blood, all of whom lived honorably in this town, don't you dare claim that she could have come anywhere near your bed, barbarian, you who came off your mountain only yesterday!" he shouts. He's found his ebullience again. "Don't you dare!" he yells, taking a theatrical step forward, and in a broad, grand gesture throws the chair far into the street.

"You won't believe it!" the other one exults. "Oh, you people who see us here, you should know that this man's sister is in my house and that I do with her what I want, just as if I were paying her. Last night, I took her once, ripping her skirts and blouse off her, pulling her by the hair, the way lions go at it, and she was screaming in pain and pleasure, I assure you. Then I took her a second time . . ." he bursts out laughing. "She's my wife, after all, isn't she?"

"No!" the other spits out, "She wouldn't even want you as her servant!"

Chicou the brother-in-law is triumphant:

"Didn't you yourself give her to me before the *cadi*?"

Within the circle that formed as soon as the second rejoinder was uttered, leaving just enough space for the final brawl as usual, the real Chicou takes another threatening step, and this second time he knocks over the table. As he growls, "Barbarian, just off your mountain!" he is able to glimpse the sky in front of him in a flash, as if the purest part of his rage and fighter's joy had been lost there.

A skinny, brisk young adolescent dressed in blue jeans and with a beret on his head tries to force his way through the onlookers standing there, including the two waiters who've come close, yet one more time, so as not to miss a thing of the conjugal night whose details the brother-in-law publicizes in insulting fragments intended for the real Chicou. ("Defend your sister's honor, I ask you, your sister who's a whore, I tell you, on her back in my bed night after night!"—"My sister is a virgin, a white dove of paradise who soars far above you and your scum, you poor wretches who know nothing but prickly pears!") The young man, hearing the last few words, stops. "My sister is a whore too," he states coldly, out loud, and feels himself brimming with hatred.

When Cherifa reaches the end of the street, leaving behind the rumble of voices whose sudden explosion she doesn't understand, she hesitates. In front of her lies what they call the *place d'armes*, the town's central square, where soldiers parade on national holidays. Which way should she go now?

Around the *place d'armes*—a square with a kiosque where an old and venerable palm tree stands, unsteady in the wind—are many "European cafés." A few Muslims patronize them—they're known by the town because they drink alcohol—but if they do, they stand only at the bar, alone. Besides these surreptitious customers with their guilty conscience there are some Europeans at the tables, dozing off a little at this hour. Behind them in the room they hear the booming noise of the jukebox that the young are playing; to them it's a reassuring sound. They could stay there for hours, watching, not tiring of their place, their kiosque, their palm tree, ready to jump up at the slightest worrisome sign, and they wince in the depth of their soul where fear, the warm companion, lies crouching. From time to time, soldiers from France, just disembarked the night before, pass by; they roam around, erect and stiff, uncomfortable in the crushing noontime heat: the café customers stare them down coldly.

One more minute of waiting: people will surge before their very eyes when the stores close. One more minute of being at ease to dwell on the results of the latest harvest, the latest business figures, or future plans if . . . But there won't be any if. "The war, the mountain," a mere flash of madness to be cured like any madness. Oh, just to sit here, stay here forever in the sun, "in the peace of this sunny square! There won't be any if." One man in the group takes out his pipe, "Never seen that *mouquère* before!" "She walks differently from the others," another man answers, lowering his head to scrutinize the figure, then he leans backward with a wide yawn, and when a popular melody reaches him from the back of the room he listens to it, happy to know that he'll hear it again from the lips of his daughter when he comes home. "I know all about women like that!" the first one goes on arrogantly, "Her veil is made of silk, a lightweight silk. She's not just some cheap little kitchen maid!"

Cherifa cuts across the square diagonally. She didn't hesitate for long. She remembers that the business district where Youssef's shop is lies on the other side. She hurries on, measuring the emptiness of the square with her eyes before charging ahead.

Facing her on the other side, between two cafés, is an ice cream shop. By herself, with her knees crossed, Touma sits at a table in front of a pêche melba. She is out of breath from her walk from the police station. She likes this place and comes here almost every day—nice and obvious, easily visible to the customers of the cafés on either side; she can picture how the desire of the men sizing her up grows sharper from being able to observe her. "An emancipated Arab woman" ("Yes, with high heels, short skirt, a permanent wave, just like our women! And well stacked, too, an enticing little brunette; she could be from Marseille or Arles . . .").

Touma likes being raped this way by these men; she sees it as a form of respect. The others make their face a blank when she passes. "The others," she corrects herself, "the Arabs," and pronounces the word as she lifts her head. She shudders with hate. She opens her purse; with a tantalizing nonchalance her gestures become drawn out. A noisy bunch of young men has entered the café on the right. Without turning her head, Touma hears their laughter, the splash of their voices; from within, a shrill American song reaches her ears and makes her feel like dancing, wiggling her body with exasperated motions right in the middle of the square. She takes a pack of cigarettes from her bag and a silver lighter, a gift from Captain Martinez. The group settles down on the terrace; the American song continues, nostalgically now. "Arabs, I hate them!" Touma mutters and light her cigarette with an easy hand motion, a gesture learned with childish perseverance whose mastery has become necessary to her every time she comes to sit here, at the same table, and wait.

"Will he come today?" she wonders. Her head bent backward, she smokes, arching against her chair. Shortly, one of the young men will come over to her, perhaps; she'll invite him to sit down because she likes to take the first step; she'll exchange a few lighthearted pleasantries with him, just enough to have the comfort of some dialogue and to tell herself that after all, one of these twenty-year-old Frenchmen will seek her out, even in this town where the two communities allow no mixing whatsoever (with one or two exceptions, and they seem to exist merely to make the drama that centers on them more measurable)—to tell herself that, should she want to . . .

"You want to go dancing with me this evening?" he says and smiles, boldly timid, showing all his teeth. ("I've never asked such a thing of an Arab girl before . . . If my mother knew . . .") In a husky voice, leaning a little on the consonants of the language she learned rather late:

"I go dancing sometimes, but not here, only when I go to the big city."

"Not here, not even with me?" Delighted with the beginning banter, amazed also to feel stirred by this girl ("she has to be fiery, she has to be quite sensual"), the young man goes on bluntly: "So, what's your name?"

Touma bursts out laughing, a laugh that streams out in a long ribbon, ending on a somewhat sour note. She is surprised: "You don't know my name?" then starts laughing again, with a touch of madness, and like golden sand her laughter seems to scatter to every corner of town.

"You have a lovely laugh. I like you very much, very much indeed," the young man stammers.

Now reassured, Touma's eyes wander across the square. She dreams; she's far away and her musing softens her face. Suddenly a veiled woman passes by. "You see," she says abruptly, "I could have been just like that woman, veiled—no, disguised—" She has an evil look. "Would you have liked me that way?"

The young man casts a rapid glance at the "Moorish" woman. When all is said and done, that word means little to him. All that matters is his desire, which fills him with a kind of cool drowsiness. "Do I have enough money," he wonders, "to take her out and catch the next train to the capital? Over there, we could really have a good time . . ." and he counts his fortune.

Passing by with her head down, Cherifa heard the laugh. A quick look aside and she recognizes Touma. "Damn you!" she says but without any hate, more out of habit; her attention is fixed on one goal only, Youssef, and that obliterates all other feelings. Then, with the same indifference, she notes, "So, it's really true what people say about poor old Doudja's daughter. Curses on her, she must be informing on us!"

"Would you like to take the one o'clock Micheline with me?" the young man asks, pleased with his suggestion; and he has a gentle look, the look of his sudden infatuation. "I really want her! I like her kind of beauty," he thinks in a rush. He knows that his friends are watching him from the terrace next door, with irony and envy. It makes no difference to him. He feels stifled here. Touma and he could spend a wonderful day together in the big city, far away from everyone, from the others. He starts to explain:

"Next month I have to go into the military. So you see, I'll have all the money I want from my parents. I'll take you wherever you want, I'll buy you whatever you want . . ."

"Really?" Touma asks, thrilled at first; but she isn't laughing anymore. She isn't talking anymore. Her eyes are riveted.

"Will you come?" persists the boy, whom his friends now address with a "Hey, Bob!"

"Say yes!" Bob insists. "I'll go and get the money from my house, as much as you want!"

"Really?" Touma repeats, but she isn't listening to him, she can't take her eyes off another young man, in blue jeans and espadrilles, who seems to be coming in their direction, very slowly.

She looks back at Bob.

"Your name is Bob, right?" And Bob hovers over her, smiles, insists again:

"Please say yes!"

Touma returns his smile, lights another cigarette, thinking, "It's so nice to see yourself reflected like this in a man's desire, a man's or a child's, it doesn't matter, but especially to forget the contempt of all those who judge me when I pass by, if not actually insult me under their breath, 'Bitch, bitch's daughter!' if not actually spit on the ground in front of me before moving away. God, desire laid bare is so much better, even in a boy who's going into the service next month!"

She turns her head toward the square again. She doesn't need to look up. The boy in blue jeans approaches them.

"Go away," she says to Bob in a changed voice. "Go away!" Still happy, Bob says, "I'm going to get the money right now! I'll see you back here in a little while, in an hour at the latest, right?"

Touma nods. Her heart is pounding.

"Yes," she mumbles, then adds roughly, "Go now!" Bob stands up. He doesn't go back to his friends. He leaves, almost at a run. "Father will give me ten thousand francs," he figures. "He won't refuse." He runs.

"I'm warning you for the last time," the young man in blue jeans says calmly in Arabic, standing in front of Touma. "I'll give you this one day to get out of town; it's your last chance. Or else you run the risk of not seeing another day."

Touma looks up; she appears unruffled. She smiles and answers, "You wouldn't really kill me now, would you?"

"You're the shame of this town! You deserve to die a hundred times over!"

"You'd dare kill a woman?" she says, staring at him sarcastically, and then with a touch of empathy. "You're still so young."

"It's the last time, you've been warned!"

The boy disappears.

Touma smokes a third cigarette and her eyes wander around the square, now emptying out. "Tired, yes," she says to herself, surprised at the sudden dizziness she feels inside, urging her to leave and go no matter where, far from the square, the town, the sun, no matter where, by herself—"Yes, I'm tired this morning." She thinks this cautiously, fearing the weariness that threatens her. "It's the heat I can't bear today; an August heat, but it's only May," and she closes the purse she had started to open for another cigarette.

Cherifa, with her back to the square, enters the business district near the Arab market. Youssef's shop is here, but she doesn't know the exact place. "What if I get lost now," she thinks, feeling distraught. "What am I going to do?" She doesn't dare ask directions; in the street, her veil isolates her. "If only I'd see a child . . ." and she takes the widest street. "I'll be wasting time, I could get lost," and she keeps on walking at her slow pace so that Bob passes her, takes her for a stroller. "True," he thinks as he moves on, "Touma could have been veiled like this and I would never have seen her, never asked her out . . ."

"What if I get lost," Cherifa repeats to herself in a panic but keeps going, with only one purpose in mind: Youssef. "He must be warned in time! He must . . ."

5 ··· HAKIM

Hakim hoped in vain that for the rest of the day he'd be able to immerse himself in the paperwork that with Chief Jean's tacit approval has been his refuge for the past several months. Right now, however, Jean looks distracted as he listens to the report. Repeatedly, Hakim has to restate a question, an observation; each time, the captain seems startled to be drawn out of his preoccupations. "Tired, sir?" Hakim expresses his concern. "No! . . . No, it's nothing really." The voice hesitates. With studied coolness Hakim takes note of these early symptoms. He has been preparing for this for a long time: change is in the air. He's even more convinced of it when, as he's about to leave, Jean calls out to him briefly but hurriedly, "Stop by Martinez's office! I think he wants to see you!"

At thirty-eight, Martinez is a police captain. He's stocky, with the shoulders of an athlete, but he moves gracefully, catlike; his eyelids are fleshy, his look piercing. The self-assurance of a social climber. He made his career in this town, where he was born (his Spanish mother was a laundress in the military barracks), and now he bides his time. The events of these days are in his favor; so he believes. The longer the war goes on the more they'll need him and his consummate knowledge of the local population, the politicized and suspect elements in the region. His confidence is growing. With the addition of one or two more political allies, he'll have an excellent chance of becoming chief commissioner before he reaches forty. A success.

He watches Hakim come in; he dislikes him. He's wary, obscurely irritated not to be able to pinpoint a reason for his dislike. Perhaps it's only because Hakim is the protégé of the "old man," of whose methods he disapproves. It's naive, he thinks, to persist in not using violence; violence, before anything else, overt violence, is the only policy that pays off in this country. He despises the detached, disembodied manner in which Jean directs an interrogation, as if to say, "I act the way my conscience tells me to." Fuck conscience! The old man would have made a fine school principal; he would have grilled the little Arab boys in the same polite way for their final exams. "The result," Martinez continues to himself, "is that the town's nationalist cells are staying intact. By the time some important information might be obtained, it's usually too late."

Meanwhile he listens to the report Hakim is giving for the second time.

"So, according to you, there's no point in arresting Youssef, because, as it happens" (he utters the words smugly), "he's your neighbor! Your relative? No, no relation, but you're sure of his work schedule." He waits.

"Yes, Captain, I am."

Hakim senses the other is showing his claws. "He hates me," he thinks. "He has no idea what to think of me and has just two ways of dealing with people: as servants or accomplices."

"The other suspect is in the building. You'll handle him yourself. I'm putting you in charge of the interrogation."

Hakim doesn't answer, salutes, and leaves. Martinez follows him with his eyes as he closes the door. "You're the one we're testing," he says to himself with satisfaction. "I want to know what sort of instrument you are, because I'm afraid you'll turn out to be a double-edged sword." He continues to give out detailed orders, as is his wont. He sends two men to assist Hakim, "in case he proves to be a sensitive soul," he adds, without trying to hide his skepticism from them.

When he is finally alone in his large, bright office, he sighs deeply. He's hot. He wipes his forehead, opens his shirt collar, and turns to the window. Outside the sun is almost at its zenith. He throws it an affectionate glance; he's feeling good so early in a summer that promises to be sweltering. Then resolutely he gets back to work.

The two policemen join Hakim in a large room above the prisoners' quarters. Hakim doesn't say a word to them when they enter; he is facing Saidi, the suspect. The room is empty; a door at the back opens into areas where noisy preparations are in progress. On a sign from Hakim, one of the two policemen goes into the other room.

Hakim interrogates the suspect in Arabic: "I recognize you. Your name, Saidi, meant nothing to me, but now I see, you're the former manager of the Baghdad Café, aren't you?"

"Yes," the other man mutters.

"Listen, here's a bit of advice. You'd be better off telling us everything you know . . . You've been through quite enough so far, don't you think?"

"I don't give a damn! You're not here to feel sorry for me," the other one comes back with, stifles a curse, then abruptly decides not to say another word.

"I believe you have many children. After the years you've already spent in prison, wouldn't it be better to live a quieter life . . ."

"I don't give a damn," Saidi thinks but says nothing.

"If you won't speak of your own accord, you'll be going next door. You know what that means."

"I already know your procedures. And I don't give a damn!" Saidi grumbles one last time and then falls silent again. He says no more. He listens no more. He doesn't even look at the policeman, who seems endlessly patient, who states his questions without a frown: "I advise you to tell us what you know! Besides, we already have quite a lot of information about last night's meeting. If you give us details, you'll come out of this clean, I promise you that."

"God," Saidi thinks, "he's whining as if he were the one about to be tortured!"

The man sent by Martinez checks out the scene with an irritated look.

"Let's get down to business, Inspector. He's wasting your time!"

Without turning around, Hakim hesitates. He understands—this man has been sent to spy on him. Hakim justifies himself: "I'm just trying to talk some sense into him. He's stubborn; I know him. It's not a given that he'll talk in there."

The agent bursts out laughing.

"Starting off in such an optimistic frame of mind, Inspector! No, really, it's obvious you aren't used to this yet, Inspector!"

"Inspector!" "Inspector!" Hakim suppresses an angry gesture, shakes Saidi by the shoulders, and begins questioning him again, in Arabic; but now he doesn't plead, he yells, he shouts. Saidi remains immured in silence; Hakim, beside himself, thinks, "But is he a complete idiot?"

"Who was at the meeting last night?

"The name of the political leader who came down from the mountain to make contact, who is he these days?

"Where was the meeting held?

"We know a lot already but show us at least you're willing to cooperate!

"Idiot, you prize idiot!" Hakim now growls; a desperate energy rises inside him to grab at something, but what . . . for it really is he who's doing the pleading while Saidi unrelentingly ignores him, with his dead stare and the crease across his forehead. "An idiot," Hakim mumbles, shaking powerlessly.

"You're really taking too much time, Inspector!" The policeman, who doesn't understand Arabic, is openly sarcastic; he's bored. Then, as all three of them leave to go into the room in back he exults, "He'll talk! He'll talk, you'll see." Hakim has once again become impassive.

Saidi glances briefly at the place, the furniture. He actually thinks the word *furniture* and coldly notices the electric wire, the buckets, a generator (the first thing he recognizes), and a movable bathtub against the wall. Hakim no longer speaks. On his signal the two men approach Saidi. "Take off your clothes," one of them begins in a dull voice. Saidi doesn't understand French. Hakim, with his back turned, makes no effort to translate. He stops in front of the window, whose shutters have just been closed. It looks out over the northern part of the town—the river in the distance, where the white trail of its dried-up bed is visible, the black hovels near its banks; next to it, the gray mass of the new building that was intended for the families of the police force when construction began. "I'd hoped to get an apartment there," Hakim daydreams. "My application must lie forgotten somewhere in a dusty old file; in the end, they don't want to put anybody there; and those who could afford the rent want no part of the neighborhood. Soon, though, with all the officers' families that are to arrive in large numbers, there will be a housing shortage."

The two policemen rip off Saidi's shabby jacket, then his pants. He lets them. "We're his nanny!" one of them mocks. But Saidi seems indifferent, absent. Lying down now, a huge body, white, just slightly thick-set, the pleasing shape of an athlete. Hakim still has his back turned as if he's decided to show no interest. One of the policemen winks at the other in the direction of the inspector.

"Let's get started," Hakim says at last, curtly, as he turns around.

• • •

Once, for three days, Saidi had been the hero of the town. The Baghdad Café, which he managed, was located just above the *place d'armes*. It was also the competitor of the Palais d'Orient, in the next street, for the center of Arab life. One morning, the Baghdad remained closed; the regular early customers couldn't get over their surprise. At ten o'clock they began to form a silent semicircle around the lowered metal blinds. In ten years—no, twenty—the café had never been closed. "Excuse me," one man had said, "it did close once, on May 8, 1945, but that was a special day." Saidi's young brother, just an adolescent, stood out front looking scared, unsure whether he should try to disperse the curious. In response to the questions some of them asked ("Where is Saidi? Gone to the capital? Sick?") he shook his head no and seemed panic-stricken. Mute since birth, he only mouthed rough groans.

Moved by the mysterious sense that idle masses feel when they sniff an upcoming event, especially if they know when to be patient, and now resigned to the fact they wouldn't get their usual spot, all the jobless waited in eager anticipation for the expected show. A man in the crowd, one of the spectators, suddenly asked in a clear voice, without the others knowing from whom it came, "Maybe Saidi is here, inside the café?" And because Saidi's brother began to shake his head too vehemently, the anxious crowd immediately knew that Saidi was definitely holed up inside. Therefore, the event would be Saidi's exit from the café—there was no other way out.

The questions began again: "What's he doing in there?" "What's happened to him?" "Why is he hiding?" "Is he alive?" but then they stopped abruptly when Hakim passed by (he didn't have a car yet) on his way home. With a friendly look, as if he were merely a customer (he was off duty, after all, and on his way back from work), he asked warmly, "Is Saidi sick?" Then he moved through their collective silence, and nobody knew whether he had lowered his head because he was lost in thought and had instantly forgotten his question or whether he was already speculating on the oddity of the closure.

The crowd dispersed as if the inspector's passage and question, reminding them of the hour ("Noon, I'm going home for lunch . . ."), indicated that quite a bit of time would yet go by and they'd have plenty of opportunity to wait some more. Saidi's brother was still in front of the entrance, now sitting on the curb in the dirt, absorbed in some incomprehensible monologue, which he interrupted from time to time by shaking his head; then a sudden silence dissolved over him like a whirlwind of terror. He stayed there, stunned, turning to look around at the lowered blinds.

In the afternoon the same crowd gathered. In tacit complicity, the curious avoided crowding together so as not to attract the attention of the authorities; Hakim had passed by again and then two police officers arrived, one of them known as the Corsican, obviously to watch the place. They stopped, lingered a while; they had tried to question the brother but he had fled. Finally, clearly suspicious of something, they went away.

A number of innocuous old men, who normally didn't frequent the café until evening, had ordered chairs to be brought out to them from the Arab pastry shop across the way. Not wanting to give up playing a lengthy game of dominos or to lose their habitual setting, they sat down at the other side of the street, hoping they, too, would witness the event. Comfortably installed, they pretended they were playing. Others came and went in small groups, stopped for a moment without asking any further questions, and compassionately watched Saidi's brother, who'd come back. As soon as the crowd grew too dense they scattered and went back up the so-called rue du Bey, which in fact bore the name of a conquering general from the previous century. There they reached a rather charming little square with benches. They sat down pensively, no longer curious, just resolved to wait for the outcome.

The same crowd appeared the following day, but when he passed by at noon Hakim found only a few people strolling and the mute brother still sitting on the curb. Hakim stopped and asked him casually, "Is Saidi traveling?" The boy raised distraught eyes, began to shake his head violently. Taken aback, Hakim repeated the question. The brother noticed Hakim's uniform, lowered his head, now terrified again. Hakim looked around: at this hour the rue du Bey was inexplicably deserted, all the way to the pastry shop run by Slimane, who was closing his store in an awkward hurry. Then Hakim went over to Slimane, intending to affirm—so thinks Slimane, who is then obliged to answer him—that as a policeman his vocation is to protect and watch over those who share his religious beliefs. A pastor—and why not—Slimane thinks to himself and is overcome by cantankerous hostility, which he sifts deep inside his myopic eyes while he answers Hakim's questions:

"I don't know, Inspector; yes, the Baghdad is closed; Saidi must surely have gone to the country; perhaps there's a death in the family; he's from one of the mountain douars originally. No, the mute is often like this—very strange. Yes, I always close at this hour, that way I can be on time for prayers. May God keep you, Inspec—Si Hakim!"

"Peace be with you, Si Slimane!" and Hakim pronounced these words amicably, went back up the rue du Bey, happy with the formulaic phrases exchanged in Arabic, which made him believe (though deep inside he knew very well this was an illusion) that he was just like the others. Just like those men who—at the same time noticing how odd they seemed—gathered in the square in spite of the midday sun. "May God keep you, Si . . ." "Peace be with you . . ." "May God fill your home . . ." No one spoke those words as he did, with the same thirst for transparency.

In the afternoon, the curious in the square intermittently sent out a scout, who came whistling down the street with a watchful eye, stopped, and checked. "Yes, the mute's still there, Slimane is still in the doorway of his shop, and the Baghdad is still closed." Then he'd come back to tell the others to be patient. Suddenly a collective quiver of excitement ran through the crowd as the two police officers of the day before, one of them the Corsican, and an unidentified civilian were sighted in the distance. ("Who is that? Do you know him?" "No, I haven't seen him before." "Isn't he the Spaniard from the bar?" "No." "I recognize him; it's the owner of the little hotel near the church, some sort of fancy brothel for the officers from the barracks.")

He was a short, obese man whose shirt hung out from his pants. He was gesticulating, arms in the air, ahead of the policemen following him at a fast pace, in a frenzy, their hands almost on their weapons. The group was heading for the Baghdad. Then a strange rumor, whose origin nobody knew, circulated through the crowd in the square: "It's the husband," they said of the civilian. They retraced their steps, the policemen dragging Saidi's brother, the hus-

band behind them. He was unfolding a large white handkerchief
with which to wipe himself off, even though the hottest part of the
day had passed. The mute boy, half crazed with fear, stopped a few
times, refusing to budge, at which point he was knocked down so
hard that he sprawled in the dirt; he got up again, opening his
mouth wide in shouts that would never be heard. Behind them, the
man went into a jumbled diatribe that those out-of-work men in the
square who understood French could make out:

"I'm telling you, my wife isn't at her sister's! No, she doesn't have
anyone else! No, she never leaves without telling me. Run away?
What else can you come up with? You dare to insult my wife's
morality while she's in danger, while she has to fight off that dirty
brute . . . If the police can't even protect us anymore in this country—" And he shouted other things, stopping for a moment in front
of the crowd in the square that turned away its collective head in
unison at his approach, as if to contemplate the sky or the mountain. The man couldn't silence his rage before the anonymous mass
that spurned him but by which, it seemed to him, his wife—whose
moral values couldn't have allowed her to run away—must have
been overpowered and then violated.

From that moment on, the story of the mute brother, hauled off
and pummeled by the police, and of the cuckolded husband who
with the help of the authorities was in search of his wife made the
rounds through the entire Arab quarter. The men talked among
themselves in their homes about Saidi, but not with their wives,
although the women already knew every last detail ("Saidi has
always been a hothead." "Yes, and since the war's begun . . . real
debauchery, he's all too free, no ethics . . . Shame on him!"). The following day the word *rape* appeared in the police report (the brother
had been interrogated all night long and told the story, as best he
could). Then it was on the lips of the women in the shops in every
street close to the market and in the words spoken by the aimless
youth hanging around the European cafés who'd swarmed back to
the area near the Baghdad. Not needing to take any further precau-

tions, the men on the square, too, had returned to their earlier observation posts, though they didn't mix with the Europeans waiting on one side, held back by a police cordon, while at some distance another force with weapons in hand surrounded the Baghdad.

The wait began again. Among the first group there was now an agitation mixed with dull fear; among the jobless, Saidi's friends, a mocking, happy silence.

"He must've had a good time!" one of them sighed.

"He's always having a good time . . ." said another, and a third muttered between his teeth, "Now there's a real woman! She should be congratulated. She couldn't care less that it was an Arab! When you look at Saidi with those shoulders of his, that body, his fine mustache, and you compare him to the husband . . ."

"It's as if he'd slept with every European female in town . . ."

Finally, they all stopped talking. Hakim had arrived noisily in a jeep; he got out, made his way through the crowd and went straight to the door of the café. "Saidi! Open up!" he calls and in one wave the crowd tries to surge forward, ill contained by the now overwhelmed police. "Saidi!" Hakim continues his entreaties in Arabic. "You're surrounded! If you try to resist it'll be worse for you." Then he tried to knock down the door with hard thrusts of his shoulder.

A few moments later—Ali told Lila (they'd just been married and she would listen to Ali's lengthy accounts about his town that was hers as well, but whose street face she never knew, just the murmuring, the silences, and the shadow of the old houses, bristling with the life of women alone, all day long)—Saidi came out, handcuffed, massive and noble, surrounded by Hakim and two other guards. The European boys began to scream, to struggle with the police cordon: "Kill him! Kill him, that dirty Arab!" while the terrified shopkeepers, not seeing the "unfortunate lady" come out, already imagined her with her throat slit, disemboweled at the back of the Baghdad. She was made to wait for two or three hours until siesta time, when the rue du Bey was once again deserted (except for Slimane, who had pretended to close up his bakery but was hiding behind his

shutters to watch the woman). She came out, escorted by her husband and a policeman, huge dark glasses masking half her face and a
white scarf covering her hair. Behind his shutters and rubbing his
hands, Slimane muttered, "What a behind! The big, generous chest
of a mare! He knows how to pick 'em, that sly Saidi!" Her head lowered, she follows her husband straight down the street in this town
where she's suffocating, where she'll die of boredom after these three
days of overindulgence. She sighs, "He made me drunk . . . drunk
with passion, with love, with . . ."

The following day, Saidi's photograph appeared on the front
page of the town's weekly and in the local-news column of the capital city's daily papers. "A Three-Day Rape!"—it was a most unusual
incident. The Baghdad was now permanently closed and there was
no other café where they could sit around all day without ordering
anything, as they had at Saidi's. So in the square the unemployed
showed each other the French newspapers with the portrait—an
identity picture in which Saidi, with bare neck, jutting jawbones,
and a frozen stare, the way simple people look into the camera—
now with the expression of a "dangerous brute" as the caption stat-
ed. As a result, he had become famous, and for several days everyone
talked about the photo as about an enviable victory, although, of
course, it would cost him dearly. The trial took place a month later.
Saidi was given only ten years in prison, reduced on appeal to four,
but the Baghdad had to be sold, to a European who turned it into a
garage. A few months later, Saidi's family—an elderly mother, his
wife, his eight children, and the mute brother (the only man)—had
to move from the town's former Arab quarter to go and live near the
river, in a clay house next to the shantytown. It was a wretched outcome.

Thus did Ali recount the incident to Lila. He also explained how
arrests and police surveillance had followed the demonstrations of 8
May 1945. The life of the nationalist parties could now only survive
as surface foam. Theirs was not a deep reaching task anymore, no
longer like driving a mattock into the crust of an earth hardened by

ordeals. An apparent inertia had settled over the town and throughout the land, a false sleep, a deceptive night in the mists, from which the spirits of men nonetheless began to emerge to save themselves from slow asphyxiation. A crushed earth, an earth opened by the people to a secret light. And through wakeful summer nights like this when, infused with enthusiasm, neither of them could sleep, Lila would listen passionately.

"The foreigners," Ali continued, "expected our submission to go on forever. But can you say you're sleeping when you know you're sleeping? In true inertia you disintegrate."

Then he'd recount other events; scenes in which awakening took the form of sexual ecstasy were his preference. He spoke about the Chicou brothers, who at the Palais d'Orient had been fighting each other day in and day out for years, tossing the wife's body back and forth between them, their obscene curses trampling her like a dog, the dishonored sister above whose head they hugged, jostled, and made up again. He told her about Hamid, the son, who ran one of the most flourishing trades in the Arab community. After a good season he'd suddenly fly to France, stay just long enough to spend some time in a few brothels, and come back home with a beautiful girl yearning for a holiday. She'd be as provocative as a movie star, a splendid doll, stay at the fanciest hotel in town for a month or two, and stroll down the *place d'armes* on the arm of her protector under the watchful gaze of the European population, shocked at this "whore from the metropolis" who permitted herself to be paid by an Arab to come and brazenly challenge them, or so it seemed. When Hamid's savings ran out, she would vanish the next day. Hamid would earnestly return to his wholesale business (he supplied all the grocers in the villages on the plain) and be completely immersed in it for many months to enrich himself anew, dividing his time between his store and home, which each year saw a new baby, until the next trip to France, the next girl, the next venture. When he hadn't saved very much he'd travel no farther than Marseille or Nice. His competitors in town could always tell the state of his financial affairs from the origin of the new recruit who'd serenely come to profit from him.

Lila was long accustomed to a family life from which the slightest allusion to the flesh was excluded, where every woman had to be careful to keep her arms above the elbow and her legs down to her ankles covered. She vividly imagined how magnificent, even anonymous, pride drove men to cut through this sensual torpor. For her it was "animal" pride; because, with ridiculously naive disdain, she applied this epithet to everything connected to sexuality, the driving force that would grip them and spur them on, to blistering attacks beyond constraint and bourgeois prudery. Ali thought this interpretation false and romantic. Patiently didactic, he explained why those who took refuge in no matter what form of ecstasy (he despised the word, in contrast to Lila) were nothing more than victims themselves. "One can only be liberated by consciousness, and what our country needs most of all is political consciousness." The speech would begin and then spill over into the future. Lila was no longer listening; she couldn't be interested in the future, hers or that of others, settled as she was inside her abounding present. Ali became irritated with her absentmindedness, rapidly waging war against her animal self-centeredness, as he said accusingly, throwing her own words back at her.

The argument would broaden, feeding the sequels of previous quarrels, those of the two years of their engagement, the last one on the very eve of their wedding, when Lila had had to run across the big city to the wharf, where she finally found Ali and begged him to marry her the next day anyway. (The motionless cranes in the port seemed to stiffen with the vitriol they once again fired off at each other.) Touching in his dedication and sincerity, and after a destructive two-hour analysis (that's "his ecstasy," Lila thought, but didn't dare say so, because her irony always proved to be inopportune), Ali had explained—between passionate embraces that suddenly gave him back some of his calm—that they should, yes, be united and never separate, as she desired, but with the goal of "one day making those things that would be useful to their country come true."

At that point the war of liberation had not yet begun. He would go on and on about the inevitable day when the struggle would be unleashed; Ali himself could not have suspected that their wedding would take place just two years before the historic days in November when the first lightning, the first true hope, flashed across the sky. No, he hadn't foreseen that the country's independence, the intoxicating future the battle would provide for him—for him, for Lila, and for so many other young people—was so close at hand. He'd seen it in some distant future that he, for one, through each of his actions strove to deserve. That's how he shaped his life, with immutable will but also with imagination, which as a function of the collective goal allowed him to justify the slightest choice in his personal life.

So it was for his marriage. So it was for the impossible discussions with Lila where he managed to see a glimmer of hope, in spite of the outbursts and breakups decided upon in a bluster of anger. Too soon would he proclaim them over for good, because he was always astonished at the pain he felt, noticing an inner open gash that seemed shamefully weak to him. And still he found the patience to search for a flickering light in the ruins that had come crashing down between them (Lila was hardly any help, frozen in silent resentment or in remorse, manifested through puerile tears)—to search for the path he would take again on his necessary march toward the horizon desired by everyone, with her by his side, his holding her, too frail, protecting her—so that the mysterious wound disappeared, scarred over, leaving only its strange memory.

That is how Ali had acquiesced to suffering because of her, Lila thought, trying in her present solitude to understand his earlier behavior. Apparently he suffered in silence because a rigorous honesty drove him to make his slightest actions productive and in some way useful to his ideal. Never had Lila valued Ali's scruples, his profound wholeness, more than now, while she contrasted it with her own fatal taste for lyricism, whether that lay in drama or happiness. Perhaps that's where the fault lay, in her determination to hang on to the style of her exhilarated adolescence; she, the "romantic," as Ali used to complain, the romantic gliding by, mostly so that she wouldn't recognize her image in the eyes of a mature and serious Ali, a real man such as the mountain demanded, the mountain that had subsequently taken him from her.

After Suzanne left that day, Lila noticed that a slow, barely defined rhythm had come to disturb the immobility of her time and she began to live differently. She straightened out her belongings to make the room look less gloomy; at the bottom of her trunk she found her reproduction of the only painting she really loved, in her habitually exacting way, Carpaccio's *The Courtesans*. "The most beautiful painting in the world," she used to exclaim, and because of it she wanted to see Venice, she admitted with such sad passion that she was never accused of being a snob. She hated traveling because she couldn't stand the initial contact with people and things, but she still wanted to see Venice. There, she imagined, the colors of the original Carpaccio, even if they were located in the chilly antechambers of some museum or empty palace, would undoubtedly match those of the streets of this woman-town, the oriental past as noisy as the Arab souks, whose exoticism had finally been smothered in favor of a secret splendor.

In the painting, now hanging on the wall, as they sat among their dogs, their parrot, and their parakeets, cold as one is when on the verge of fainting, the two courtesans brought their disenchantment into the room. Finally, Lila took out the photos of Ali, of which she kept only one, an old one dating back to the time when she first knew him. He had just graduated from the lycée in town, was in his first year of medical school, and would take the train in the morning to go to the university in the city and return in the evening. He met her, younger by two years, when she had just taken the final exams for the baccalaureat, swept along with other young girls in a joyful group, feeling bold and excited because of the exam period and the end of the school year in their small town, reverberating with the summer heat and the uproar of students on the boulevard lined with bitter-orange trees. Ali approached to reprimand one of his cousins who was there as well—she already frightened at the mere sight of him. Then Lila, irked by the intrusion and always ashamed when she saw anyone grow scared, had exclaimed to the girl with impudent fury:

"What are you afraid of? That spoilsport?"

Ali forgets his cousin, his family responsibility, and confronts the young girl, tall, thin, with her disheveled hair and proud look.

"Defiance looks good on you," he says vaguely, not realizing he's paid her a compliment.

"Lila!" and he learns her name when another girl, shocked by the incident, calls out to her: they are young Muslim women, right here on the boulevard, talking to a young man! Foolhardy behavior for which the exhilaration of an examination period is no excuse whatsoever.

"Lila . . ." Ali repeats and stares at her, amused to see her blush and pout furiously at the same time, as she makes every effort to maintain the fierce glare in her eyes (yes, he was right, it was defiance). With Lila facing him alone and suddenly aware of it, the long battle that was to become so necessary for them later on had already begun. Lila, wanting to leave but also to hide her bewilderment from the young man's half-ironic, half-tender smile, brusquely runs her hand through her rebellious curls, to some extent aware of the timid grace of this gesture, behind which she instinctively hides from other people; then she turns her head and leaves.

"No, I don't really like him," she had thought firmly for the next few days, then throughout the summer months, while she sought every little pretext for going out, claiming to get a book at a friend's house, hoping to meet him. When she did run into him, she saw it as a positive sign and welcomed it as confirmation of their destiny to connect. Each time their eyes would meet there was anger in hers to find herself so clumsily approach the mundane paths of first love. But the following year, when she, too, was a university student, she met him again in the Muslim student center, now as an old acquaintance, which is how they quite naturally began their first tête-à-têtes.

Now, in her room, she wanted no sign of the five years that had left her with nothing, or so it seemed to her at times. Nothing, she thought, unless it was her self, for imperceptibly she was beginning to live again. What was she, after all, at the age of twenty-four? She didn't have a clue and found the uncertainty painful. She gradually regained her taste for the tiny facets of a daily life of emptiness (sleeping, reading, sleeping some more, dreaming as she looked up at the sky in front of the open window, listening to the same symphony ten times over and loving it ten times more, suddenly breaking out into song in her dusk-lit room, letting her cleaning lady tell her about her life, complaining about her husband and then philosophizing, laughing alone just to hear herself laugh, and a thousand other solitary follies that seemed to spring forth from every stage of her previous life, all the way to tragic sorrow). During those days, she was often overcome by the sensation of slowly crawling out of a well, at the bottom of which she thought she had noticed an ice cold, dead present time, much like what the two Carpaccio courtesans in their boredom tirelessly contemplated.

•••

When her lawyer's visit ended early in the afternoon—he had come to town on the one o'clock train, arriving as soon as the prison opened, to meet his client who had agreed to see him and receive his first council—Salima was taken back to her cell. The sight of the bed comforted her; she expected finally to sleep for several days, because it seemed they would now leave her alone. But she couldn't fall asleep so quickly. Khaled, the lawyer, linked her to the outside world, which up until that moment had disappeared. She asked him about her mother, her family, but he knew nothing of them and promised to visit Salima's mother immediately afterward; it was Suzanne who had informed him of her detention, he told her. "Suzanne?" Salima had trouble masking her surprise; they had never been close at all; she hardly knew Suzanne, having met her just two or three times after Suzanne had married Omar (Omar, whom Suzanne's family, which was related to Salima's through earlier marriages, had refused to have anything to do with since Suzanne's wedding).

Yet she does remember that Mahmoud had once expressed great respect for Suzanne, which had left her, Salima, pondering. Maybe annoyed as well—she now dares to admit this and her body on the bed begins to relax at last—annoyed as she always is when faced with young women who have not experienced unrelenting, paralyzing difficulties (that she herself constantly had to overcome) and who seemed, nevertheless, to succeed at being happy and fulfilled, at protecting what Salima values most—energy. Without working outside the house, Suzanne had the appearance of an active and independent woman; though she wasn't happy, she breathed harmony and serene confidence. She laughed so joyfully, she was so affectionate in communicating with her little daughter. Above all, and this was what Salima had immediately perceived and even envied, in all of this Suzanne was graceful and radiated strength. These qualities should have brought them closer. Salima felt happy, and before she sank into sleep, her last thought was that the circumstances, this imprisonment, would allow them to accept each other later on.

She wakes up later—thinking she's slept for many hours without feeling rested, but only an hour has passed. She finds herself bathed in sweat, her heart beating fast as if she's come out of a nightmare. She needs a few seconds to orient herself, to hear: from the floor above, long screams reach her. They're torturing a man, she thinks, and is panic-stricken, because since the lawyer's visit, she had thought she was sheltered from all this. She covers her ears, and in a gesture recovered from her childhood she begins to pray for the first time: "My God, my God! . . ." Snatches of Koranic verses rise to her lips.

She stays that way for a long time. Finally she gets up, stands erect in the middle of the cell, facing the skylight, and begins to listen, carefully, sorrowfully, clenching her teeth; the screams form a long chant, a threnody. She trembles as if she were cold, but clenches her teeth again, stretches her willpower to stay upright, her hands now glued to her thighs as she listens. Why run away from it? One should listen! She is seized by a wild exaltation. "This is the song of my country, this is the song of the future," she whispers, an upright silhouette in the center of the empty cell, quivering with zeal and joy—and why not (how distant now the little teacher, stiff in front of her students, in front of the men who run into her in the street, bowed down in the evening over her notebooks and corrections, locking herself away in hypersensitive desiccation). "This is the song of my country," she repeats, trembling all over. Later, when the man falls silent, she is overcome by fear. She is careful to wait, wait for another scream, another sign of life and horror at the same time. "The song of my country," she says again, as the man, too, begins again. Jerky, brief groans at first, which then swell anew into a single endless scream, immense, and Salima rides it with all her willpower because it seems to her that at the end it will open a door into the heavens. Blue landscapes she sees, instead of the cell's gray wall, the noontime sun that blinds you, or the evening sun that reconciles, faces of smiling cherubs . . . of children in her class she recognizes, of Suzanne walking . . . of the man. "Who is he?" she wonders, shivering again, yet from the first moment on transported well beyond compassion.

With teeth still clenched, in the grasp of the effort in which she perseveres with such tenacity that she's emptied, she continues throughout the entire day—so it seems to her—to accompany the man's long, loud screaming. Long after the screams have ended for good, Salima still resonates with their echo, before wondering whether it is the end of the man's torture or of his life ("No, his life"). Suddenly it seems she knows him, has trouble tearing herself away from him as if she lived in his shadow for years on end, like the women in the homes of her neighborhood who, every night, encounter the worried faces of their taciturn husbands returned to the silence of their room.

•••

Elsewhere in the prison, Martinez exclaims, opening the door, "He sure made a lot of noise!" while in the room, Hakim and his two assistants are trying once again to revive Saidi. It's Martinez's second visit; he had come an hour earlier. After leaving his office to go out to lunch, have a short siesta, then briefly help his young son who was having a hard time with high school math, he returned to the station at three o'clock, punctual as always. He was supposed to stop by the old man's office but chose to check in on Hakim's interrogation. As he makes his steps resonate down the hallways, dark as a convent's, he cynically admits to himself that the result of the interrogation hardly matters to him at all.

When earlier that morning Touma had provided him with the names of Youssef and Saidi and the latter was then brought in to him, he figured they would get nothing out of this man; he would undoubtedly have nothing to say, even though Touma's information was generally good. Martinez's intuition was rarely wrong, so in principle he would only attend an interrogation when he smelled prey at the first questioning. It happened frequently, in fact, that confessions were extracted at the precise moment that Martinez came in, for through the fog of his pain and from among the faces of the tormentors he knew, the victim would swiftly glimpse the cold face of that man whose single question would sometimes weaken his resistance. Martinez knew this and used it to elevate his prestige with his subordinates.

This time, when he had given the order to put Saidi through the procedure of questioning, he was driven by no hope at all; he just resigned himself to habit. The gears of the machine needed to be kept oiled.

When he first opened the door and looked in, Hakim hadn't seen him, although he was facing in Martinez's direction. He was leaning over Saidi, fierce determination in his constricted features; between the two policemen, one with the generator, the other holding the electrodes to the man's body, he was questioning Saidi in Arabic. Martinez understood, "Talk! Talk!" and then gradually the curses followed: "Son of a bitch, son of a whore! . . ." Hakim's voice was curt, not a trace of irritation. After long observation, Martinez admitted to himself that he would have to alter his earlier reservations: Hakim seemed weary but persevering, catching his breath only when Saidi lost consciousness. Martinez appreciated the patience, which he saw as one of the essential qualities of police work. ("It is tenacity," he liked to tell himself, "that progressively, without our thinking about it, without our rebelling, helps us overturn all the usual barriers, prejudices, and other taboos by which our usual duties still seem to be surrounded." In contrast, this profession used no disguises and Martinez liked its truthfulness.)

He was about to leave quietly when Hakim noticed him. A quick flash in his eyes, "No, not of surprise," Martinez thought, "but of hate, I know I'm right." Then, after a friendly sign of approval to Hakim, he shut the door, headed for Jean's office, and was filled with fierce satisfaction. He'd been so right to entrust Hakim with this job! He knew that Hakim had once refused the task on the pretext that the Arab baker they were then questioning was one of Hakim's acquaintances. Jean had given in. He, Martinez, on the other hand, had plunged Hakim right into this current assignment without his daring to object. Martinez saw it as proof of his authority.

As he enters Jean's office and greets him, Martinez bursts out in laughter that is purposely vulgar. "I've been telling you all along, sir! All things considered, to be more successful in our battle against the *fellaghas*, we might as well use their brothers. I'm not coming up with anything new!" He is triumphant; Jean doesn't answer.

Now, at the second visit, Hakim notices Martinez the moment he comes in.

"You've been at it for four hours, Hakim!" Martinez uses a thoughtful tone. "Still no results?" Then, as if it were a compliment meant for Hakim and his men, he continues:

"He sure made a lot of noise! And he's got a lot of guts!"

Hakim is bent over Saidi, then straightens up, throws a last glance at the naked, motionless body on the floor, and finally addresses the waiting Martinez:

"He's dead, Captain! His heart gave out."

While the two policemen dress the corpse and Martinez goes to the window to open it, now that they no longer need to conceal the screams, Hakim says a second time, dully, "He's dead." Then he takes a large handkerchief out of his pocket and wipes his forehead.

6 ••• HASSIBA

Twice a day the Micheline, the railcar that was the pride of the town
when it was first put into service a few years before, comes in from
the capital. It arrives in the afternoon, at one o'clock and then at
seven, and instead of stopping at the station, which is too far from
the center, it goes right to the *place d'armes*—so that the patrons on
the terraces of the surrounding cafés can watch departures and scrutinize newcomers. It's fodder for their conversation.

Khaled, whose reputation as a lawyer has only increased among
the local population for the past ten years, arrives at one o'clock.
When he gets off the train and reaches the square, he glances at its
palm tree and in painful wonderment sees again the little town
where he spent his secondary-school years. Since then he has been
back only on rare occasions. He immediately takes note of the fact
that Suzanne is not among the people waiting; she has followed his
advice. He'll pay her a visit after he has interviewed his client at the
prison.

As he crosses the square he smiles at finding it unchanged, still as
it was when, as an adolescent, he used to spend his Sundays wandering around, penniless and friendless, to kill his only free afternoon in
the week. He runs into a young man and is quietly amused to see
the boy's resemblance to the shadowy figure that this place has awakened in him. "Bachir!" he says as the other shakes his hand a little

stiffly. "It must be at least three months since I last saw you in Algiers. Why aren't you coming by anymore? How is Si Abderahmane? And what about your studies? Not yet on vacation?"

His mind elsewhere, Bachir answers; the encounter displeases him.

"Stop by my father's place, he'll be delighted to see you. You can spend the night at our house. I'll let him know."

Bachir thinks, while spouting the expected formulas of politeness, "Of course it's to be expected that my father, the petit bourgeois whose bakery is gradually making him richer, would have boundless admiration for the great lawyer from the big city, apparently a simple shepherd's son who's done well. That's the model he'd like me to emulate!" His resentment toward his father is growing.

"No, really, no, but please apologize to your father for me. I have urgent business here!"

Khaled bids him good-bye, noticing Bachir's vague look ("Was I that sad or shy at seventeen?"). He watches him go toward the Micheline with long strides and then stop. Khaled turns away. It's very hot. Intuitively reverting to provincial habits, he feels reluctant to enter the European cafés, but notices an ice cream shop he hadn't seen before, heads there, and goes in. He looks at his watch; he has half an hour before he must go to the prison.

Having stopped a few yards away, Youssef had seen Khaled crossing the square; he observes the man's tall, thin frame, his slightly stooped shoulders, the short hair, the glasses. He knows him, he's sure he knows him. While he continues to examine the travelers leaving the train and dispersing, Youssef suddenly remembers: he had just seen the man who had defended him at his trial more than ten years ago. "A fine lawyer," he thinks. "In his profession one has to have a lot of courage right now." The image of himself as a seventeen-year-old returns, obstinately professing his nationalist faith in open court and against his defender's advice, not yet understanding that he was dealing not merely with individual judges but with a whole system. "Such naïveté," he thinks. In spite of his blunder and "on account of his young age," he had been sentenced to twenty years, twenty years of deprivation of his civil rights, twenty years of "loss of citizenship." Then, some twenty months later, he had benefited from the amnesty granted to a certain segment of the "1945 political prisoners," 8 May 1945 . . .

Youssef walks along the square, taking care he'll be recognized (his signals are the newspaper under his arm and a beret on his head). He is aware of the young girl cautiously following him with resolute steps, a slender figure in a white dress. He would like to share with her—as he often does with his wife, Cherifa—not just the events of that historic day, but their glow, which gave them all such high expectations. The same square, as tidy as it is in his memory; the same cafés, closed then for the festivities, since everyone thought they were celebrating Armistice Day. The day looked as if it would be a spirited fair in which everyone had a role to play; "Everyone was there, so why not us," Youssef would say to Cherifa, beginning to feel enraged. "We, the oppressed, the subjugated, the 'lowly Arabs,' we whose blood was used to water the fields of their 'great war.'" They came from all directions, the various political parties' call to action serving first of all to set hope free. They came from the shacks by the river, from the neighboring *douars*, a joyous multitude of almost-city dwellers who also believed the war was over, even women, their veils slipping off as they tried to hold on to them with their teeth, and children, some on the hips of their mothers, running briskly, and others (out-of-place sons of bourgeois families taking the day for a wild vacation). Then a cry of unguarded joy erupted from the crowd, throbbing at the sight of the flags that had appeared. "The emir's green flag," an old man said in an undertone, weeping with happiness, invoking the national hero as if he had died only yesterday and not a century before, in exile. "Our country's flag, our honor," Youssef would continue to recount, "unfurled in joyousness and hope for the first time in a hundred years."

Was it cries or silence? Youssef no longer knew, and toward the end of his account he would feel helpless to express the violent emotion that had then overcome him too—and would continue to shake him up every time he told this part of the story. The first flags had been brought out to the very center of the square near the kiosque and were then borne above the waves of the ever thickening crowd. They streamed on through the nearby streets and came to the front of the church's wide esplanade, where a huge number of policemen in closed ranks awaited them. Sheltered behind the police, tense with panic and hatred, stood the world of women in their Sunday best, hats on, and the husbands in their starched collars, who thought they were celebrating—according to the usual protocol— the armistice of a war they'd never fought, the defeat of a regime that, for the most part, they had supported. The green flags of Islam, of the rediscovered dignity of the people, kept advancing. Youssef, whose only true love was for this shifting reality, this flood tide of wretchedness, would continue his tale. Then his jaws would tighten and he'd add, "Of course, they were simple rags, bits of sheets patched and sewn by the women for their luminous songs." "Filthy rags!" the police yelled, giving the first warning that they'd have to disappear. The flags kept moving forward.

Then a second shudder went through the crowd, the grunt of a collective retreat across from the church where that morning a service had been held. Surrounding the esplanade was a police cordon from behind which the women's veiled hats and the men's dour faces had abruptly vanished. Chaos had begun: the first gunshots from the police, the first dead man (a greengrocer whom Youssef knew and had seen just a few minutes earlier, with bare arms and chest, laughing with joy because he undoubtedly loved the songs and noise), a pushing and shoving in the front ranks that had unblocked the center.

Behind them, the women stopped singing and were suddenly busy, armed with the same zeal they used at home when rolling semolina dough for the evening meal. They brought out old baskets, filling them with stones, putting some of them in their skirts and veils, and then they, too, entered the fray. A laughable battle—people using their bare hands against bullets.

A second man had fallen. In the rear beyond the square, and still unaware of the drama that had begun, the demonstrators had hardly come to the end of their first outbursts of joy, so that several young men, one of them Youssef, had to pass among them to give the order to retreat and thereby avoid carnage. The *place d'armes* was already sealed off by the paddy wagons that had come speeding in with blasting noise. Already…

Youssef would stop there; Cherifa wanted to hear the conclusion, how he'd been arrested. He would respond but in a suddenly indifferent voice. He'd talk about the lists the authorities had immediately drawn up: more than thirty young men hauled away that night or early the next day. At daybreak he'd been taken away in a jeep, flanked by two policemen, one of whom he remembered was Martinez. Perhaps a comic detail, but he couldn't forget it: throughout the ride, Martinez unfeelingly emptied his pipe on Youssef's skull, tapping it with short little blows.

"What about the prison, what was that like?" Cherifa wouldn't stop questioning him.

"I was lucky; that's where I discovered my Arab brothers, where I became a man."

Thereafter Cherifa could dream of the adolescent who for twenty months, which had seemed short to him, would listen to determined men in their cells speak about earlier struggles and the battle yet to come. That same day, massacres had taken place in martyred towns: Setif, Guelma, Constantine. Young Youssef was discovering that a native country is not shared land, not even shared misery, but blood, shed together on the same day, the same songs interrupted.

By the end of the story, Cherifa would remember with tears in her eyes that by some curious coincidence that day of bloodshed had been the day of her first wedding. For her, too, a gray dawn had risen—she had remained silent at the questions of prying women: "Do you love him?"—and since it was necessary to know whether she loved the stranger who had the right to take her that first night, and not wanting to scream no, she had grit her teeth, not knowing at seventeen if her disgust and empty heart were not, after all, the lot of every woman. But she tried to forget the man with his broad hands who had become her husband and instead asked about Ali, her young brother, who'd run off the night before to join the demonstrations. That anxiety alone had linked her to the town's passion.

•••

Youssef quickly turns his head—at a distance, Hassiba is still following him. When she came off the train, she'd instantly recognized him, thanks to the agreed-upon signs. It's her first time in this town, but for her it's the beautiful day she's been anticipating for so long. She looks at nothing as they pass the rue du Bey, the square where it ends, the alleys of the Arab quarter with the whitewashed houses where children hide from her as they do from every passerby, a kind of shocked surprise in their black eyes. At the end of a cul-de-sac alley, Youssef stops ahead of her and turns around, ready to retrace his steps. The gate of the only house in the cul-de-sac cracks open. Hassiba keeps going and enters.

Youssef then calmly returns to the center. After its usual half-hour stop, the Micheline leaves, gliding along the boulevard with the bitter-orange trees. Youssef moves nonchalantly, just as if he'd been home for lunch and is going back to work. "We're in luck," he thinks, "there'll be no raid today."

At this part of the siesta, the square, ossified in its calm, seems a hundred miles away from the mountain, where operations continue. The last customers, who were dozing on the terraces, now rise and leave with heavy steps, smoking a last cigar. They'd only have to raise their eyes to make out the planes that keep circling above the burned slopes on the smoke-filled horizon. But it's enough for them to hear the muffled sound of the convoys that since early morning have been heading for the battlefields by the back avenues. They hear them, forget them, and think only of sinking deep into the sleep of their siesta. Behind them, peace settles over the now abandoned areas. Only the waiters, bleached shadows in their uniforms, remain standing, each in front of his own door, vaguely saddened by the virginal hour. They exchange a few words from one terrace to another about the new faces the Micheline has spewed out, the only thing that prods the indolence of the hour.

That's when, indifferent to the silence and the heat, Touma passes by, escorted by a group of young men, Bob and his friends.

"Bitch's daughter!" one of the waiters calls out. "Bitch's daughter!" he says again, louder now, in the direction of his colleague. "If she's going to hang out with ruffians like that, she could at least do it with her own kind."

"They wouldn't think of looking at her, they wouldn't even touch her with a fingertip!" another replies, happy with his retort, although it's not particularly directed at Touma.

But she's heard. She unhooks her arm from Bob's, approaches the waiter, and hisses full of resentment: "You'll be sorry for that vicious tongue of yours, old man, I'm telling you! First thing I'll do is tell your boss!"

The waiter, a man of about forty, narrows his eyes. "There's a job gone," he thinks. "What came over me? Just for that piece of trash? Why didn't I stay quiet in my little spot? I should know this is a time to be silent as the grave. Losing my job, oh, Lord!" He doesn't move, stares at the girl, but then can't restrain himself.

"I'm only saying out loud what your brothers think to themselves when you walk by! What's vicious is not my tongue, it's you, who reeks, you bitch's daughter!" Then more quietly, "Is this the time for every kind of garbage to surface and stink up heaven and earth?"

Touma threatens out of habit. She doesn't really have enough hate left in her to persist in showing off her power. Bob has been following her ever since she, at the last minute, refused to take the train, only moments earlier. Just as the train was about to leave, she had decided unexpectedly to say in a loud voice, "I'm staying," looking around with a defiant expression that had mystified him.

"Now? Just after I went to get all this money?" he complained. But with a high-pitched laugh she retorted, "Well then, let's spend it here! And with your friends over there, too, if they feel like it!"

So she invited the whole little group that had been following them in order to watch their departure and was now ogling Touma from afar. Since Bob, who was usually so timid, had approached her, she'd become an exciting prey for all of them. Disappointed, Bob would have preferred to have had her all to himself, but the only thing left for him now was to go and get his friends.

"What's vicious is not my tongue!" repeats the waiter, shaken by a terrible fear. ("If I lose my job! Poverty again. And the kids, what do I do with all my kids! And my old mother in the hospital!")

Touma hasn't answered back yet. She raises her arms in the air, then lifts her head, bursts into bright laughter: her sadness is dissipating, though at the ice cream shop it had covered her with its black wings when she'd been confronted by the threats from the boy she calls Blue Jeans. Done with the challenge, done with the fear in the eyes of others, which she engenders! As if the day were barely rising, she wants to live, live . . . put out the fire that's choking her. Her arms in the air, she cries out happily:

"I don't care! Insults, curses, I don't care! People like you, the entire town for that matter, I don't care!"

Youssef's been following the whole scene from a few steps back, from under the shade of the awning on the terrace next door. He hears Touma's laugh slice through the tranquillity of the square as she leaves, balancing on her high heels in the middle of the group of young men, who haven't understood the exchange of words in Arabic and whose pimply adolescent faces darken with the beginnings of mistrust.

Youssef approaches the waiter. "Would you please avoid this provocation!" he grumbles. "This isn't the first time you've been told."

The man begins to explain, to apologize, troubled by Youssef's presence and, at the same time, relieved that Touma is gone. Disgruntled and moving off in the direction of his shop, Youssef says to himself, "When will we learn to keep our composure, bite our tongues, and keep silent? Defiance is too easy."

"How about that!" exclaims another waiter, who has seen Youssef but not heard his words. "Si Youssef must not have taken a siesta today." He takes a watch out of his pocket, checks the time. "He's half an hour ahead of his usual schedule!"

His eyes wander all across the square.

"Not a single customer at this hour!" he says, not noticing that his colleague has already gone inside. "Or rather, just one, a stranger," he notes as he observes Khaled at the ice cream shop, now paying and getting up. "It's so hot! The south wind will be here tomorrow. I can always feel it a day in advance."

He yawns lazily, swipes at a few tables with his cloth, and then slowly retreats into the rooms of his empty café.

•••

After having left Khaled, whom he had not enjoyed running into, Bachir stopped beside the Micheline. A girl in a white dress appears, her hair worn in a long braid down her back; her delicate face lit up by a look of youthful frailty. As she comes down the steps, she smiles a little, undoubtedly with pleasure at the welcome the entire town extends to her, she, the ephemeral guest. Surprised, Bachir watches her. "How lovely she is!" he thinks, taken aback, while at the foot of the train steps Hassiba almost bumps into him, not having noticed the flustered, shy young man. "Pardon me," she says, her eyes elsewhere, then takes a few steps and moves on. "How lovely she is!" Bachir repeats, his eyes in the distance, already pursuing the image of the furtive smile on the thin lips of the girl who has vanished in the sun.

Other young people are gathering beside the Micheline, which is about to leave. Bachir waits, forgets he's waiting, dreams. Suddenly a touch on his elbow. He jumps, remembers he is there to meet someone.

"Let's walk!" says the other, an adolescent about his age. He doesn't introduce himself. He speaks first. His tone is lively, his speech fast, and he seems to speak with some disdain. "A student," he says to himself, "the son of a bourgeois, we'll see what he's capable of."

"They told me. Are you sticking by your decision?"

Bachir has forgotten the girl and his disarray. He is besieged by an unrestrained resolve, precipitated by the excitement of finally having made that first contact he'd been expecting for so long, ever since the day at the cemetery when he didn't want to return to school in the city anymore, his mind jolted by an emotion that was boiling over because he had had to control it for so many months.

"I'd like . . ." he begins to tell his story. He wants to say it all. For twenty months now—several times he repeats "twenty months" with a sigh of regret as if he were saying "twenty years"—the revolution has been happening. And he, at his age, what's he been doing? Nothing. The lycée, his studies, that's all well and good. Yes, being at the head of the class to show, as his father says, that "an Arab whose brothers manage only to polish the conquerors' shoes is capable of fighting them with their own weapons." "I believed that, too. But that's not what matters anymore. Now . . ."

"Now?" the other asks with a frown. ("Sincere enough," he judges, "We'll have to wait and see. What we need is men, 'hard ones,' not romantic fanatics.")

"What do my studies and all the rest of it mean to me now? Nothing. I want to act, like the others, like the brothers." (It's the first time he uses the language of a militant. He blushes slightly, hoping the other hasn't noticed.)

"What about your father, what does he say about this?" the unfamiliar boy asks, toning down his earlier sarcasm, interested now.

Bachir stops, faces the young man (barely my age, he notes with both surprise and respect). He feels awash with—what to call it?— love, faith.

"When I tried to explain it to my father, he answered me, 'You're lucky to be studying. You're lucky to be doing so well. Don't waste it.' He thought he'd convinced me. In his head he could already see me going back to my books and my boarding school. I told him I wasn't. Having so much luck is not any luck at all right now. Now . . ." (he stammers, hesitates—helpless, and painfully aware of it—not know-

ing how to express the progression of his new certainty), "now . . .
it's all about the revolution, the liberation struggle. No, I'm very sure
of it, having all that luck is no longer any luck at all right now!"

"Not so loud!" the other says and starts to walk again, beret on
his head, hands in his pockets.

• • •

No matter how far back she goes in her memories, Lila remembers
that her mother's death had put an end to a slow-paced era, which
lay at the bottom of her memory like an August lake of light, a cold
wellspring.

In the town's traditional Arab society where marriages comply
with the inescapable choice of the head of the family, the fact that
such a choice—inspired only by the group's values—can inadver-
tently produce a mad love, as it had for Lila's parents, who were married off to each other, was actually a true marvel. Lila's father,
Rachid, had fallen in love with the young wife they had earlier presented to him according to the well-established protocol, in a house
that was too large and that was inhabited by a veritable tribe
(Rachid's three brothers, already married and each with many children; a widowed sister; and several elderly women, grandmothers
and others; and presiding over them all the omnipotent master, the
father). Lila remembers her mother as a languid young woman. Was
she beautiful? She doesn't know. At the time, women were not pho-
tographed, to prevent even their images from leaving the house. She
had died of tuberculosis when she was not yet thirty and Lila could
only fill the void of that pale presence with the image she had of her
father at that period. That was easier for her.

She loved him so much, that man who had discovered himself in
his bliss, who used to forget everyone else to the point where his love
began to seem scandalous and immodest to the rest of them. "So
irresponsible!" they used to say. "So unseemly!" they would whisper
when they saw him preferring to spend each evening alone with his
wife in their room to being with the other men on the family patio.

"Such a foolish father!" they'd grumble when he spent hours and hours cooing over his daughter rather than intuitively understanding that the role of wife and children is merely to better establish the earnestness and authority of a man.

"Yes," Lila was in the habit of saying to Ali, "what has made me vulnerable is that early presence of happiness and the memory of what's left of it!" Although she wouldn't admit it, she also thought at the same time that happiness had provided some grace.

Apparently nothing set Rachid Selha apart from the other sons in the several dozen families of few means but great pride, in this town where the only form of aristocracy consisted in the ability to assert one's ancestry back to the arrival of the French in the previous century—or sometimes further back, to the period of the Turks, when, in the name of the dey of the capital, the bey of Titteri was the region's governor. The town is the gateway to a plain that was once primarily used by caravans and had now become the richest of the country's regions, a place where foreign settlers ruled over an inexhaustible wealth of harvests and vineyards. When the colonizer climbs on his horse or into his truck to survey the wretched fellahs whose sweat he needs, these workers in their subjugation occasionally forget that there was a time when they, nomads or farmers walking leisurely, used to roam the stretches of the wild plain. Tightly squeezed like a closed fist and always seeing the countryside as resembling some immense hull shipwrecked by history's cruelty, the old town, set beside the plain, prides itself on being the only one that follows the roots that connect it to past generations. But frozen like this in the middle of the drift, the people in these families don't notice that they have been forced to close in upon themselves, in the silence of their houses and their women, to be saved from the shipwreck.

Like some others, Rachid Selha had been able to go to the foreigners' school and learn their language. Then, at age sixteen, he was obliged to stop his studies (and abandon their horizons, he thought) to come back and help out in the family business and, like his brothers, strive to permanently ignore the world the immigrants had established and developed, those foreigners who made the laws, enriched themselves, built ever larger villas in their neighborhoods, homes in the styles of the French provinces—when not Tyrolian or Scottish—that stood in stark contrast to the minarets and terraces of the Moorish quarters.

Following custom, Rachid had agreed to marry the daughter of a family of equal rank to his, one with solid traditions and with a religious education fraught with the usual puritanism. But since his marriage, this youngest and favorite son had defied his father. As befits the long-standing order of the family hierarchy, everyone bows to the father: brings him his prayer rug, kisses his hand every morning and evening with the sanctioned formulas of greeting and respect, remains silent when he is absorbed in his meditation; his sons must abstain from smoking in his presence, never begin a conversation before he does, and never interrupt him. Before this patriarch, whose only dream is to one day have enough money to make the pilgrimage to Mecca and, if it pleases God, to die there, now stands Rachid. He wants to live alone with his wife ("Alone? Why alone? Impossible!"). He wants, shockingly, to take his wife—always his wife!—to the capital ("To look around? What a flight of fancy!"). He wants . . . what else does he want? "Yes," Rachid says, "that's precisely it, my daughter will go to school. This time, father, I won't give in."

"She's a girl! She can perfectly well attend Koranic school, just like the rest. It'll be quite enough for her to say her prayers and understand the Koran."

"No, that will not be enough for her!" Rachid raises his voice. "Times are changing and even girls will need to be properly prepared!"

Weary, the father pretends to give in.

"She's your daughter, do what you want! But when she's a woman she must be the repository of our honor!"

Lila remembers that her father used to carry her book bag and, her hand in his, take her to elementary school. He'd wait for her after school every day, alone among the European mothers, who couldn't understand the young man's pride (he was no more than twenty-five at the time). When they'd come home, Lila remembered, the woman with the same eyes as hers couldn't help smiling indulgently; but she was also somewhat confused by her husband's enthusiasm, suddenly making him an exalted adolescent in his touching desire to show how happy he was with the new customs (that "French style" that people criticized).

Lila always had to laugh when she remembered the shocked reception she had provoked at the family table, presided over by the patriarch. When she was about seven or eight, with that authority peculiar to children who are too pampered, she began to describe how her father would kiss her mother on the cheek in their room, every morning and night, and then she added happily that it was exactly how her schoolbooks described the perfect family. Rachid had to leave the table to go and laugh by himself, and the insolence of that crazy laughter had seemed even more serious to everyone than his ridiculous—no, worse yet—his Western habits. She also remembered having said quite loudly one time, confronting the dreaded grandfather with childlike calm, "My father and my mother are my only family, that's it!" She now repeats the phrase of her childhood. (A drama had ensued: her grandfather had slapped her, and when he found out, Rachid had forbidden anyone ever to lay a hand on her. "I have my own ways of raising her," he used to say.) She believes this gave her the chance to reject attachments and restraints. She used to say blatantly to a smiling but disapproving Ali, "I have no ties, no constraints! Thanks to my father, thanks to happiness, I was able to escape from mother, grandfather, aunt, second cousin, the cousin's son-in-law, and so on, with all their opinions, principles, fears, and cowardice—in short, from everything that remains of a clan, tribe, and a dead past!" That painless liberation did, indeed, seem fortunate to her.

Then death struck. For one more year Rachid escorted his daughter to school, closely followed her schoolwork, participated in her games, inundated her with dolls and then books, and spent his evenings with her. But more and more often, at night while she pretended to fall asleep, she heard discussions that set Rachid against his father—because he didn't want to remarry, because he was becoming involved in political activities outside the house, "reckless ones" the patriarch decided. One day Rachid disappeared: he had gone to live in Algiers. A few months later he returned to insist that Lila go on to high school. He was no longer afraid of being in open conflict. "Don't count on her joining your harems!" That is what he'd said, or maybe something a little less aggressive. In Lila's mind it became confused with the long conversations she had with him later—"My father," she thought, "my only friend." "She will be free," he had added, before he left for France for good.

For two or three years there was no news of him. He wrote only to Lila at her boarding school. He'd send her brief postcards but didn't give an address. During that time the old patriarch was aging rapidly, as if the departure of his favorite son had opened a breach in time's ravages. He shrank, mellowed, became reticent, only talked with and smiled at Lila when on Sundays she'd come back from school. She was an adolescent with awkward manners who'd grown too fast. To reach the family home, she had to go through the central streets of town, where it seemed as if every passerby whom she ran into was saying, "That is so and so's daughter, the family that . . . she goes to high school . . . she walks in the streets by herself . . ."; and another: "Now our girls are dressing like Europeans, without any veil, good God! What has happened to the modesty that used to protect our women?" She'd keep moving, anxiety in her heart for feeling so alone and as if undressed, but then, gritting her teeth, she'd raise her head and think of her father, "the rebel, the agitator, the hero." At the time, that is how he'd appear to her.

The patriarch would ask, "Has your father written to you?" Pity for the old man washed over her. "No," or else, "Yes, here is his card," and then she would take the map of France and patiently indicate the place shown on the postcard.

One Sunday, Lila, the daughter of the prodigal son, was the first whom the patriarch told that he was finally going to realize his great dream: he was leaving for Mecca. He then pleaded, as he had for forty years, "May God let me die on sacred ground!" His departure became a celebration. At the end, he took Lila aside and softly began, "You'll tell your father, should he return . . ." and he gave her instructions as if he were leaving forever.

Lila had relayed these words to her father in the first letter she wrote him (at last, he had given her his address). Deeply moved, she told him how happy the patriarch had been, then informed him of his death as it had been told to her: he had died of sunstroke on a Friday, the very day of the pilgrimage; died of gladness and plenitude, Lila was convinced of it. Rachid did not come. "What good will it do for me to attend the family's disintegration?" he wrote. For it was disintegrating, suddenly plagued by forces that until then had been underground. Lila's three uncles were arguing over the modest inheritance, each driven by competitive wives now showing their claws in the house where they'd lived for so long, packed together with their broods. With the financial share that fell to him, Rachid bought himself a small hotel in a working-class neighborhood in Paris. Lila's letters to her father became longer as she described her loathing for the family's decline and her nostalgia for the time when the patriarch's presence had at least given the family some style.

Lila was then finishing her years in high school. She was close only to Suzanne, in a friendship that needed no words or speeches and consisted of an intuitive coming together in which each kept silent about her milieu, but recognized the other in the books they exchanged, in athletic rivalry in the stadium on Thursdays, and in a similar unbridled lack of discipline that each squandered in the same way. Lila passionately threw herself into her correspondence with her father, in a long monologue of blind aspirations (for six months she held forth to him on purity and the ways in which to achieve it) and versatile, mystical incitements (she discovered that Islam was not merely her family's and society's way of conforming but also, in the past, a source of innumerable adventures for visionaries mad with audacity and exultation). She wrote him a solemn and absolute declaration (that she would never marry, because her independence and freedom were to be devoted entirely to her country). With each letter, her unfettered lyricism would fill ten pages, which Rachid read attentively, but all he managed to retain from the chaos was her impetuosity. "My daughter will be a liberated woman," he would say and loved her with an outpouring of what had once been his own happiness.

Lila saw her father as someone who had attained every goal she had set for herself: independence, liberty, purity—for she understood Rachid's departure to be a victorious revolt, without recognizing its inevitable uprooting. She also felt a cruel shock when, from a letter whose embarrassed wording irritated her, she discovered he had remarried, with a French seamstress. Rachid said that in the early years when he found himself on foreign soil, jobless and without any friends, this woman had helped him. At seventeen, Lila didn't accept disappointment; rather than give up the image she had created, she interpreted his disclaimer as weakness: so her father wasn't perfect. Therefore, like anyone else, he was forgetful of the great love of his past, unfaithful to the morality of the absolute and uncompromising, which had ended up shaping her by continuously finding confirmation in Rachid's life. Six months later, eyes shamelessly aglow, she met Ali on the boulevard with the bitter-orange trees.

During the year that followed, Lila settled for an exchange of brief missives with her father. She was too busy noticing that in discovering love she was discovering her own truth, her own secret face, which she recognized with passion when leaning over Ali's. One day, panic beset her: frightened, as if facing a venture whose risks or outcome she didn't fear as much as she did its excess—wherein she would certainly founder—she suddenly wrote a letter to her father, her long-ago friend. The letter was no longer the river of dazzling ramblings of her adolescence; it was a call.

That's how Rachid interpreted it. He was now a forty-five-year-old man, gray-haired and lean, with slightly bitter features, and so one day, leaving his wife and friends behind in Paris, he set out on a journey. He was returning to his own country for two weeks. With the exception of the two days he reserved to visit the rest of the family in his hometown, he would come to wait for Lila when her courses at the university were finished and together they'd go for long walks in the suburbs of Algiers. Filled with emotion, they went back to their old habits, to their complicity that, they now each clearly recognized, came from their close resemblance. Completely taken with her, he noticed for the first time that the tall slender girl with the green eyes and shy smile, who in her defenseless beauty so resembled her mother, seemed armed in spite of her fragility with the same stubborn determination that he, without any false modesty, admitted was his. Every day as she came toward him he would study her and say to himself, "How proud she is!" At the first embrace she didn't dare look him in the face, as was her wont. With the caution that prolonged the emotion of their reunion, she was getting to know him all over again, this man who, for so many years, had been a beacon to her. In the stiff body, the slumping shoulders, the hard look in his eyes that would sometimes soften with brief moments of light, she saw a man separated from her by all kinds of bitterness and an itinerant life. Still, in him, in his laughter ("I haven't been this happy in a very long time!" he'd say), in the detachment with which he evoked his memories, in the principles he presented with a steadfastness she admired ("I'm so lucky to have a father I respect"), she also found a youthfulness that undoubtedly was a form of naïveté inseparable from his nature, a kind of innocence that his misfortunes had not changed.

They became infatuated with each other. In the two weeks of his visit, during which she saw very little of Ali, Lila was transfigured by the rediscovery of her father. They would linger in the small restaurants by the harbor; they'd both burst out laughing when a waiter took them for a couple; she'd accompany him to his hotel, and as they walked she'd listen to him speak at length, and a healthy exhilaration would come over Rachid for being able to look back, together with his daughter, at the years behind him. He would describe his years in exile, and it seemed that it was thanks to Lila that the break with his environment, whose drama she had never suspected, was beginning to form a scar.

He brought up the reason for his departure: "One day I said to myself, 'I'm thirty years old and I'm still not a man; always in the shadow of family and father. Sure, I would oppose him, since I wasn't always prepared to bend to his wishes, and yet I was living off him . . . So I left! Nothing here was binding me to the future; all of it was linked to the past. So I left! Then I found myself somewhere in a godforsaken village in France without any money. I looked for work. It was really difficult. Thank God, there were some fellow countrymen. They're found everywhere, like waves of locusts" (he laughs briefly). "I had to go all the way to France to discover what the men of my own country are like! That is when I really knew what solidarity of the people means. Then I went up to Paris."

"What did you do in Paris at first? Where did you work?" Lila wanted the stories to go on forever.

"I arrived with an old man from Kabylia who had been working in France for thirty years. Every three years, he'd go to visit his wife and children at home, then he'd go back to France, often changing places because he liked being on the go. He knew all the old-timers; thanks to him, I was hired to work in a factory."

Rachid would go on talking about the many North African laborers in Paris, the organizational work to be done, the foundations that had to be laid for it, struggles in which to become involved, the awareness of the laborers' strength, their strikes. He'd explain and continue. Lila listened to him devotedly, finding that the earlier image she once had of her father, when idealizing her own dreams, had been very meager. Emotion seized her, not only because Rachid's words were a window opened onto a new world, but also because she now began to desire a boundless life, as she was often to repeat to Ali later, one that through the years would gradually expand until it reached infinity. "I'd like to reach the point one day where reality is both a vast field and some earth nearby, very near, which I could gather up at any moment and let run through my fingers. With what kind of feeling?" she'd ask herself, trying to particularize her ideal. She'd reflect, search for what she was missing, "with very great care, because being mindful of others must be the one and only inexhaustible passion," she'd conclude.

Rachid also talked about his minuscule hotel: ten rooms for ten working-class families; the husbands had resolved to bring their wives and children over so they could take advantage of the government's aid to large families. Then he mentioned Alice, his wife, and the things that kept her busy—she helped these women who ended up one day in Paris in their peasant dresses, taught them how to get around, how to deal with the Metro, recognize numbers, register their children for school. There was so much to be done. Lila stopped asking questions, intimidated by the presence of the unknown woman whom in her seventeen-year-old self-centeredness she used to hate, and from now on would respect because her father's face mellowed when he spoke her name. "He loves her," she thought. Embarrassed, she said nothing.

During the last few days of his stay, she scarcely had the courage to stammer, "You ought to see Ali," and blushing she quickly changed the subject as Rachid, jotting down the appointment, answered: "Of course I'll see him! I came because of him, didn't I?"

Rachid and Ali spent the following day together; Lila stayed in her student room and slept, so she wouldn't have to wait in fear, but fear of what? She sighed with relief when later at dinner Rachid finally said: "I'm really glad I saw Ali. I can leave with a calm heart now."

He left for France the next day.

"Not so loud," the other boy says and begins to walk again, beret on his head, hands in his pockets.

At the bottom of the boulevard, he gives Bachir his instructions: no question of his joining a cell; in any case, he himself isn't from this town nor can he stay.

"I'd really like to be part of something here," Bachir sighs sullenly.

Unreadable, the other says, "Well, we can always try!" and then with a note of empathy, "Rest assured, this is just a small job without much risk."

He sets a time for that very day and disappears into an alley. Bachir continues on by himself. Without thinking about it, he heads home.

Si Abderahmane has just bought a two-level Basque-style villa in the European district, where until now no Arab has ever lived; it was one of the first houses sold by the French who left the country. He is waiting at the back of the living room, its bay windows open to the lawn, standing near a tall fireplace, which won't witness any more Christmas celebrations. He's downhearted about the son who'd been his pride and joy, his hope for the future, and for whom he now helplessly has to wait! Out of breath from rushing through the heat, Bachir comes in, confronts his father, remains silent.

"You're not even apologizing!" Si Abderahmane explodes. "I

warned you just today: there's always a risk of raids or arrests. Did you have to choose this very day to loiter around town? And what about your studies? Your school? Am I now supposed to be thinking about that instead of you, I who . . ."

Bachir isn't listening—he observes his father, whose face is streaked with rage and whose wrath is making him stutter; he has a vague sense of sadness. Behind him—he doesn't need to turn around—the entire household is listening at the door, his six sisters and his mother, who, in tears, must be raising her arms toward heaven yet again, to invoke God, the Prophet, and every local saint, the way she's been doing recently.

The father continues his diatribe. Bachir is overcome by a profound sense of emptiness. Si Abderahmane is completely beside himself: Bachir looks at him, an agitated shadow on the edge of a foreign land. Seized by weariness and imbued with the satisfaction of how easy it is for him to feel detached from paternal shouting and the tirades of the women behind him, he slowly smiles with a quiet grace.

He will still wear that smile when the flames rise before him later on, the beginning of a magnificent fire that will light the town throughout the night. The same absentminded smile of joy penetrates him as though it were a given. At the far end of the plain the sun goes down and takes on the colors of the fire that prolongs the sunset. The farm adjoins the station; the thirty carloads of straw that were to leave the following day, lined up near the sheds close by, are burning well.

Bachir had escaped from the house at dinnertime with the same fervor he once displayed in his childhood games and in his carefree adolescence. After a long trek to the edge of town, he found the companion assigned to him. Together they waited until the farm's caretaker had made his last round; together they prepared the torches to be thrown into the cars, lined up in the back of the freight depot, closest to the farm buildings. While a third accomplice was cutting the telephone wires, Bachir and his companion moved away to wait for the flames to grow larger.

Bachir is watching calmly, it's a grandiose spectacle. The sun has disappeared below the horizon; as the day pales in early abeyance, the night seems intent on casting about its darkness, when the beaming fire pierces it with its bloody cracklings in the sky.

It's time to leave; they signal Bachir. Filled with the year's harvest, the nearest sheds are beginning to burn. They've succeeded.

"Time to make our getaway! We've got just enough time to get to town before curfew," the boy says under his breath.

Bachir follows him; he wishes he didn't have to rush. They take side streets and climb over barricades; Bachir turns around; the flames are high and the fire grows ever bigger, like the heart of wanton joy. As they walk along the river and approach town, Bachir tries to put a name to the excitement raging inside him: "Beauty is so cruel!" he hears himself mumble without understanding. Casually, he repeats the words like a mantra whose meaning emerges through mere repetition: "Beauty is so cruel . . . cruel!"

"Watch out!" the other one whispers. They both leap into the shadow: police cars, followed by fire engines, noisily pass by. "Let's part here," his comrade says softly to Bachir. Bachir turns to him. He saw him for the first time just this afternoon; he'll undoubtedly never see him again. In a surge of emotion, he thinks, "My first comrade, just for a moment, the time of a lightning flash . . ."

"Good night," he says in response.

"Beauty is so cruel." The phrase dances inside him—intuition, anxiety? He remembers the young girl in the white dress, her evanescent passing, her vanished reflection. Is that, too, existence? A series of shadows that are erased? That, too? The fire, and others that will follow? The sudden vertigo in him when the flames illuminated the plain, the plain he was seeing for the first time, streaming at his feet like a farewell? "Let's hope this is a fire that won't end but will last, will resist . . . that's what I want (so I can live) . . . that's what I want . . ." At his age, he feels haunted by not yet being able to dive to the bottom of reality, grasp it as something permanent yet blinding, a rustling below the surface that can be heard in spite of the world's noise. As he walks along he makes every effort to plunge into the truth of his problem. "We shouldn't be blinded by beauty, nor by passing 'froth,' but . . ."

A small laugh. The surprised voice of a woman. "Bachir!" she says happily.

He raises his head, absorbed as he had been in his impassioned search. He almost bumps into the couple. He sees Khaled.

"You know him?" Khaled asks, giving the smiling Lila a long look.

"Bachir!" she repeats and is happy, then to Khaled: "He's my cousin; no, he's more than that. Bachir, what're you doing out at this hour? What a pleasure to see you!"

She easily convinces Bachir to come home with her; they're two steps from her apartment, and to give him an excuse, she assures him that he'll never get home before curfew at the rate he's going. Then Khaled leaves them in front of the large building.

"Farewell!" Lila says to him, and it truly is a farewell. Khaled smiles elusively before he turns his back on them ("So young, just children, those two," he thinks). As he reaches his hotel, he cannot avoid telling himself with bittersweet sadness that meeting this woman, whom he hadn't even known a few hours earlier, will be a permanent open wound for him.

"What a pleasure to see you today!" Lila says again when they reach the sixth floor and she opens the door to her apartment, lit up at night through the open windows by the glare of the nearby fire.

It's been a very long day for her, a leap taken into unknown space. The time up to now seems to be a black lake, a stagnant body of water in which she sees herself surface slowly as if surprised by the passing of the hours. It seems to her as if meeting up with the young man whom she loves like a brother turns the end of the day into a rebirth. But the awakening has been difficult and faltering.

"I went out early this afternoon," she explains to her guest, who settles down while she closes the blinds and turns on the lights in the room.

"I went out and was liberated," she thinks, so obviously preoccupied that Bachir notices.

"Is this where you live?" he asks, and in a gentle whisper she replies:

"This is a stopover."

• • •

For a long time, Cherifa had wandered around the Arab market. All the merchants are closing up, some of them earlier than usual, frightened by the day's operations on the mountain and of not making it home for lunch. They leave in clusters, avoiding the square. In the silence that has fallen over the area normally so animated at this hour, even the children coming out of school instinctively walk like sad thieves; they scatter into the alleys, appearing rigid and strained.

Cherifa has finally found Youssef's shop—after stopping two boys of around ten who were on their way home from school, book bags under their arms, and asking them for directions. The first, whistling insolently, took her for a prostitute and let out a cheerful series of obscenities. A few steps later, breathing hard, she begged the second boy, who smugly gave her the information: of course, he knew Youssef's carpenter shop! She showered him with blessings and thanks, hurried on, and arrived at the shop a few minutes later.

"I have to stay here till one o'clock, when we normally close!" said Yahia, Youssef's helper, a suspiciously prudish young man. "If Youssef doesn't come back, I'll close up," He's about to shut the door in her face: no women here!

"I'm his wife," Cherifa protests, and then in reaction to his incredulous look, adds,"May God strike me blind if I'm lying! I'm his wife and I must wait for him."

She slips into the shop and insists on staying there; then at one o'clock, she says: "You can go and leave me here! Lock the door and, since he's expected back, he'll find me here."

Yahia doesn't trust the situation. He's sorry, he can't do it. He's sure of himself and his principles: a veiled woman in the street at this hour who told him that she's just crossed the whole town? That can't be Youssef's wife.

"No, I'm sorry!"

Cherifa gasps with powerlessness:

"Can't you wait a little?" She begs, implores; her face is still veiled, with only an eye showing through a triangle. Without turning his face to her, without even catching her eye, the young man counters, "I'm chaste." He thinks, "Both in body and spirit." He remains adamant. He no longer responds. He forces Cherifa to leave; a glance, a single glance, at the young woman's ankles, in spite of himself. Then there is uneasiness in his soul, remorse, he moves away with his head down. He doesn't live very far away; he'll be home just in time for prayers.

• • •

In the square, Youssef is unhappy about the incident he's just witnessed and heads rapidly for his shop. "The undoing of many men in town," he thinks, still disgusted with the waiter who insulted Touma, "is the joy they take in being defiant. What good is venom? It's an illusion for the weak, the satisfaction that comes from cursing and surliness. In the struggle, one forgets all that." In his secret organization, he prefers to work only with those who show complete self-control.

A beggar dressed in rags stops next to him; he's out of breath.

"What's the matter with you?" Youssef asks, having recognized him; he enters the hallway of a building to talk to him.

"I've just come up from the shantytown by the river. I thought I'd find you in your shop."

"Quick, what is it?"

"They arrested Saidi at ten this morning. We've only just heard the news. I was told this information could be useful to you."

"Thank you."

Youssef leaves. How did they get to Saidi? Do they know about last night's meeting? They must, but what exactly is it they know?

The leak must be found. That's absolutely necessary! Under torture Saidi might talk. How long will he be able to resist? Youssef is about to open his door when he's startled by Cherifa, who'd been crouching on the curb, a white mass inside her worn veil sitting in the sun, now standing before him.

"You, at last!" she cries out; the veil slides off her head and reveals her anguished face.

"Come in, quickly!" Youssef helps her inside, closes the door, and leaves the blinds down. "You!" Cherifa repeats, exhausted from her wait, and then explains: Hakim came home that morning to question his wife about Youssef. Amna, a true sister, said nothing. But the danger's still there. Did Hakim believe Amna? Won't he know the truth this evening when he comes home? All he has to do is ask the children. And besides, since when do they really need any proof to arrest people? Anything suspicious will do.

"So," Youssef says, "they didn't get just Saidi's name but mine as well. Who else is on the list? All of them need to be warned right away."

"Saidi?" Cherifa whispers, "So someone else has been arrested?"

Only then does she realize how imminent the danger is. Since that morning she'd been living in a state of intense agitation: the need to alert Youssef and, to that end, leave the house, be exposed in the street, and run through town. She'd been determined not to feel humiliated by the looks of the men in the cafés, to find her way, no matter what, to curb Yahia's mistrust. All the violent emotions that had fed her increasingly strained willpower and that had revealed her temperament had pushed her beyond herself.

She'd forgotten the danger itself. In truth, it's perhaps not that which drove her, but rather a gnawing desire to suddenly know whether she could really spend her life waiting in her room, in patience and love. That's why she crossed the entire town, bared her presence to so many hostile eyes, and at the end of her trek discovered that she was not only a prey for the curiosity of men—a passing shape, the mystery of the veil accosted by the first glance, a fascinating weakness that ends up being hated and spat upon—no, she now knows that she has existed. She's been inhabited by one inflexible thought that has made her untouchable. "Get to Youssef! He's in danger," she had repeated. "But is he, really?" she ended up wondering when she found herself alone on the curb, surrendering to, or even beyond, the same fruitless waiting. "Won't he first of all be shocked to see me here, out in the street?" No, the danger is real.

Now she is afraid. Real panic. She forgets everything, her racing, her audacity, and she doesn't even think of looking at the shop, although for five years she's been desperate to have a precise image of the place where her beloved husband works.

"They've arrested one of your friends? You see, you're in danger!" And she cries out, "You've got to leave! You have to!"

Youssef takes her in his arms and quiets her down, beginning to feel tender. But he also calculates the time he'll need to take the necessary precautions: in the next two hours the others must be alerted; in case Saidi talks, the place for the meeting with the party leader has to be changed; then he must locate the girl who is joining the resistance in the hills, find a different hiding place for the coming hours, and, of course, get away himself.

"You must leave!" Cherifa sobs.

"Go home," he tells her as they embrace. Vulnerable and demanding in her anxiety, she begs him, "You'll leave, won't you? You're going into hiding, promise me that, I beg you . . ."

"Of course," he reassures her; then as he looks at her ("How beautiful she is, so resplendent, and I'm going to leave her"), he says, "There's a contingent leaving for the maquis tonight, I'm sure of it; a girl arrived today, a few boys who've been waiting. Maybe I'll go with them as well . . ."

Soothed, Cherifa instantly seeks to justify her panic. She's afraid Youssef thinks she's weak.

"I'm not weak, Youssef; I have plenty of courage, I assure you, but . . . but I can't live without you. Never before have I trembled like this. Now I'm afraid of being afraid for you."

"In the hills I'll be safe!"

"I know!" she says as she tries to find her calm again, then all of a sudden, without having thought of it before:

"A girl, you said? A city girl who's joining the resistance?"

"Yes, a young girl; she's not the first one!" he replies, surprised at her question whose meaning escapes him. Cherifa is in his arms again; hope glimmers in her eyes:

"Youssef! Oh, Youssef! I'd like . . ."

"You'd like? . . ." He doesn't understand at all. He's in a hurry. Only two hours and so much to get done.

"You'd like . . ." Although he's trying not to show his impatience, his briskness is obvious to Cherifa.

"No, nothing," she whispers. "Time's going by, you should leave."

That's how a step traced outside the shadows can allow a glimpse at the route and at the path to the goal marked in stone; but the light failed to dawn in the same burst for the two of them.

"What I wanted to say," Cherifa now explains to Lila, who has come to visit her—a happy surprise on this day that she must somehow bring to an end. "What I wanted to say was, 'Take me along too, since there are other women up there . . .' But I didn't dare."

Lila listens intently. "Do you regret it?"

Cherifa is sitting on the mattress, facing the door, just as earlier this morning, open to Hakim's unexpected arrival.

"I don't know! It's probably better this way. There are moments when certain things seem so near, so easy, but then a minute later, a second later . . . it's not the same anymore, and those same things become, how shall I put it, extraordinary and distant? But he—" her tone changes. "He?"

"Do you think he would've accepted it?"

"I don't know. Perhaps that's what I regret. He's been my husband for five years. God is my witness to how much . . ." (she was going to say "I love him," but traditional virtue prevents her from using the words), "to how attached I am to him. I know him through and through. I know everything he wants, what he's going to say before he says it. And yet, in this case, I don't know what he would have done. It's odd. Besides" (she sighs, is getting tired), "he seemed in such a rush, he had so many things to do, to alert the others . . . It wasn't the right moment!"

"As for me," Lila says suddenly after a silence, "he would've taken me along, too, I'm sure of it. Only it wasn't the right moment for me either. I was . . ." (she hesitates), "I was too late."

She also thinks, though she doesn't say it, "I should've woken up earlier, even at the moment of his leaving. I would've gone with him and he wouldn't have had to 'take me along.'" She keeps quiet. Faced with Cherifa, she suddenly understands what it is that separates them: Cherifa is now actively preparing herself to wait. But for Lila, waiting is merely another form of sleep.

Lila had just arrived; an unforeseen desire had impelled her to finally leave her apartment. Rather than pay a visit to her many aunts and uncles scattered about town, she wanted to find a refuge, no, find herself by finding her own world again, the most familiar one, at Ali's sister's house. For the two women, Cherifa's story became an unexpected bond; when confronted with her sister-in-law before now, Lila had always been intimidated by the tranquil perfection that beauty had bestowed on her.

"I've only just come home," Cherifa had said as she welcomed Lila, and the gentleness of her tone had struck Lila, making her think, "She's trembling; she too is alive!" and with simple spontaneity Cherifa continued:

"Now I'm alone. I'll be living alone. Youssef will not be home tonight. He won't be back again . . ."

While Cherifa talks about Youssef's departure, Lila is thinking, "Here I am, finally emerged from my solitude, here I am alive as well, but undoubtedly not in the same way as she . . ." Cherifa is talking. Her tone is serene: Youssef is gone; in a single breath, in the last embrace in the shadow at the back of the unfamiliar shop, like a drowning person she had inhaled a life force; from now on everything can be endured—the days of the spectacle when they remain seated on the floor to watch the war, and the other days of forgetting, of waiting, of killing boredom, and sometimes of despair.

"I must get outside of myself," Lila thinks again. Suddenly she confesses: "I arrived two weeks ago! I've rented an apartment."

"You're living alone?" Cherifa's surprise isn't only from politeness. Yet she doesn't immediately add, "You ought to come and live here," for which Lila is grateful.

"Yes, alone, and nothing to do" (some anger, some resentment still there). "Not going out, thinking of nothing!" Then she tries to make Cherifa understand, make herself understand.

"Since your brother left, I've been telling myself: he left me behind, alone; fine, then, I'll stay alone, I'll live alone! But I don't know anymore. I can't find myself anymore!"

Cherifa says nothing.

"You, who are so full of love, you're going to think badly of me: because he left me, I told myself, I'll forget, I'll destroy everything from the past. It's so easy for me to forget. But then, like cut flowers, I wasn't able to live. I was bound to him and he abandoned me!"

Cherifa finds these recriminations childish.

"He hasn't abandoned you, you can be sure of that! He hasn't abandoned you," she repeats, as though giving a lesson to this young woman who doesn't yet know how to love.

• • •

As she crosses the square, her eyes on Youssef ahead of her, Hassiba begins to recount her life in a private monologue. She's been waiting for this day for three months. From her vantage point she can see the mountain's blue-tinged peaks; keeping Youssef in sight, she thinks, "The mountain! I'm going to the mountain!" and it seems to her as if every step moves her closer to the moment when she'll encounter that immense existence, calm with collective strength, riches, and songs. She will present herself as if to Judgment Day, when you arrive with faith in your heart. A voice inside her whispers, "I'll have to explain all this to the brothers." All the time she'd been waiting, she'd repeated to herself what she felt she must say. She perceives truth as a light; she believes that all those who arrive at the mountain must speak their own truth.

"I've been saying it from the beginning: I want to go there, to the resistance, I want to work with those who fight! Last year their answer was, 'You're too young, you really have to think this through.' Now I'm sixteen. I've thought about it a lot: the revolution is for everybody, for the old and the young. I want to shed my blood for the revolution."

The small voice inside her stops. She's repeated these and other, similar sentences so many times. One day a brother had asked her, "What can you do?" and she answered, "Nothing." Then for three months she learned how to nurse, make bandages, give injections. Finally she was told, "We need a nurse. If you're still willing to go . . . But life on the mountain is hard. You'll have to travel on foot every night. Night is our time. And we walk."

"I can walk! Barefoot if need be. I want to walk with the fighters. I want to suffer with the fighters. Night and day."

Youssef passes the *place d'armes*, goes down a straight street, and then turns at a square. The young girl in the white dress is still dreaming. "Of course, I'll tell the brothers on the mountain everything. I've thought it through. I'm not a child. I'm sixteen. I want to do my part for the revolution."

But that evening as he joins her in the shelter from which they will soon be exiting, Youssef looks at her youth, her bright eyes, her shoes (his first words to her are, "You expect to walk like that, later on?" and, talkative despite the gruff remark, she says, "No, but they told me not to stand out during the train ride . . . that I should pass unseen . . . It's the first time I've worn high heels. They're new . . ."). Baffled by her humble goodwill, Youssef attacks Hassiba's first words:

"You want to work for the revolution—do you have any idea what that means?"

Hassiba is well prepared; no other thought has occupied her mind. She never questioned the cause. Never. Images file rapidly past her, she's looking for the answer: her father, a railroad man in the capital, came home after his accident saying, "France has fired me." Then poverty followed, the father's death, her mother forced into cleaning the homes of other people in the better areas of the city, in despair when her son, at an age when he could be working, was arrested by the authorities as soon as the first troubles began. "Condemned to death," they told her. "The day I went to see him," Hassiba remembers, "the guards sent me away. They sent my mother away. They sent all of us away. That's when I went to see the brothers for the first time. 'I want to work!' I said to them." She reviews the past but is still searching. She's silent.

Youssef regrets his question; why harass her? Perhaps he wanted to say to her, too young, too fragile, "The revolution is not just leaving home and having faith, it's also adversities, massacres, death, all of it to be confronted head on . . ." But she had found what she'd wanted to say and is proud of it, reciting slowly, listening to herself ("It's so good to know, search, and then understand, too!")

"The revolution," she says solemnly, "is the whole country's battle against colonialism, and colonialism is France, which doesn't want to recognize our rights!" She then concentrates, reflects, and adds what she had heard one day from the mouth of a brother, a doctor who was teaching her how to be a nurse, "There are French people who do recognize our rights. They understand us because at one time they, too, had a revolution. Now it's our turn . . ." "The revolution," she repeats seriously, raising her head, "is everyone's battle."

"Yes, everyone's," Youssef says, staring at her, but his mind is elsewhere, as night approaches and the hour of their departure draws near.

• • •

"What about me?" Cherifa, who wants to convince Lila now and upset by her sadness, picks up again. "Am I not also alone? But I'll never think that it's because he's left me, oh no! Separations no longer count now; wherever we are, we're still together."

Lila gets up. She promises to come back. Maybe tomorrow. Without a doubt. She crosses the courtyard, passes the closed door of Lla Aicha's room ("So she's dead now! I can't remember what she looked like," she confesses). Cherifa walks her to the front door. From behind the closed curtains of her neighbor's room come squeals, as of piglets.

"Your neighbor? Does she beat her children?"

"Yes, that's Amna. She has two boys. Twins." Then with a sad smile, "She usually doesn't hit them!"

"Such pointless noise!" Lila sighs, looking beyond the terraces at the smoke on the mountain. She says, "You don't hear that from down there."

"That?"

"The war, I mean . . ."

Slowly, Lila has left, crossing town. It's the beginning of day's end. A soft coolness is released in imperceptible waves along the streets, just above the ground, where the torpor of the hot hours has deposited its halo of dust. In the center, around the kiosque with its tall palm tree that spreads its slight, ragged shade across the square, the cafés are filled with listless customers, groups of Europeans with their six o'clock anisette, their unbuttoned shirts showing their hairy, broad chests; they take off their hats and put them on the zinc table to start their daily card game. ("The sun is going down," one of them says, yawning, then laughs stupidly, as when a woman passes who is too young for him.) In the next street are the taciturn Arabs who patronize the Moorish cafés, where soon the radios will shriek ecstasy, emit the sobs of the Orient that pierce lost souls and the emptiness in which motionless dreams unravel—a single cup of Turkish coffee to end the jobless man's day and then he'll go home, near the river, expecting his wife's unchanging question, "Did you find any work?" He won't answer; why bother to look when there's never any work to be found. Just one coffee. The dominos are brought out; soon the daily cigarette will be rolled between callused fingers. On every terrace, one across from the other, the music will weep over love and the night and the solitary lover. Lila moves along, straight and a little stiff, weaving her way past them. At the Palais d'Orient, the Chicou brothers, behind schedule because of their unexpected morning session, are immersed in their game, deep in thought, covering their earlier furor. It's the beginning of day's end.

Silence. The palm tree's net of shade is about to disappear from the square; after the anisette, the card game will begin, and the Orient's laments will gain entry into the languid souls. The real Chicou will spit out his first insult—he has already stood up and, with his usual broad gesture, made stately because it's habitual, given the chair such a violent shove that it has tumbled onto the sidewalk. There he is, an inspired orator standing in the street to address the town and throw his obscene prophet's flames in its face. A moment of silence is suddenly outlined in the sky while, over there, the operation on the mountain ceases; the soldiers prepare to come back and their convoys to descend from the mountain—where, still invisible to the town, the fire they've left behind in the forests of chestnut and wild olive trees overruns the thickets and the underbrush. Like so many others, Lila welcomes the respite with mute attention. She stops at the end of the street. "It's ugly in a strange way, this colonial square with its subprefecture," she thinks, searching her memory for the path her frivolous adolescent figure had taken when she had blushed at chance encounters with Ali. Then she had disappeared in a dreamlike light, much like this evening's light. Just as then, at this hour the square sleeps languidly.

A scream. A sharp scream, the scream of a woman flayed; the silence ends in terror, in the melee of those who come running. ("There, it came from there, next to the kiosque, just beneath the palm tree." "An assassination attempt! A girl. She's dead!") Lila cuts through the crowd that surges forward in a single wave toward the body, toward the blood they're looking for—"But she's lost no blood," someone notes. "Killed instantly; a bullet right in the heart!"—and then the speaker recoils in fear and anger. "That's him! There, right over there, that's the assassin!" It's Bob who shouts.

Lila now stands over the dead body: a young girl, maybe twenty years old, half lying on the ground, having first crumbled to her knees before completely collapsing on her side. Her refined, olive-skinned face is uncovered for the town to see, as if there, in front of everyone, she had first wanted to lay her ear to the ground to listen to something . . . to seek something, far from the others and the world. Lila reconstructs the slow movement of the end that she hadn't seen, can't avert her eyes, painful fascination forcing her to look, even though there's a lump in her throat and she feels almost as if her heart is bleeding in the face of the girl's pallid death.

"Who is she? Who is she?" she exclaims in unrestrained anguish. She cries it out in Arabic; a man with a churlish look indifferent to her mysterious grief, has heard her and whispers:

"A bitch's daughter who was betraying her brothers! For her the hour of justice has come!"

Then Yahia moves away, before the police arrive, straight ahead without seeming rushed, carefully avoiding the central streets. Since Youssef has left, he is now alone in the carpenter's shop and has decided to continue being punctual. "The hour of justice," he grumbles, then puts it out of his mind: this death, just an incident; the days of fear and trouble now beginning are just fleeting moments. "God, the Only One, the Merciful One . . ." he begins, before his prayer rug, while he readies himself, for the fourth time that day, to bow down in the direction of Mecca and its black stone.

"What's wrong?" Suzanne immediately asks Lila, who has knocked on her door; but quiet and cold, Lila says:

"I'm visiting people today. You're my last stop."

Suzanne doesn't press it. "Something's wrong," she says to herself, "and not only because she's pale. Her eyes are transfixed and there's no emotion in her features . . ." She invites Lila in, introduces her to Khaled, happy that, thanks to the unexpected arrival, she can insist he stay for dinner. "I was planning to leave this evening," he'd told her. Now Suzanne can keep him here. Without consulting him, she phones to make a hotel reservation for him.

Khaled would rather have been alone with Suzanne. He has no interest at all in new faces, polite questions, and the time-consuming necessary preparations it takes to reach that point where one chooses either to completely ignore or else desire to get to know the other person. After the day's work (his visit with Salima, then her mother; going by Omar's office; familiarizing himself with pending issues for which he is now responsible; then all those women who came to him as soon as the news of his arrival had made the rounds, all their complaints, their distress . . . What can he do all by himself?), he's yearning to relax. Suzanne is made for bringing him peace. Since Khaled's arrival, she's been gathering information about how his work's been progressing; she's remembered the importance of one case, the urgency of another. She knows every drama; after her husband left, she studied the active files. She's happy she's been able to make Khaled promise that from now on he'll return once a week. The rest of the time, she'll do the filing, she'll lighten his load. "If I hadn't had Nadia," she smiled regretfully, "I would have done an internship as a lawyer after obtaining my degree; I would've been prepared for the work today." She says "the work"; nowadays her resentment has crystallized around those words. Omar was gone and "the work" was left hanging. But she's made her decision: the time has come for her to take charge of it.

She comes and goes, sets the table, leaves the room and comes back again, asks a question from the kitchen, returns to hear the answer, then rushes back to her stove. In a good mood, she says, "Children, let's eat!" First Nadia has to be put to bed, must say good night to everyone and be taken to her room.

Lila is alone with Khaled. She hasn't said more than three words since she walked in. She's sorry she came.

"Are you from this town?" Khaled asks with only polite interest.

"I'm from here." She falls silent. Not another word, but inside herself she continues, "This is my town. I was born here. My whole

childhood, my years of study, and my dreams. My meeting Ali . . ."
For two weeks she's been slowly drifting in the dangerous waters of
her recent past, trying to pick up the thread again somewhere
beyond it. She's aware of it and has also discovered a new desire to be
in harmony with the town and find herself a place here.

"Still in your apartment?" Suzanne asks as she comes in and leads
her friends ("My friends," she thinks serenely) to the table.

"It's an eerie place," Lila answers, making an effort to communicate this detail to the stranger. The beginning of a smile on her face,
politeness—Khaled wonders but is grateful for it—or else a token of
coquettish timidity. He then notices how, in spite of her smile, she
seems distant, unfathomable, "her charm consisting of uncertainty,"
he assesses after another brief look. "Could this be a disguise?"

The conversation is halting. As if by accident, Suzanne says,
"Omar wrote me; he went to see your father in Paris," and her cheer-
fulness disappears. Lila doesn't answer. Even the image of her
father—she still has that fierce if childish attachment, Suzanne
thinks—can't break through her distraction. Suzanne listens to
Khaled talk amiably about general topics and is grateful to him for
that (Lila, too, is listening but says to herself, "How ironic to end
this day with a dinner that feels so social, how boring . . ."). Suddenly Suzanne, who used to be mindful of Lila's mood swings, concludes to herself, "Lila is busy coming out of the cocoon that her
unflagging sense of happiness made her weave—thanks to Ali. What
can possibly emerge from her, her inexperience, her awkward
naïveté, the lack of attention to everything unless she recognizes her
passion in it, and then she goes about it with such enthusiasm . . .
What a difficult prison happiness is," she thinks again. And because
she likes the dinner atmosphere this evening, Khaled's arrival, which
is a real help to her—she will tell him that later—she takes advantage of a moment's silence to think out loud:

"I was thinking," she submits, and Lila raises her head, "is it really happiness that matters? I—and I've always believed it to be difficult for me—" (too strong willed, Omar used to say, an inflexible

and uncompromising nature), "to ask the question with a good deal of detachment, heaven knows . . . It should be approached this way." She smiles; Lila listens. She's always loved Suzanne's simplicity and the way she manages to talk about herself without any false modesty. She admires her for the equilibrium she exudes, not knowing much about the stoicism it sometimes requires. She says nothing.

Khaled responds, "I don't know whether, in this country, we have the talent to be happy. It needs . . . how should I put it, a vocation." ("Not too pedantic for his age," Lila judges as she listens to him. She'd made note of his somewhat terse expression from the very beginning.) "But," he goes on, "what's happiness?"

"All the women I know," Lila intervenes in a tight voice, rediscovering her pleasure in contradicting, "are happy. But they're asleep."

"Is that really so?" she wonders instantly, once again closed in upon herself. "Cherifa, was she sleeping this evening? She was preparing herself to wait. But," Lila asks herself, no longer listening to the continuing conversation, "is waiting not the same as killing everything inside yourself, with patience and somnolence? And what about me? What have I done until now? What did I do during three years of marriage, of happiness? What am I doing now with my solitude? Nothing, nothing . . . and yet, others struggle, others die, others . . ."

"Throughout our history," Khaled goes on, "we've always had to resist; our people have been shaped by throwing themselves into battle or locking themselves up in pride. Now a tremendous challenge begins and will go on, but at the price of enormous slaughter!"

He was trying to rattle Suzanne's optimism. She protested; she spoke of the French people who also wanted no part of this war, of the principles of democracy, of the elections to come, of other countries being liberated "without any slaughter," of the imminent end of the nightmare. Khaled began to get up, muttering bitterly, "The prisons will never be full enough . . ."

Sitting on the rug, Lila was watching him, trying to understand why he put so much anguish, a kind of cold fever, into his prophesies.

She didn't say anything. She had no opinion that she deemed interesting enough for this level of conversation. Still, one expression from Khaled's speech had stuck in her mind: "the challenge"—she knew it well, even to the point where the challenge challenges itself. Before, she used to practice it with Ali: using her willpower to murder the rebellion inside herself, to deny herself the sense of "tremendous challenge." Ali would forbid her to do something—they were engaged at the time—"You won't attend that course; I've been told that such and such a student goes there just to see you, to make advances to you, and so forth." Annoyed, she'd say nothing, although a month earlier she would have laughed teasingly and gone to the class with wild satisfaction. He'd also said, "I want you all to myself," on the day she'd counted on working with some girlfriends, and she had stayed home, but glumly, only to confront him silently for hours and hours on end, while she thought inwardly, "You think you have me under your thumb . . . you think you're my master." And unruffled hate went through her like mad laughter. Hardened and ambushed, that was how she had later fallen head first into happiness—a flat calm, a morass. "No," she corrected herself, "later, but much later: there was light."

She was thinking of all that, taking a certain distance, released from these memories without any warning (she understood it the moment she found herself beside Khaled, who was walking her home). Suddenly old, sharply and lucidly indifferent, she wondered in amazement, "Is youth nothing but a set of bombastic and suffocating events?" She also thought of her people, her country. No, she wasn't seeing her country as young, as always ready to stand up just for the excitement of standing up, no. And to Khaled, pursuing the earlier conversation, she said softly:

"My people are my grandfather (died in bliss and plenitude, I'm sure of it), this town, these houses at the foot of the mountain that haven't ever changed . . ." She doesn't dare add, "My people are my happiness with Ali, from whom I've been banished"; she hesitates and then understands.

"My people," she starts again, "are all my roots."

Silence as they continue walking. They had to go all the way across town: a wide boulevard lined with chestnut trees, then a series of alleys that end in the road leading out of town in the direction of the villages on the plain. Only then would they arrive at Lila's building. They should have taken a taxi. They were moving along slowly.

Khaled was quiet, feeling intensely how Lila's last sentence had touched an old wound in him. Since her sharp words provocatively offered during dinner, he was finding her beautiful, her face lit up by some secret energy, which had chased away her initial coldness. He would have liked her to repeat those words with the same fierce pride filled with tenderness; "My roots." What splendid words!

Why did he then tell her his life? How important could it be for her to have him explain, for instance, how uncomfortable he was that he spoke his mother tongue so badly, which conferred an anxious approximation on his contacts with compatriots. Or to have him tell her that he had no family. The son of a Kabylian shepherd who had died in poverty, Khaled had practically been adopted by an old teacher from France who had mentored him in his years of study until he too died, in solitude. How could she be of help to him, when with his detached bitterness he admitted to her that his only years of real happiness had been those of studying in Paris; for ten years now, only his profession had kept him from drying up in Algiers. He was hesitant to marry a former mistress, who had wound up in the city, in this country, on his account, because she wasn't the solution, although he valued her. "Feeling marginalized," he continued, and since Lila hadn't said a word from the beginning of his ill-timed confession, he kept going on about the drama of men thrown between two civilizations, a rather mundane situation.

They were still walking at the same slow speed, now leaving the shade of the chestnut trees. It was completely dark. Lila had said briefly, "Let's hurry up! We're close to curfew time," and as they were rushing along, Khaled, suddenly irritated with her sentence as if it were her escape route, wanted to know precisely "where things stood." He thought in those very terms and then, in his agitation—was it merely wounded pride?—he didn't hide the crassness of the thought from himself. "What is she really?" he wondered aggressively and, at the same time, noticed the grace of the young woman whose profile would appear to him for brief moments when they'd leave the shade of a tree, cross beneath the pale light of a streetlamp, only to be newly immersed in the darkness under the next tree's foliage. Yes, he recalled later, when in his hotel room he spent hours smoking in the dark, suffering from an insomnia that wouldn't loosen its steel grip until almost dawn—he remembered the violence that hit him and that he later saw as his powerlessness in truly reaching other people, because of his morose proclivity to believe invariably in irreparable failure.

"Are you faithful?" he had therefore asked her out of the blue—because Suzanne had indicated early on that the husband of this dreaming beauty was in the resistance, such a romantic introduction.

"To be faithful, must one think about it or believe it?" she answered, and since they were in the shade, he didn't see her smile, both shy and somewhat ironic, faced as she was with his crude maneuver. Right afterward, forgetting about it, Lila continued with a concentration that Khaled suddenly loved passionately:

"I'm changing, I'm changing every day, I'm trying to find myself across the strands of time, and yet I'm always the same person. Ali" ("So his name is Ali!"), "is a man and to me that means someone deeply grounded in the earth, like a tree rising high in the forest, endlessly growing to reach the peak from where the view is the finest. I need him; without him, I feel I'd flounder. Is that need what we call faithfulness?" she was asking. "Perhaps." Khaled stops. What is he? Not a tree deep down in the earth, high up in the sky, but cut off and left abandoned on the embankment. Lila's intuition was not deceiving her in her behaving with him as she was, a barely congenial stranger.

"I love you," he said straight out and gave a short laugh to cushion what he believed to be preposterous. "I'm head over heels in love . . . at my age."

Silence. They keep on walking. They now reach the main road; already they can see the tall block of the building.

"I'm sorry," Lila says after a long moment. She turns her head (is her voice terse, hesitant? Khaled wonders).

"Do you see the fire," she continues in an impersonal tone. "It's very close to town. Maybe sabotage. There're so many large farms in the area. All the settlers are afraid these days."

Is she afraid, or only afraid to hurt him? Khaled has stopped fearing being ridiculous—he is well beyond that now, at the deepest point of exile, behind an ocean. At the same time, a dark sorrow overcomes him. But when he leaves Lila, the smile she gives him in the presence of Bachir whom they meet at the end of their walk, is of such brave tenderness that he gratefully understands that, before, she had only sought to spare him.

At daybreak, when at last he was able to fall asleep, a strange dream disturbed him: Lila was standing before him, though he couldn't reach her, and with that same smile of hers was handing him her own entrails, pulled from her half-open belly.

8   ...   BOB

The operation on the mountain is not yet over when the jobless, who are killing time on the benches in the square above the rue du Bey, are the first to see the tribe of the Beni Mihoub advancing in a mute throng.

At the front by himself is the patriarch, Sheik Abdelkrim Ben Mohamed Ben Ali Ben Mihoub, a direct descendant of the holy man who, according to the town's memory, arrived one day from across the mountains. As this saintly figure contemplated the land around him—where gazelles and jackals then used to sleep as well as the few remaining lions who out of laziness hadn't been able to find their way back to the southern steppes—he caused multiple springs to spurt up for the new town. Gaunt, sad old men, dressed in white robes and bearing the same majestic look as the sheik, trail behind him. And then the women follow, children on their hips, chests high, without veils, their full dresses, whose print has long ago vanished, dragging through the dust raised by their bare gypsy feet. Little girls at their side, their dirty golden hair draped over their shoulders, let their eyes wander over the first gardens they see in the town.

The sheik walks and sees no one. He has one burning thought: "We abandoned our seed and we left. We've given our men to the mountain's battles and the enemy has burned our homes. I addressed myself to God, 'Since from here on in our lot is all fire and ashes, help me, oh Lord, to bring those of my blood for whom I am responsible, across the plains and valleys.' We abandoned our seed and we left."

The throng goes down the long rue du Bey, passes Saidi's former café now transformed into a garage, and causes a traffic jam in the square because the patriarch insists on walking only in the road. A few men stand up on the terraces of the Moorish cafés to watch the procession; these are not the first refugees. "Someday," a man says softly, "we'll all be like that, nomads in our own country . . ." The others listen, motionless. Without a word from anyone, all the radios that had been broadcasting their songs have stopped playing. It is the beginning of a great silence.

Ferrand, a settler who is seated alone at a table in the square's main café, averts his eyes from the wretched group passing by. He is happy today. His harvest has just been finished; the hay is in the sheds; he's paid all his farmhands, and then at dusk he came to town. Just before, he had attended to the departure of his seasonal workers, fifty strong-armed young men. Because the harvest was good and Ferrand is reputed to be a kind man—he knows the workers think he's a "good boss"—he suddenly suggested driving them halfway in one of his returning trucks. Their expressions of thanks flattered him; he knows a little Arabic and he likes the fact that the simplest formulas of the language are solemn blessings.

The tribe of the Beni Mihoub and its leader have moved on. One of the customers at the table next to Ferrand's comes over to greet him respectfully. "We're fighting this war against a handful of agitators," Ferrand begins as always. "We should get it over with fast!" (But he also thinks, "Will I be able to keep refusing to pay them bribes so they'll leave my property intact?") "Just recently I was discussing the situation with our deputy . . ." Leaning forward toward Ferrand's table, his conversation partner nods vigorously and Ferrand, the wealthiest landowner in the area—although not comparable in any way to the despots of the plain—pleased with himself, his town, and its customs, continues his speech loudly enough to be heard by the other customers.

Hakim passes in front of them to enter the room inside. He greets no one today. He has just left the police station. The guards on duty had noticed with surprise that the inspector had left his car parked in the street and gone away on foot at a leisurely pace. On the way Hakim stopped in every bistro in the area frequented by Spanish, Maltese, and Italian workers, the Mediterranean masses who, since the conquest, had been arriving in waves to find employment in the warehouses near the station. It has taken Hakim an hour to reach the *place d'armes*.

Until this moment, nobody had ever seen him so openly enter a European café. Before, he used to be respected because people saw that he abstained from alcohol and observed the public Friday prayers like the good Muslim he was or wanted to give the impression of being. Today, Hakim stands straight and silent at the bar; the sounds of the jukebox reach him from the back of the room. He has one drink, two . . . He sees the kiosque from there and the curious who watch the tribe's procession, which he had also quickly taken in from a distance a few minutes earlier, while standing on the sidewalk. The silence is beginning to weigh heavily almost everywhere; most people confuse it with the indolence of oppressive afternoons. "It's the end of the day," Hakim thinks from the bottom of the well into which he'd been feeling himself gradually sinking ("Another one, please"). "Why the silence? What are they waiting for?"

Ferrand has paid for his drink and that of the customers at the next table, then he gets up with difficulty—he is now in his fifties and arthritis bothers him; fortunately, in another month, he'll be going to France for a cure. He walks down the boulevard to his driver in the parked car. He's not returning to his farm this evening; he has alerted his personnel. He'll be going to the seaside resort nearby where his wife and children are. He's pleased with his short walk. It has suddenly become quite cool. In front of him, a cloud of dust shrouds the parade of the disappearing tribe.

Ferrand is careful to move slowly, greet everyone he knows. He gives his driver a friendly tap as he sits down beside him. He's happy. From his large new car he watches the town slide by.

• • •

The office that Omar had opened four years earlier is not far from the *place d'armes*, in an alley at the corner of the Palais d'Orient. Mahmoud—wearing a loose coat, the season notwithstanding, and a hat that changed him completely—had been late this evening leaving the meeting that the party had set up a few days before. He felt the reckless desire to take a short walk through his town, which he hadn't seen in the almost two years he'd been underground. He took streets he knew would be deserted at this late hour; he'd end up at the wide beltway where the shade of the chestnut trees would help him avoid the risk of an ill-fated encounter. He had half an hour before he needed to be at the appointed place where he was to be picked up; he saw that moment as a true departure.

Working in obscurity in the capital had hardly given him the opportunity to share in the pride of real danger, even if it did offer the satisfaction of calculations and strategy. Moreover, in those locations where Mahmoud used to hide for months on end, he all too often had to overcome a sense of purely physical strangulation. Now, the proximity of life amid armed men, nighttime marches, combat, and brushes with death were exhilarating—especially, Mahmoud wished for the experience of "his faith and determination" (words he had once used with Omar) rushing at him when he was surrounded by rural and mountain people, the immense conflagration he considers to be the true source of the future. He saw his present actions and the immediate importance of his responsibilities as just a minuscule part in the effort ("superhuman," some thought) of an enormous task. He deemed them necessary to set in motion the flowing construction of a new order that would spread far and wide. Although Mahmoud was well past the age of easy romanticism, a glow of happiness came over him—and for him happiness always surfaced like this: on the eve of an undertaking, when circumstances granted a reprieve from the excitement of approaching peril, the calm of decisions made, all those all-too-unwavering feelings, for a split second made room for the soul's strange jubilation at perceiving the future as a field, unexpectedly unfolding. Mahmoud walked along, mindful of the joy to which he yielded in all its breadth, and which he then suppressed.

He was mistrustful of his feelings (in spite of everything, he was satisfied with the discipline he had imposed upon himself by not planning to see a single member of his family here, despite fifteen months of separation). He was especially mistrustful of too vigorous a tendency toward passion and he now thought back to the interview he had conducted some time ago with Omar. "That was a waste of time," he'd said dejectedly under his breath, for he had been deeply disappointed.

He had put too much hope on that meeting. Although every report received had clearly concluded that Omar was unlikely to join the battle, Mahmoud had thought it might be a misunderstanding, undoubtedly some conflict between Omar's quick-tempered nature and the local organization. After all, they had studied and had taken their first steps in the political struggle together, which could only have united them, in spite of Omar's recent withdrawal from politics. Mahmoud was not ignoring that; indeed, he had used it as justification by referring to the slump in which the parties had then found themselves.

So Mahmoud had contacted him again and believed that his argument would quickly help Omar change his mind. Nevertheless, he'd made it clear that he wasn't soliciting Omar to join up; they simply wanted to know to what extent they could count on him. What he had found instead were flight and poor excuses ("Where was the revolution going?" "Hadn't they triggered it too soon?"), a pessimism whose true nature Mahmoud wasn't able to detect right on the spot. He'd gone on the attack:

"Afraid?"

He suddenly had doubts about him; why not? Omar might be

growing fonder of his creature comforts, as had so many others. (Mahmoud hardly had any illusions on the proletarian origins of this or that intellectual; if the onset of old age or a solid position didn't incapacitate a man, his wife was sure to take care of it.)

At Mahmoud's question Omar had flown into a rage. Surely that was not it; nor had four years of a comfortable life or marriage spoiled him. What was it, then? Mahmoud still had some hope left: after fifteen months of war it was easy to show that enormous accomplishments had been achieved and that overall awareness had vastly increased. And wasn't that what they, they and many others, had been after for so many years? Omar kept on making excuses. At that point, Foudil had harshly cut him off; after all, they certainly weren't short of men, it was, in fact, the only thing the country wasn't short of. Mahmoud had left, telling himself that Omar couldn't accept that the crucial activism hadn't come from his accustomed periphery, his familiar framework of thought and argumentation. For years, he hadn't believed the solution would come from the people, from the obduracy and will of the masses; and at the present time he no longer had the courage to recognize his mistake.

Mahmoud now continued walking, carefully surveying the area but still seeking to understand what had happened, not because his friendship required it, but it seemed to him that it would help him better understand which point he himself had reached. Omar didn't just represent the typical case of the intellectual that reality leaves behind; if he wasn't sinking into middle-class comfort, he was moving onto a much more dangerous path—a path of solitary arrogance that shows itself in the best possible light and chooses the isolation of a desert to do so. A temptation that Mahmoud suddenly sensed as being permanent for so many former comrades. The struggle for them had so often been a never-ending challenge, a mad defiance because of which they would accept prison, exile, or certain death. Oh, so many simple, tough men were at this very moment facing the thrill of confronting their torturers. And yet the essence of the struggle was not merely discovering oneself to be more and more ferocious when resisting the enemy's force. After all, now that all eyes were open and each body was mobilized, the enemy as such mattered little.

Leaning against a chestnut tree, Mahmoud smoked, to kill the few minutes he had left, utterly happy that he could depart for the maquis from the town of his birth. A couple was coming in his direction; lovers, he thought; he didn't want to move away and thereby attract their attention. The young girl was moving slowly, swaying her hips, her head on the shoulder of the man, whose military uniform Mahmoud didn't notice until they passed him. As she walked, the girl was offering him her lips, but her eyes, open over the man's shoulder, looked at Mahmoud. Engrossed in his thoughts, he turned his head, threw his cigarette down, and disappeared with long strides into the dark.

●●●

On her way home this evening, Touma was vaguely surprised that she hadn't encountered contempt or anger in the passerby whom she knew to be a Muslim but who had been totally unaware of her in a way she didn't understand. She laughed soundlessly; but her laughter died quickly. The soldier kissed her lips again in the full light of the streetlamp, in his fervor almost crushing the frail curving body that pretended to abandon itself to his embrace.

Perhaps she was also playing at being casual, while fear was whispering deep inside her; perhaps, in spite of the squabble with the waiter, she was trying to abandon herself to Bob, to the others who were at their heels, to the insolence of pleasure, the noise, the lacerating laughter. "Have fun! I want to have fun!" Touma's voice was hard. Bob was surprised, "What's the matter?" He felt tender toward her, despite the noisy presence of their companions.

"I want a drink," Touma continued. "Get drunk . . . how do you say it—" she was searching for the words, "'whoop it up,' isn't that it?"

One of the boys heard her and repeated it, louder: "Get stinking drunk, whoop it up, those are the young lady's orders!"

They all cheered above Bob's bewildered silence, their hurrahs rising around the kiosque, breaking through the inertia of the siesta that had turned the place into a desert.

A moment later, the bar of the hotel-restaurant behind the church was invaded by the "youngsters," as the proprietor and his wife called them. She was a flabby woman with a face that was still fresh, "the same one who five years ago now . . ." One of the boys in the group began to whisper like an old gossip.

"Who what? What did she do?" Touma, suddenly awakened from a dream, asked too loudly. "What exactly did she do?"

Silence snuffed out the sniggering, but Bob, as if to take revenge for the solitude he'd lost, said coldly, "She went off with one of your compatriots. And, because that went on for three whole days right here in the center of town, in a café, it became quite a scandal."

"Ah." Touma is indifferent, and then brazenly adds, "It seems to me that it's almost the same now, but just the reverse, isn't it?"

They applaud. They clink. The sound rises. So does their boldness; one of them asks the waiter, "Is it true this is a brothel?"

Another says, "Look here, it's reserved for officers who'd probably be bored if there weren't one . . ."

Touma doesn't say a word. She drinks. She has ordered a whisky; a second one. She's a sad drunk.

"You seem tired; is it the alcohol?" Bob questions her. His intonation is tender; he's worried about her. Touma stares at him as if she's seeing him for the first time.

"I'm afraid!" she says in a soft voice. Bob leans over. In the middle of the uproar, he has trouble hearing her.

"I'm afraid," Touma repeats, her eyes lost in the distance.

An hour later, Bob has managed to get Touma away from the bar. The others, most of whom—like Touma—have had too much too drink, follow them. Bob has the idea of hiding in the "sacred woods," a park not far from the river that is reached via a maze of alleyways. After running breathlessly—the streets are coming back to life again, and forgetting they're chasing Touma and Bob, one of the group stops to launch some ripe insults at a dignified woman passing by—the escaping couple succeeds in getting away.

Touma looks sick. The woods are deserted, with the exception of two or three children from the shacks by the river who are quietly playing marbles. Silent witnesses, they approach and gravely observe Touma, who's doubled over, vomiting, near a spring. Bob takes out a handkerchief, wipes her face with careful motions, has her lie down on a nearby bench, takes off her shoes, and sits down beside her. When she falls asleep, he holds her bare feet in his hands. He lets her sleep like this for more than an hour, from time to time checking her rapid breathing, her clammy brow—she has a fever—then looks around at the shadows of the foliage, the silence. Quickly bored, the children have gone back to their game. A dark-eyed young man slowly passes them, his eyes staring at Touma's stretched-out body as if Bob, beside her, didn't exist, then he hastily disappears without giving Bob time to wonder about him. Bob is feeling calm. He's no longer sorry they didn't make it to the city. All his money has been spent on drinks for the whole group. He doesn't have a penny left. Touma is still sleeping. He imagines that this day won't have an end.

She wakes up, her face crumpled, feeling completely lethargic; it is as if someone had replaced the usual Touma of the frayed voice and provocative look. Passive, her mind elsewhere, she lets Bob kiss her. Desire makes him stammer; he caresses her face. She keeps her eyes open, dreaming, "I just wanted to have some real fun!" she sighs. Her head feels heavy. "Is that what being drunk is like?" she asks Bob, who keeps going on about how he loves her. She'd imagined it to be more festive.

Suddenly she pushes him away, sits up. Seeing her terror, but still wild with pent-up desire, Bob asks, "What's wrong with you?"

"Nothing." She gets hold of herself, answering curtly, and puts her shoes back on. Bob, who's still hesitant, still happy, sees her go back to the hussy ways she's been imitating.

"Really? Nothing?" Bob says, turning his head and noticing the back of a boy who's just disappeared. "Is he the one you're afraid of?"

he asks. She smiles, amused by his already protective courage. But when he insists again on trying to understand what's bothering her, she answers sullenly:

"I'm never afraid! What're you thinking?"

• • •

"Is it because of my sister?" Tawfik had said when, for the second time, he was told that he should be more patient before he'd be able to enter one of cells of the underground organization. He was too young. "Too young? I'm sixteen, seventeen next winter! There are some in the resistance right now who're younger than I."

He went home; he shared a small room with his mother in one of the white houses in the old quarter. "Your daughter's a whore," he grumbled as a greeting. The old woman lowered her head. She was used to it. Bad luck continued to pursue her: Touma, her oldest daughter, was gone, although she was the one whom, before he died, the father had sent with great enthusiasm to the French school—belatedly, true, but had the father not died and had she then not decided to go to work as a secretary in an office, Touma could have continued her studies. A year later she was quarreling with her brother, then barely twelve years old: he couldn't tolerate the fact that she was hanging out with Europeans in public, all the more because she was seen at their dances. Coming from the big city for this sole purpose, some of her uncles had intervened and locked her up in the house. She'd vanished two months later. Since then, three years had gone by. God only knew what had become of her, and to spare the mother, her name was never mentioned.

The mother, however, was more concerned about something else: for many months Tawfik had not been looking for any work at all, spending entire days lying on his bed in silence. When he did say something it was only to insult Touma, although they could have gone on pretending to forget her. She herself dared think of her daughter only when she was alone at night, sitting on the threshold of her room, her eyes filled with tears, no longer hearing the neighbor women's gossip. Then she'd lament: "Oh, Lord, what have I done to deserve this fate? I thought I'd exhausted my share of misery, but now dishonor has been forced upon me."

There she'd stay for hours on end, her head swaying back and forth, forcing herself to murmur, "God be praised that her father died with peace in his heart! God be praised!"

Tawfik, who'd hoped to get a job as an accounting clerk at the court, was no longer taking the necessary steps (a middleman had already cost them their savings), collecting the papers needed, or putting his file together. He'd go out early, wander the streets, sit briefly in a Moorish café if his mother had been able to scrounge up a few coins that morning, and come home for lunch without having exchanged a single word with anyone at all, not even nodded to his acquaintances. He'd eat alone and his mother would wait until he was finished to claim the leftovers in the corner that was their kitchen. Sometimes he'd throw the plate down or else turn the table over and shout, "Always this damned couscous! And nothing on it either!"

In the courtyard, neighbor women would attempt to console the quietly weeping mother: "Be patient! He's possessed by a demon, he was so gentle just a few months ago! Pray and be patient, spell God's name!"

There were times when he wouldn't go out during the day. He'd lock himself in his room while the neighbors took the old woman in. He'd lie on the mattress with open eyes, "That whore of a sister," he'd growl. "I'm sure it's all because of her!" They could say whatever they wanted, he could find no other explanation for their reservations about him. They didn't trust him. Everyone knew that Touma went out only with Europeans, her conduct was more disgraceful than that of the lowest prostitute. "Prostitutes!" he'd often roar at his mother as if with her silence she were defending the absent daughter. "At least prostitutes are still patriots; but your daughter! . . ." He'd shout loudly, then more loudly so the neighbors would hear, so that the whole neighborhood would hear. "Your daughter, you don't even know what she's done, do you? You see nothing, you're aware of nothing, and she's betraying the cause, she's a traitor!"

But what good did it do to shout? He wanted to work; for a long time now that was all that mattered to him—not to rot away in an office, keep the books, bend over papers—no, to work, to be useful, to feel he was part of a family, set free from shame, from the weight he'd been dragging around for years. He wanted to prove to them that, in spite of everything, in spite of her, he was worthy of their trust . . . and he was beginning to understand that he had to take matters into his own hands. Yes, it was up to him to prove to them that he was pure, that he was a man, that he was not too young.

Thoughts like these preoccupied him for days on end. He was no longer grumbling. He was no longer flinging insults, but was enclosed in his silence under the loyal gaze of his motionless mother, who, from the other corner of the dark room, would watch her son as if he were being attacked by invisible dangers. All the while keeping them hidden from view, she'd take out her prayer beads and, like her son, would refuse to raise the curtains to contemplate the mountain on days of military operations.

During the same period, his mind muddled, Tawfik began to spy on Touma and follow her around. He very quickly figured out what her habits were, since she was still working as a secretary in an insurance company. He'd wait at a distance, hiding behind one of the pillars of the arcade across from her office; she'd come out and go to her place nearby in a street with new buildings. He'd stay there for a while and would note the arrival of Martinez. Sometimes Touma would go out with him. One day, as she was about to get into Martinez's car, she walked away from him, crossed the street, and confronted Tawfik. For several days she'd been saying to herself, "I want to see who that boy is." At first she'd taken him for a suitor.

With hate in his eyes, he'd begun, "You dirty whore, bitch's daughter, spawned by dogs!" He'd inundated her with all the evil curses he'd been holding in for months, for years. Touma wasn't listening, but staring at his eyes, his thick eyebrows, his sleek hair, and finding the adolescent beauty somehow familiar, she suddenly realized:

"Tawfik!" she whispered to her brother, whom she hadn't seen since he was a child.

In the car, Martinez asked: "Who's he? Someone who wants to hurt you? Is he threatening you?"

Touma, just a little pale, was smiling. "No, not at all, that's my brother! Every now and then he brings me news of my mother."

The second time, she'd been sitting on the terrace of the ice cream shop, as she frequently did; he approached her, head down, wearing the same blue jeans, which she noticed before she looked up at him. "Is there something you want? Money perhaps?" She was smiling at him; he was her brother, and a foolish thought crossed her mind: it pleased her that he was so good-looking.

"I want you to leave!"

"Leave?" She didn't understand.

"Leave town! So we don't have to see you again. So we can finally forget you!" She looked at him, dumbfounded, still happy to see his handsome olive face, flushed with contempt, and then she burst out in laughter, exploded in hate:

"You seem to think you've a right over me! You poor idiot! Why don't you earn some money first and buy yourself a new shirt and pants that aren't so threadbare?"

He'd disappeared. "Bitch's daughter!" were the only words that lived inside him from then on. He avoided everyone, the few friends he'd made when playing soccer, and also those he used to harass all the time so they'd convey to anyone concerned that he wished to participate in the struggle. He was now certain that the organization would want nothing to do with him as long as his sister continued to parade around like this, openly going to the police station to supply them with information, wandering around at night with young noncommissioned officers from Paris. His only chance, he thought, was to impel her to leave. He tried threats, kept on pursuing her for weeks, until the day he handed her his ultimatum. Did he believe in it? He made every effort to, fired off the words *last chance*, and reminded her there were two trains leaving town, two opportunities for her to disappear.

When, after following her to the woods a few hours later, he passed by the bench a second time—his mind made up—he no longer felt any hatred, just a vague pity for the girl whom at first he was surprised to find asleep and who then appeared as a stranger to him, even when intense fear showed in her gaze. He went away whistling. He roamed the town until dusk, his step light. Finally, he was going to live, struggle, die in the only desirable way: giddy with revenge. He thought of Touma, no longer to mentally insult her and spit on her shameful image from which he was setting himself free, but as a victim (her terrified eyes had expressed it) exposed to the stroke of fate.

That day Tawfik didn't go home. For the first time, his mother raised the curtain of her door and, like her neighbors, became immersed in watching the war.

• • •

Hakim puts his last glass on the counter and pays. He goes out into the astonished silence that's fallen over the square since the passage of the refugees. He moves slowly, as he used to when he didn't have a car and enjoyed stopping and greeting every acquaintance he saw. Now he doesn't stop anymore. Chaos reigns over the café terraces amid the toppled chairs; the half-finished orders wait for the customers to come back to their tables. The few who haven't budged are watching Hakim. Already, the news that they've seen him leave the bar is making the rounds, but no one can confirm that he's drunk. When she runs into him, Lila, after some effort, recognizes him. "It's the neighbor's husband, the policeman," she says to herself as she passes him, her mind dwelling on the situation. "How difficult some professions must be right now . . ." She doesn't delve any deeper, stays away from judging, from the drama; she doesn't know how to worry about others, thinks about them only to situate them in relation to herself. For an instant, Hakim has appeared to her in full light; then she immediately forgets him again—a shadow among so many others.

It's late when Hakim reaches his house. Once Lila left, Cherifa lowered the curtain to her room; that way she won't have to get up when Hakim signals his arrival with a loud cough as he opens the front door. He crosses the courtyard, plants himself squarely in his doorway, facing Amna and his children, who're surrounding her. They're worn out and sleepy after the blows Amna had dealt them in an eruption of cold fury. Amna doesn't move. From where she sits she smells the alcohol on the man's breath because the room is narrow. She raises her eyes.

"He's been drinking!" she says to herself, and hate, the night bird deep inside her soul, surges up. "He's been drinking!" The children are falling asleep. She sits up, turns her back on Hakim, who's not moving forward. ("This is my wife," he thinks, "these are my children. This is my house . . ." In spite of the descending darkness his house seems drowned in the same pale light as that in the room where Saidi lay.) Amna leans over, picks up the twins and carries them one at a time to their sleeping place beneath the marital bed; their slack bodies entwine in their sleep. She doesn't kiss them. She never kisses them. But this evening she looks at them a little longer before lowering the bed curtain over them. Then she puts the baby in the cradle, whose cord drags on the floor so she can rock it from any point in the room without tiring or paying it any special attention. The child isn't sleeping; he begins to moan, faintly at first, then more and more loudly. Standing before Hakim, Amna lets him scream.

She's very close to Hakim; there's no expression on her face, with its broad cheeks, heavy eyelids, and almost scarlet complexion. "My master, the father of my children, the protector of my days" an inner voice repeats; she doesn't say a word. She stares at Hakim, can hardly make him out, for he's darkened what still remains of the day. Her eyes dwell on his strong shoulders, his slightly corpulent, straight body, his tall frame, but she sees nothing of his face.

"What's the matter with you?" he exhales; she remains motionless, says nothing. Behind them, frightened in the dark, the baby is crying desperately.

"What's the matter with you, woman?" Hakim repeats and his voice has risen like a sea. The child screams. In the back of her own room, Cherifa is surprised by the noise that reaches her.

"What's the matter with you, woman?" Hakim says a third time. "Your child is crying!"

Amna doesn't move, stricken with bewilderment, "My child? Is that my child who's crying?" She questions herself with difficulty. The man takes a step forward, approaches her: "My lord and master, the father of my children," she says again to herself when he touches her, when he takes her in his arms, shakes her violently, and then, with a blow right to her engorged chest, causes her to topple onto the mattress. At the first blow, Amna screams, her voice mixing with that of the unstoppable cries of the baby; she shrieks, she's not in pain but she shrieks and then, as the blows follow one another, she is unexpectedly silent: she understands. Hakim strikes the body on the floor. He has killed a man today. He hits. Saidi screamed for a long time, too, and suddenly stopped just like this. He hits.

Once more it is only the child's jarring voice that pierces the night, which has fallen over the house, has reached Cherifa, who's shivering in her room and settling down in her bed on her side, half naked in the semidarkness.

• • •

"Saidi is dead, they killed him!"

"Saidi?"

"Saidi, the former manager of the Baghdad Café."

"Captain Martinez and his men just returned his body to his wife . . ."

"Death by torture, you think?"

Among the onlookers, who come here every evening at this time to stop on the boulevard lined with bitter-orange trees, right across from the *place d'armes* and the evening arrival of the Micheline,

Tawfik has heard the name Martinez. From where he stands he tries to learn details, while keeping an eye on the approaching train. It will leave again in half an hour. There aren't many travelers for the second departure. From his observation post Tawfik can see everything. "Martinez?" he asked. They repeat the little bit that's known: the police car had arrived with much noise in the river district; the twisted body of Saidi was thrown down in front of his wife and children. One policeman came out of the car to offer some explanation, to which no one listened. Tawfik turns away.

The Micheline starts up soundlessly, glides along the boulevard, whose streetlights will shortly be lit. Tawfik is calm.

"What time is it?" he asks some unperturbed onlookers, who are hesitant to leave.

"Seven o'clock," one grumbles. Night sets in.

Tawfik drifts away, crosses the road, and approaches the square.

Touma is sitting on the far end as usual, though she's never stayed at the ice cream shop this late before. Bob hasn't left her side. For hours he's been holding forth to her about his love. As he speaks, Touma finishes one ice cream, then eats another, nibbling in childish pleasure. Bob is laying out his plans to her: in a few months, he'll be leaving to do his military service. He doesn't know where they'll post him, but wherever it is, he'll write her. She orders a third cup of ice cream, laughing at her own gluttony. Her shoulders are cold beneath her light dress; she thinks she'll need to go home soon. Her room is so small . . . Bob is still talking; what's he saying? Over and over again? "I'm not asking you to wait for me but I'll be back with every leave I get . . ." She smiles at him; he's sweet, she thinks. She interrupts him to tell him so, to add that he's the first sweet boy she's ever known.

"There's some ugly talk that you hang around with Martinez . . . I'm not asking you to account for yourself . . . I know you're not that interested in me . . . that you're probably not even listening to me . . ."

Touma isn't listening. "Wait for me," she says forcefully; she gets up so suddenly that Bob stops in midsentence, repeats, ". . . that you're probably not even listening to me," then rises to follow her.

In a short while the waiter will have to testify before Martinez; he'll tremble because he won't know what statements to make, what he saw, what he should have seen, what he should or shouldn't say. He isn't sure. "Yes, that's the girl, she went up to him first." He isn't sure, he corrects himself: well, the boy saw her first, but he himself had not turned around to look. He was standing in front of his terrace, dishcloth in hand; he was about to wipe a few tables clean—exactly, the one where Monsieur Ferrand had been sitting . . . yes, of course, that's of no interest to anyone. Well, then! There he was, standing, busy watching that brief moment when everything on the square is silent, just before nightfall. He was there . . .

"The girl came forward, seemed in a hurry, was almost running. I said to myself, 'What's come over her, damned girl, she seems furious.' Only then did I turn my head. No, I don't know him . . . no, I wouldn't recognize him . . . yes, I'm sure of that . . ."

That was how, right in front of him, brother and sister met each other: a couple stopping at the center of the square; they seemed to exchange a few words, not in a violent way. Then the waiter clearly saw Tawfik take out his weapon; what he heard first was not the gunshot but the scream. Then everyone who'd been there since the Beni Mihoub passed through came running, rushing to the kiosque and thereby, in the melee, allowing the killer to get away. No, the waiter didn't see him escape . . . no, he's seen nothing . . .

Touma's body remained on the ground, resting on its side; the circle of men ("Her brother!" "Yes, it was her brother! He avenged his honor! May God have mercy on him!") had time to examine the slaughtered victim at leisure. Then they began to retreat, their ranks growing thinner.

"It's none of our business." "A family matter." "Let's leave, it's safer." "I didn't see a thing." "So many dead right now, so many murders! These are strange times!" "No, it's the time of justice !" Words everywhere. The last witnesses turn their back on Touma, on the square. It's time for them to go home, before it's dark. They can already hear the military trucks coming down toward town again in a muffled rumble. The operation on the mountain has come to an end.

Bob is alone now with Touma at his feet. The waiter is in the same place, still holding his dishcloth, still watching. He hasn't budged; he didn't mix with the crowd that, in the final throes of a perishing beast, has slowly but surely left the place. A siren in the distance: the police, at last. Two jeeps; at the wheel of the first is Martinez, who's just been alerted.

While the strident screeches of the cars unravel the silence, Bob, in the middle of the desolate square, bends over Touma and lifts her up. Before going back into his empty café, the waiter watches Bob circle the kiosque blindly wandering around with the girl's body in his arms, stretched out as in supplication.

• • •

On the road near the shantytown, the tribe of the Beni Mihoub has stopped. The doors have opened before them. The women briefly sit down in the doorways. Water in moist, fresh jars is brought to them. They drink, bless the homes, rise, their children still dozing on their hips. "It's time to leave"—the sheik has spoken.

"Stay and rest here for the night! Our humble homes are open to you. Please stay!"

The little girls with their dirty hair aren't listening as they let their gaze wander across the facade of a large empty building.

"It's time to leave!" the sheik has repeated, sounding more forbidding.

The group forms again. At the front, the sheik sees nothing, not the falling night or the beginning plain, where shelter is harder to find. "We abandoned our seed and we left" hammers away at his thoughts, like the inception of a new rage.

9   •••   ALI

"You know Khaled?" Bachir said irritably in front of Lila's door. "I don't particularly like him."

"He is . . . I think he's sincere," Lila pouted. She made a gesture with her hand as if to drive away a thought. She turned to Bachir and smiled her usual smile with doleful candor, and they entered.

Bachir had left his house before dinner. "I'm hungry," he said and headed for the kitchen. Lila was happy to be able to take care of someone: she got him settled at the table on the only chair she owned. She served him an omelet, salad, and olives. He ate heartily, would look at her from time to time, and smile.

"I didn't know you were in town."

He knew nothing of her present life, not even of Ali's departure. He didn't dare ask any further questions. Throughout the previous year he'd been close to the young couple, often going to their home on Sundays when he had the afternoon off. He got along well with Ali and felt a deep affection for Lila, more than for any of his own sisters; but he knew nothing about Lila and Ali's relationship, for in front of a third party they would adopt such reserve with each other that no one ever ventured to make assumptions about the harmony or distance between them. Instead, people would make believe they were addressing them as one person, which didn't come very naturally.

"Have you been in this place long?" Bachir was looking around at the uninviting walls.

"Two or three weeks, I'm not sure," she smiled wanly. "I'm trying to live alone. I'm having a hard time getting used to it," then she sighed ostentatiously, "I'll never be a modern woman!"

Together they burst out laughing, both of them happy to have run into each other. Then there was a problem: Lila hadn't anticipated having a guest, or anything else for that matter. She had only one bed. She suggested bringing the mattress into the other room for Bachir; this room was still empty and was a place where, every time she entered, she felt as if she were in prison. She herself would make do with the boxspring and a blanket. Bachir laughed at these schemes and they cheerfully resolved to stay up talking all night. "All night?" exclaimed Lila, who loved to sleep. "Why not?" Bachir was pacing back and forth: for him it was the end of a magnificent day. He knew Lila well—she always had to be dragged along, she could never arrive at a decision by herself. "Sure, I don't mind," she said, afraid only of being sleepy, but Bachir was convinced that sleeping was a waste of time. She didn't agree: sleeping was one of her voluptuous pleasures and, besides, she was never stingy with her time. "Sure, I don't mind," she repeated, smiling submissively and turning on another lamp.

They talked so much about so many things—the future, them- selves, life, their country, everything—that the idea of sleeping never occurred to her once that night! Speaking honestly, with passion, in the deep of the night—those were beautiful hours she realized, later on, much later. They had a kind of cold clear furor that makes time stand still, so that to her the night, the marvelous pause, began to mean happiness, oblivion, and more . . . It was like the secret moment in which one finds oneself in profound unity, in a move- ment of the self where all currents, normally so chaotic and diverse, suddenly come together, a unique flow of the soul—but also a moment in which one discovers oneself and the other at the same time. Later on she amended her thought to "the others." For, until that moment, she had believed indisputably that for her there was no way to know herself other than in love—and love was the cluster of links that enslaved her to Ali. After that night she told herself she was wrong: one can find oneself with the same lucidity when one is with a friend, a comrade in arms, or an equal. This also came with Bachir's disappearance—she didn't dare say "death" because her former terror of death was tenacious. For her, Bachir had simply vanished, the same way youth, innocence, and so many other graces vanish one day.

Sitting on the floor under the light, Bachir was describing the fire at the farm and the revelation it had brought him: of living beauty that burns and is burned. He was explaining it badly but Lila was surprised that he'd been able to act. "My first act," he said with juvenile pride, which freed him from the act itself, "because without any passion."

He was thinking out loud with unexpected focus.

"Can we always act without passion, or rather without violence or hate?" Then he added, for he was thinking of himself, "Maybe it's possible only when you haven't yet suffered." And to himself he went on, "I've never been humiliated, I've never suffered any real injustice, I've never thought of myself as a victim."

"There's no doubt that when you've suffered too much you're also beyond all passion," Lila answered, uncertain, for she knew this was not a simple issue. Passion, violence, hate—these were things she'd never taken into account. She had an inborn mistrust of all feelings; she'd never hated anyone, she'd never pitied anyone, and none of this came out of her sense of refinement. Deep inside, feelings worried her—until she encountered love, which seemed to be a survival instinct, a need to feel attached, rooted—the word that had touched Khaled. So much ignorance, so many restrictions left her bewildered. The only thing that mattered to her was exhilaration and, by the same token, any feeling that could occupy her whole being, could keep her dazzled.

"You and I," she said, "have never been hungry: in this country, that is our real limitation."

She didn't want to move on to other things, but wanted to situate herself, Bachir, the people she loved, inside the space of this night as it enveloped the land of her birth. With the exception of the shantytown below her windows—she then realized it had been out of a desire for ludicrous penance that she'd come to live here, on its margins—the entire town and the people she knew were, after all, living like this, on the same periphery, without being conflicted about hunger, that atrocious animal obsession.

So much about pleasure, love, solitude, sex, about all the distorting mirrors in which writers choose to extend their personalities, had been discussed in the books she'd read. She began to dream of experiencing an attempt to grasp these apparitions through a different prism: the prism of hunger, its teeth, its belly, all its lyrical forms. What a literature could then be born, filled with passion, desires, vices, apathy, solitude, or love—why not—monstrous polyps, poisonous mushrooms in obviously frightening images.

"No, hunger isn't a stimulant! Maybe at first, but later on?" she was addressing Bachir, "Later it would surely become a kind of stupor, a form of sluggishness. Why should it be an additional resource?"

She was losing her way. Bachir and she were young, euphoric, pure, and unattached; since the nocturnal hours were destroying every worry, she gave up trying to find their other flaws. As she was listening to Bachir, she found herself receptive, liberated from the past and, for a while, from the future. The peaceable flow of moments was like a marvelous vacation. Other nights, before then, next to Ali—in their darkness, the strange lake of their pleasure, there had been another form of breathless seeking. Would she truly never again experience the wonders of that fascination? Would Ali return? Could Ali really die? She pushed the questions aside.

"I'm old," she said all of a sudden.

"Old? At twenty-four?" Bachir thought she was actually worried about it. "Not at all."

"Yes, I am," she answered with a grimace. "In a country where more than half of the population is under twenty, twenty-four is old."

She was pretending to be serious, but only to hide the extreme attraction gradually invading her of the question of old age. Youth, like all forms of uncertainty, was in the end appearing barren, tiring, difficult. She wanted to grow old, and quickly too, so she could feel ever better, more audaciously armed as she faced life, which she was undoubtedly condemned to savor only as an affront.

Bachir talked and talked, as though giving a monologue in the theater, working on his breath. Lila found him to be much like herself, exactly like herself, with his increasing momentum and intense aspirations and dreams, his fear of losing his grasp on reality. For a very long time, reality for her had been a man who loved her, had been that love itself; for Bachir it was the future with all its hesitations.

All he had, he was saying now, was this summer, to choose the direction his studies would take, and that was only one rather significant element of his present situation. Everything was tempting to him, and he knew, for that was how unseasoned he felt—he'd admit it with some melancholy pride—that once his choice had been made he'd succeed anywhere. Yet at the same time everything seemed incomplete and unsatisfactory in advance. In a profession one should give oneself and be wholly involved. Even if he were to overlook his preferences, even if he wanted to think only of the future needs of his country, he wouldn't find just one path that would lead to wider horizons. His father, on the other hand, wanted him to become a doctor, because he'd seen some members of the lower-middle class get rich that way, all the while preserving the outward prestige of intellectuals who'd been trained abroad. But this was not Bachir's true vocation, even though there was still plenty to do in that area.

What would he himself like, Lila asked. He was strong in math, he answered, with naive solemnity, and he'd like to explore that road as far as possible. But it would take time; following his leanings in that direction was perhaps too self-centered. So . . .

They discussed this at length, as if the answer had to be found then and there. Brusquely, Bachir stood up and, gesticulating, swept the problem aside. No, none of that mattered; besides, a leaning toward math was not a vocation: perhaps it would become one later on, much later, when all the rest was in order. Only one thing mattered: he wanted to feel he was needed and he wanted it now, so he could finally leave the crossroads where he felt he was standing immobilized.

"It's good to be a link in a chain!" he then said: he was thinking of the fire.

He took a few steps back and forth. Lila was turning off the lamps and opening the window.

"I'm going to join the resistance," he decided. "That's it, I'm going up to the maquis. For some people going to war is a duty, for others it's a heroic departure. For me, it's a necessity, a real chance."

Lila was listening to him, but at the same time thinking sadly of Ali. Why hadn't she been close to him, inside his head, when he was talking to himself like this, as he must have been?

"I can't pursue a vocation alone, all by myself," Bachir continued more and more fiercely. "But when death grazes me, and I feel the need to live fully every day, then I'll certainly know a vocation is a luxury . . ."

Since they weren't sleepy and nothing had been left unsaid, they began to read poetry to each other, taking turns like children and enjoying it. Bachir had a lovely voice, one that was already that of a man. He knew many poems by heart. He lovingly recited Victor Hugo, with warmth Rimbaud's *Le bateau ivre*, and poems written by young people going into battle; he then moved on to the poets of liberty—Rimbaud again, Eluard, and Desnos.

In her room Lila had only one worn school text of Apollinaire. Softly she began:

Oh, God, how pretty war is
With its parties and its long leisure times!

Through the open window, they could see the smoke from the farm, where the fire was beginning to die out.

•••

Hassiba walks in front, right behind the guide, close to Youssef; four other men follow them in silence. She has changed her shoes, wears new canvas ones that are bothering her a little, but she doesn't want to show it. She walks so fast that Youssef has to tell her to slow down so she won't tire herself out too quickly.

After a three- or four-hour march, they come to the edge of a ravine; the forest starts above it. Before them are piles of smoking ruins and ashes.

"That's the village of the Beni Mihoub," someone says. "All their men are in the Liberation Army; the women and the old people just fled today."

Youssef gives the signal to pause. Then they'll push on; the forest has not been completely burned and will still offer good cover. The men sit down. The guide, a lean, spare shepherd, remains standing. He stares at the rubble without saying a word.

"I knew them well," says the person who'd spoken earlier. "I knew them well . . . Those of us in the party used to come here and organize political meetings, and they'd all attend; they'd approach, listen for two or three hours. But afterward, they'd say, 'You don't need to tell us about poverty; we know it, we live it; that we're being exploited, we know very well they've stolen our land. All we want to do now is fight back. We want weapons! Weapons,' they'd say."

No one answers; no one questions. Youssef has given the sign to get started. The guide leads the trek again. The man continues talking as he walks. To whom? To the ruins, his companions say to themselves. But Hassiba is listening; she focuses her attention both on keeping an even pace and on catching the words, for the man behind her is not speaking loudly enough anymore.

"'With what?' they'd answer our speeches. We'd arrive in town very proud of ourselves: we thought we'd be teaching them every-thing. But instead they were ready and merely waiting for the signal!"

Finally, the man stops talking. A shroud of silence falls once again. Hassiba no longer feels tired. Two hours later, at the next brief stop, the man quite naturally begins all over again: "Men like those of the Beni Mihoub *douar* can be found in the mountains every-where. 'Don't tell us why we must struggle, but with what! We know we're being exploited; we're living it . . . All we want is weapons!'"

Hassiba would like to know what became of the women and children of the Beni Mihoub *douar*. She doesn't dare ask. The silence is pure. She feels impatient and would like to know when they'll be seeing the brothers. She's in a hurry to meet a fighter, a real one, a patriot in uniform, "a uniform that's ours." Beside her, Youssef appears to have forgotten her completely. From time to time he glances at her feet, her canvas shoes, with a look that seems to say, "She's not doing too badly." In the meantime, she's making every effort to keep up with Youssef, right behind the guide, so that they can all see she's not slowing them down.

At the top, above a valley, she turns around: the town and the plain are spread out below their feet. Far in the distance they can make out some faint smoke. She looks at it with detachment as the only sign of life in a world to which she no longer wants to return.

• • •

Night has fallen and Cherifa has raised the curtain of her room, stood in the doorway for a moment facing the silence that returned once Amna's newborn had stopped whimpering. Then she went back into the empty room and lay down on the bed. On the bedside table she's left a candle burning: she's still afraid of the dark when she's alone.

"Will he come back?" she wonders and peers through the open door in front of her, even though she can't see anything from there; just a corner of the dark sky and a few stars. In this season the night is lovely.

Tomorrow there won't be any show. Life will pick up where it left off. Life? Certainly, Youssef has thought of everything: she won't need to sell her jewelry; Youssef's assistant will run the shop by himself; every month he'll bring her what she needs to live. If Youssef dies, the organization will take care of her. "Will he come back?" It's impossible to avoid the question. She can pretend all she wants, Cherifa thinks, pretend to be confident, display her serenity. She smiled when Lila was there, she was able to say calmly, "I'll wait." Now she is alone.

She's not suffering. She's not rebelling. She says to herself, automatically, "I should pray to God, I should recite some verses of the Koran to accept my lot, to purify my soul." But she doesn't pray and her soul is vacant; Youssef isn't near her on the bed. She's no longer alive; she will not live anymore. Tomorrow, she'll go back and forth from her room to the kitchen, shake out the mattress, hose down the courtyard. Tomorrow, and the day after; what foolishness! Then stop for a whole day, maybe two, to remain fixed before the mountain on fire. But where will the real spectacle be? Death thus exposed will make faces at her, and confronted with the display, she'll only be able to let the curtain drop down again, lock herself inside her solitude, refuse everything, ultimately wait. This night, her first night alone in five years, she knows she won't be able to wait. Yet what else can she do? What else? In the dark, her hands linger on Youssef's place, on the sheets, then she brings them back to her own body, her naked body that from now on she will feel as it ages, loses itself, is silent until . . .

She gets up. The night is so luminous that she hesitates, but the pain, which is just starting inside her, is stubborn and slow. She will not sleep. She thinks about nothing. She sits down, slight and abandoned in the doorway of her room, and when she turns her head to the courtyard it seems to her as if old Aicha, a ghost her memory suddenly draws forth, has come back to wait as well, impervious to despair.

• • •

Outside, the empty shade has captured the streets of the town.
Where the plain begins, the fire has burned for a long time. "So kill
me then! It's up to you to kill me, my brother!" What else was she
saying? "You, my brother; can't you see they're all waiting, all of
them here, now, around us, around the square? They're waiting! Oh,
you, my brother," did she say that, too? Tawfik can't remember anymore. He does remember the blazing eyes and the mouth that
stopped right in the middle of a crazy laugh, no, the scream that
took its place, a long scream that since that moment has been suspended somewhere. "So kill me then, you, oh, my brother!" Tawfik
roams interminably through the alleys.

It used to seem so simple. "I was sullied and I cleansed myself. I
was carrying a blemish and I purged myself of it." He repeats the
sentences because silence no longer exists for him, something he
only now understands. His sharpened mind unearthed them, but
the words in Arabic (which he used to find so charming!) seem foreign to him. While provoking him, Touma, too, spoke Arabic. Then
her eyes rolled back, but their grim gaze seemed to hold on to him,
as he threw the weapon away, faltered, recoiled, then fled when the
crowd opened one of its paths to him, the murderer, only to close up
again instantly, to rush forward and see the victim, stretched out at
the foot of the kiosque, built to the glory of some conquering
colonel who, in the previous century, must have accepted the surrender of the town that had once been free. And Tawfik runs, runs
until the moment when, realizing he's not being pursued, he slows
down and begins his nocturnal walk through the area of his birth.

"I was sullied . . . I was carrying a blemish." As a child, he was
told that's how a man spoke when his honor was offended by a
daughter who gave herself to a stranger, on this road. It was on the
bank of the river; the shantytown didn't exist yet, misery's roots were
still buried in the protective earth: the shepherds of the wadi, where
laurel and wild mint are still picked, used to have a few clay houses
here. This is where the first people who came down from the mountain, or former nomads who'd come from the southern plateaus, had

settled, all those whom the town claimed not to know, but whose daughters, the river girls, as they were called, were as famous for their beauty as for their virtuous timidity. These are the same girls who now fill the brothels of the capital, when they aren't belly dancers in the nightclubs at the harbor.

But the girl whose memory still remains, the one who first gave her body without even selling herself, died near the river, her throat slit by her father. "I was sullied . . ." the head of the family said, before leaving town and heading toward the plains. Since then, on the same spot, the reprehensible blood has been covered by a small forest, the "sacred forest" where two young lovers come every day at siesta time—she, a girl from a good family who's supposed to be going to class at her high school, and he, a beardless adolescent in a suit. Having escaped the paternal villa early, he kisses her devotedly, while a *fatma* with only one eye visible beneath the wide white veil passes by, not daring to look at them. For protection, the *fatma* calls upon the specter of the righter of wrongs, that father who stood over his daughter, the victim whose throat he'd cut. The young couple shake themselves, pick up their books and bags, and move on, hand in hand.

Walking along, Tawfik is not sleepy, feels no fatigue, forgets the night will end and daytime will come again, that his mother, a half-broken shape on the floor, holds watch with dry eyes—Touma's body not yet washed. Her eyes are dry and her soul is at peace because Touma has finally come home. No one has told her anything; it wasn't necessary to mention Tawfik's name. The neighboring women had remained standing near the dead girl. "She's grown into such a beautiful woman!" the old mother thought. In front of the bier, each of the four neighbors placed some incense. They burned it without a word, not even a blessing, not even a prayer. Then, one after the other, they went through the door, crossed the courtyard in the semidarkness and let fall the curtains of their own rooms over themselves, their children, and their homes.

"She's grown into such a beautiful woman," said the old mother, gazing at her child. Finally she thinks of closing the eyelids of her daughter, the girl who fell on the square, meandered all over town in Martinez's jeep, and came home. All that time her eyes had been wide open, as they faced a sky plunged into the grayness of a dying evening in May.

The old woman does not weep, not a single tear. She gets up, goes to the back of the small room, where the only piece of furniture is a large trunk of black oak. With trembling hands she takes out a key she keeps wrapped inside one of the sashes of her pants; she opens the trunk, and from its bottom, among the shabby linen that's been mended a thousand times, she takes a medallion made of six Napoleon coins. Then she takes up her place again, facing her dead daughter. The rays of the moon play freely on the gold coins that are like six open wounds in her hands. The old woman is dozing; her head tilts forward; at times she opens her eyes, looks for a long time at Touma, who lies on the only mattress in the room. Then, before giving in to sleep, she mutters so she won't forget the next day: "Ever since your childhood, this gold was intended for your wedding trousseau. If nobody wants to come and weep over you out of the goodness of her heart, I'll pay for professional mourners for you. I'll pay for the mourners!"

• • •

On the mountain, death has been striking indiscriminately in dust and destruction all day long. But in the self-possessed town, it slipped in at night and chose its quarries carefully: a feral girl at dusk and then, just before morning and the splash of the sun, a happy young man who was smiling, his last nighttime offering before life started anew.

At the bottom of the staircase, Bachir saw the guard arriving, led by the concierge; the little man points to the one he'd noticed coming in with Lila the night before, the one whose whispering he heard for hours on end when he stayed listening with his ear against the door, the one he went to inform on to Captain Martinez at dawn.

He also denounced Lila, whom he'd never stopped watching since she moved in. "I told you so!" the little man gloats, with a pointed finger. Bachir was watching them, not surprised, as if, of course, they had to be there at the end of his route; at the end of happiness.

Moments before, he'd abruptly stood up. "I'm going!" Across from him, Lila was beginning to doze off, but objected to his hasty departure. "Wait, I'll make some coffee first!" No. He laughed; he's in a hurry; he feels rushed; a gladdening impatience overcomes him. Lila insists; he finds a thousand excuses: his father needs to be reassured, the cool air of dawn—and what else, Lila wonders, upset by the flurry, standing by the door that is now closed again, then opened a minute later: Bachir—his smiling head framed by the door.

"I forgot to tell you . . ." He hesitates, then begins again, "I was afraid to tell you: I'm in love."

Lila has no time to answer or smile. He's gone again; she hears him whistling on the stairs. Surprised by this final flash of his, she goes out to call him from the doorway, a sentence in the wind: "Why don't you take the elevator!"

Bachir doesn't turn around. He keeps on going. The image of the young girl in the white dress coming off the train suddenly rushes at him. "I'm in love," he says again, to himself, and takes the stairs as if, to come down from the past night, he prefers the longest way available. Upstairs, Lila watches him. He's whistling, singing, has all the time in the world. Hassiba's image inside him, without any question, without any anguish, carrying her simply like a precious burden, he repeats with a newfound assurance that outstrips his discovery, "I'm in love."

Then he hears the guard's words; he sees the little man extend his arm, then withdraw, afraid. Behind them, the sun rises slowly. "If only I'd bend down a bit," Bachir thinks, "I could see it." There are four men in front of him; he can't tell from their uniforms whether they're soldiers or policemen. He has trouble making them out. "I'll keep going," he begins, "show them my papers; I slept at my cousin's, at Lila's house; everything's easy, even in times of war . . ."

He's forgotten about the fire. He sees the mountain and its battle, like his love, as a natural continuation. "How simple life is," he says as an obvious fact, then moves ahead; his attention is already diverted, but . . .

Perhaps the concierge repeated, "I told you so!" Perhaps fear itself, arms in the air, erupted one more time, like flames, before the uniforms. "There was no signal; what's it called?" the concierge thinks, as he stays rooted in the back, his finger pointing. "No words of warning." Before the shot is heard, before Lila leans over the banister of the stairs, her eyes wide, whispering in terror, "Bachir, Bachir," Bachir has collapsed, smiling, because what he has seen before his eyes is the slender silhouette of the young girl in white descending and glancing at the town.

• • •

"The second death tonight," mumbles police chief Jean flatly, standing in front of his desk. Then he looks up at Martinez, "Not counting the one who died here on the premises, of course."

Martinez doesn't answer. He waits, thinking, "It's the hour when the boss has scruples." He notices the dead eyes, the pasty complexion: Jean must not have slept well.

"What bothers me," Jean goes on in a different tone and with forced detachment, "is Ferrand's farm burning all night long."

He stops. The other still stands there facing him, rigid and impersonal. A kind of disdainful pity seems to color his look.

"Don't worry about him," he says somewhat offhandedly, "the insurance will pay. Ferrand will even manage to get the army to watch his farm."

Jean doesn't react. The heat started early this morning. The south wind came up, the first day of this year's sirocco. There hadn't been any real spring; it will be a long summer. "This year, the year before last, last year . . ." Jean is absorbed in his calculations. "How many years exactly before I can retire . . . finally go and live in Touraine with its soft light." He's spent.

"What is it you want?" he asks roughly of Martinez, that hard man, not tired like he is, tired and ready to resign. Martinez seems grounded in this land where he was born; Martinez, always ready for the job, a word he loves to throw out, proving his vitality and almost inhuman energy; Martinez, whom he hates.

"What do you want?" he asks again stiffly.

Martinez doesn't hurry to answer. Ever since he entered this room, with his self-assured step, his fine figure, his broad shoulders, to face Jean, who each morning behind his desk feels older and older, more and more foreign, Martinez has understood he's going to win. The chief will back down, he's sure of it.

"I'd like to be in charge of the girl, all by myself."

"The young man is her cousin. What else do you expect to find out?" Jean says. His voice is soft. "He's not really protesting," Martinez concludes.

"I was able to get more information" (Martinez's delivery is rapid; the victory is just a mere formality now). "The student" (he pronounces the word contemptuously) "was first seen near Ferrand's farm, just moments before the fire. If he's the one who pulled that off, then he was part of a cell in town. As for the girl, it's very odd how she came here to live. Her cousin spent the night with her and yet his parents knew nothing about it. She's married to another student, of whom there's no trace. Finally, her father has been in our files forever. A lot of coincidences all at once, wouldn't you say? Through her, I do believe, we have a very good chance of getting to the network."

Jean isn't listening anymore; he knows all too well that this conversation is merely the continuation of the previous one about Salima a few days ago that put Martinez and him at odds. He'd sat up with a start: no, there'd be no woman tortured in his prison! Martinez had yielded, but it was just a deferral; the slightest opportunity would see them arguing again.

Martinez waits, evaluating Jean: "Maybe he's afraid of Ferrand and whom he knows; maybe he's afraid of finding himself relocated or forced to retire early . . ." Jean raises his heavy eyelids and, growling inwardly, thinks, "What's the use? What's the use of resisting?"

"Well then, take care of it," the chief finally says, "since you want to so much!" He sits down, and then giving in to sarcasm, adds, "Did you get anything out of that man yesterday, before he died?"

"Nothing, Chief, but this time I'll take the operation on myself!" Martinez snickers. "Our Hakim doesn't quite have the hang of it yet; he went too fast!"

He bows slightly and goes out. Jean rises and leaves his new office, with the large bay windows and light-colored furniture. With heavy steps he goes through the halls of the prison. When they open Salima's cell for him and he stands in the door, there's a sudden burst of tenderness in his heart as he wonders, "Haven't I saved her? Haven't I . . ." Salima wakes up. She has been sleeping straight through since the previous evening, since Saidi's voice stopped. She never opened her eyes when Taleb, the guard, slipped in during the night to put a blanket over her body, curled up with cold. In the doorway, Jean hasn't budged. She has a hard time seeing him. In her sleep, Saidi kept on shrieking. She finally emerges into the silence; becomes aware of the air's purity. "Am I alive?" She sees the man before her, emerging from where—from a nightmare? She doesn't recognize him, averts her eyes. Through the window above her, it's daylight again, perhaps the same as yesterday's, as all the others since she's been here; she can't remember anymore. She knows nothing except that it's silent at last.

"If I hear any more screaming from people being tortured, I'll go mad," she thinks with difficulty before she falls back asleep.

• • •

"So here I am, at last," Lila says to herself, as if this should have been her objective all along. "At last . . ." and she follows the guards into the new prison. Martinez had kept her waiting for many hours. She had had time to reflect. "Confess? I have nothing to say; tell them I'm alone, that I've been living alone, without even the usual ghosts of customary solitude . . . And of the bright night, when it seems that Bachir keeps his hand stretched out to me from beyond the staircase, and his fall, tell them about that too . . ."

The room she enters is empty; not a stick of furniture, not a chair. Two policemen stand there, like statues by the door. In the back is Martinez; behind him, a closed door. He watches Lila come forward, observes the slightly slanted eyes, her expression. He sizes her up before asking his first questions; a hackneyed interrogation. She responds curtly, her voice cold: her name, her husband's, her father's, Bachir's, the names of all her people, conjured up for no purpose. Several months ago, no doubt that was last year, she gave the same answers; she remembers: bureaucratic formalities to get a passport.

But now she's here, for a different passport, a different passage. Martinez gradually comes to the real questions, as if he had had some scruples about entering the labyrinth. He'll make her confess what she knows about the town's network; he wants to know. He's not mistaken; he's never mistaken. He'll make her confess. He'll do what it takes.

Lila waits; a sudden distracting thought clouds her face. It isn't fear; nor is it hatred. It is something more familiar that she recognizes by its flavor of slow exhilaration. "I don't know; I don't know anything." "Those aren't the words you want," she thinks, and her green eyes resting on Martinez remains aloof. "You want me to talk and I won't say a thing, not about what I know, not about what I don't know. What I'm most familiar with is silence, immuring silence . . . refusal . . . challenge."

No, still on edge, she is, in fact, mistaken: nothing is familiar to her. Not the exaltation of finally feeling she's reached the place where cold pain, the screams of bewildering nights, the chorus of the victims' victories, open up; not the palpitation of the new world to which she's going to belong, finally delivered from herself, from the tangles of her youth, from the plains of her solitude. No, nothing will be similar to the dizziness that once used to possess her, those magic spells. She's mistaken: she thinks she's relearning the challenge, while everything behind her has abruptly found its course. Facing the ordeal that's beginning, she thinks that one single certainty awaits her: the triumph of her arrogance and pride in the duel, while from here on in it's actually a question of her being born—of a true awakening.

What luck, she will say to herself later, very much later, in the cell she will share with Salima, what marvelous luck to finally be nondescript on an earth and at a time that are no longer so!

•••

As the night ends on the mountain, Hassiba, Youssef, and the others have stopped. They settle down in a deep cave, the very first refuge they find. They must rest there until evening. The young guide has left; another will soon be coming. Crouching before Hassiba, who has fallen asleep immediately, Youssef watches her a little absent-mindedly. Since the previous evening he'd forgotten about his wife. "Do we forget peace that quickly?" he thinks sadly and keeps his eyes open.

After this mountain there is another, then another, an entire chain that separates the town from the high southern plateaus. Somewhere in these mountain masses lies the seat of the *willaya* from where the fight for this part of Algeria at war is being organized. The forest that is its shelter is impenetrable. The enemy knows it. Sometimes, too, as if out of pure conscientiousness, an army plane passing over makes a detour to drop a bomb, a second one. Then it flies off.

In one of the vast clearings, a last village—a few huts—can be seen. At nightfall a passing plane had dropped a series of bombs on it. Shortly thereafter, Mahmoud took a few men from the *willaya* with him to investigate. In charge of the infirmary, Ali has come along as well, in case there are any wounded.

Dawn has broken when they leave the forest and approach the huts: a last house is still smoking; a donkey with its flanks open, oozing blood, and braying, lies dying.

"Anyone here?" someone asks.

A peasant woman who must have heard them comes toward them from a distance; her gait is slow. Behind her follows a little girl of barely ten, her hair spilling down over her shoulders, a staff in her hand. A herd of goats jumps around them under the sun.

"Were you afraid yesterday?" Mahmoud asks the woman when she tells them that she and her child are now all that's left of the *douar*.

"No," she answers, "why should I be afraid?" And she looks at them with trust.

"Were you afraid?" Ali asks in turn as he goes toward the little girl. "How lovely," he thinks, "in the heart of all this carnage." He's still thinking about it, he won't forget, he repeats to himself as they retrace their steps.

The little girl had given him a vague, shy smile.

"Were you afraid?" Ali had insisted.

She shook her head no. He was still looking at her, and she smiled at him a second time, more bravely, then fled at a run: she was going off into the sun to play with her goats.

June–August 1961

AFTERWORD

On July 1, 1962, Algerians were casting their ballots in a referendum to establish the nation's independence from France, throwing off a colonizer's yoke that had lasted one hundred and thirty-two years. The previous day, Assia Djebar had celebrated both her twenty-sixth birthday and the publication of her third novel, *Les Enfants du nouveau monde* (*Children of the New World*).

The July 1 celebrations followed a brutal war of liberation that had pitted nationalists against their colonizers for eight long years. The conflict had been particularly gruesome. Torture and mutilations were freely and openly practiced by both sides on combatants and civilians alike; terror was systematically used in the cities as well as the countryside. The world-famous 1966 film *The Battle of Algiers* is historically accurate. It shows insurgents coldly depositing bombs in public places, including those likely to be patronized by women and children, to maim all who happen by. It also depicts French soldiers recklessly destroying blocks of fragile century-old buildings and their occupants to get at a few suspects hidden within. The hinterlands fared even worse than the capital city. Completely devastated by the conflict, rural farms and villages endured the razing of crops, widespread famine, and the forced relocation of nearly two million villagers—out of a total population of barely nine million—into "pacification camps."

If, to an American reader, such details seem eerily reminiscent of the war the United States fought in Vietnam, this is no coincidence. France had been trounced at Dien Bien Phû in May 1954 and forever lost its foothold in Asia—a lesson not lost on Algerian nationalists. A few months later, on November 1, 1954, the Algerian insurrection began with a series of attacks on armed French outposts—including in the city of Blida, where this novel takes place.[1] Those French officers who had made it out of Indochina would soon serve in Algeria, using the same ruthlessly repressive methods they had honed against the Vietcong. But on July 1, 1962, defeated in Asia and Africa, the Empire was in its last throes. And the Parisian world of letters prepared to fête its returning star.

•••

While Assia Djebar was already well-known in France when her third novel was published in French, it would be nearly three decades before she gained similar status in the English-speaking world. In the United States, Djebar has sometimes been paired with Moroccan-born Fatima Mernissi, a sociologist who has taught in that country; or, more often, with Nawal al-Saadawi, the Egyptian medical doctor and writer. Djebar took it upon herself to oversee the 1983 French publication of Saadawi's *Ferdaous* (*Woman at Point Zero*), for which she also wrote an introduction. As authors who challenge their Western readers to disentangle their own ideological investments in the Islamic world, a culture that they may perceive as other, Djebar, Saadawi, and Mernissi do share a concern for the difficult position of Muslim women writers within the Judeo-Christian West.

The English-speaking Saadawi has more easily gained international fame through her willingness, early on, to address such unmentionable topics as female genital mutilations, her time in Egyptian prisons, and her relentless persecution by her own government. In contrast, Djebar, who is fully at ease in French but not in English and prefers to keep a low media profile, has long put her private life ahead of her professional one, and done little to actively promote her own literary work. When she decided to resume publishing in 1980 after a ten-year silence, René Julliard, the owner of the Parisian press that had championed her and tamed the media for her, was dead. She has yet to acquire a literary agent, a fact that has perplexed publishers and restricted her entry into the American market. She has also been slowed down by the uneven quality of the British translations of the two novels that first made her reputation in the West (*Sister to Sheherazade* in 1988 and *Fantasia: An Algerian Cavalcade* in 1989), undertaken much too quickly and without Djebar's final control—a fact the writer still regrets, since she reads English well. The bewildering variety of her original publishers in Paris, some with copyright policies applied idiosyncratically if at all, discouraged foreign publishers.

In the United States, general reviews tend to steer her potential readership away from literary considerations and toward social or political questions.[2] Sooner or later, they gravitate to the "plight" of "Women and Islam" (or "Women *in* Islam"); that is, they resort to a paradigm defined by outsiders, with pre-established epistemological and theoretical assumptions as to this field and its subject. This is an Orientalizing position that Djebar has refused many times to occupy. In 1987, responding to my query concerning her (and Algerian women's) debt to European feminists, she said, "Who had time to wait for them? We were already there!"[3] In the scholarly Anglophone world, interest in Djebar's work accelerated with the 1992 translation of *Women of Algiers in Their Apartment*, an experimental collection of short stories published in French in 1980, in which the writer explored the fragmented, multivoiced narratives that have since become her signature. This U.S. translation was undertaken by Marjoljin de Jager, this time with Djebar's active and meticulous collaboration. A majority of her later works have since made it into English. But for the English reading public, it is as if her pre-1980 work does not exist, a situation that skews our understanding of a major *oeuvre* that has been evolving for half a century.

Thus, the Feminist Press's felicitous decision to give us this early novel makes it possible to situate Djebar more clearly. Grasping the literary and ideological complexity that lies beneath the deceptively simple linear plot line of *Children of the New World*, we realize that this novel, dealing with a war that had barely ended, is not merely an anticolonial diatribe but a complicated text that was already posing questions on the future of a nation in the making. It allows us to move Djebar out from under her limiting position as the poster child of Western feminism and/or the daring darling of postcolonial, postmodern resentment. This profusion of labels, accurate but reductive, is the unmistakable sign that Djebar's magnificently brave corpus has overflowed our too-narrow academic boundaries. If we wish to read her fairly, in as large and as generous a context as she reads the world, we need to go back to these beginnings.

"THE NEW ALGERIAN WOMAN"

Assia Djebar had already published two novels, *La Soif* in 1957 (published in English the following year as *The Mischief*) and, in 1958, *Les Impatients* (The impatient), composed within months of the first. These were amazing accomplishments considering the fact that, in 1958, the young author was on the run; her new husband was wanted by the French police, and her young brother had already been incarcerated for several years as a political subversive. The war raging on the other side of the Mediterranean Sea made her return home impossible. By the time *Les Impatients* was published in Paris and *The Mischief* was reviewed in the Sunday *New York Times*, Djebar was a fugitive.

On that first day of July 1962, the left-of-center Parisian magazine *L'Express* penned a warm review of the new novel, *Les Enfants du nouveau monde*, accompanied by a picture of the author. A month earlier, *France Observateur* had saluted her in an article entitled "Assia Djebar: La nouvelle algérienne" ("The new Algerian woman"—or, more accurately, "The new type of Algerian woman."[4] The definite article said it all. This "new Algerian woman," as the piece depicted her, was smart, stylish, and sophisticated—in other words, Westernized. The journalist even saw fit to comment favorably on Djebar's "made in Paris" sartorial elegance, thus establishing the pattern. Parisians were still infatuated with the precocious young author whose first novel they had praised for its hedonistic portrait of upper-class, acculturated females who could drive cars, smoke cigarettes, go off to university, and stand up to their men. Although its subject matter was very much in contrast to that of *The Mischief*, *Children of the New World* reinforced Western stereotypes in a different way, corroborating Orientalist clichés about the plight of Muslim women in need of modernization. Europe-based critics would simultaneously position Djebar as a credit to her race (the token educated Arab); a credit to her gender (the token writing woman); even a credit to the French colonial school system (the token native student): no need for her to color outside the prescribed Orientalist lines. However much she might have supported the Algerian revolution, however much she might have aided and abetted the rebels, she was still praised (and marketed) as an exceptional product of French universities and French acculturation: "mission *civilisatrice*" accomplished.

In fact, Djebar had attended boarding school in Blida, the town that would become the setting for her third novel. Graduating from its high school in 1954, she moved to Paris to prepare for the entrance examinations to Ecole Normale de Sèvres, the ruthlessly competitive school where France trained the next generation of its best and brightest academic mandarins. Enrolled in fall 1955, the first and only Maghrebian student to be so admitted, she was banned from the premises the following spring for participating in the political strike called for by the FLN (National Liberation Front), the main group mounting the insurgency in Algeria. She was also barred from ever taking the yearly qualifying examinations. Unable to get back home—and exhibiting the maverick streak that would become more evident over the years—Djebar chose to spend the time writing a novel, to see, as she has often said, whether she could do it. Her first novel took place in Cherchell, the town where she was born. The second would follow a French-educated young Muslim woman from Algiers to Paris. And the third would detail how the citizens of a town she knew well coped with a brutal war during the month of May 1956, at precisely the time when its writer was being punished in Paris for her nationalist convictions. Although not openly autobiographical, these three novels represented her imaginary homecoming.

Married in March 1958, the newlyweds had escaped to Tunisia by way of a clandestine passage through Switzerland. Meanwhile, worsening conditions in her native land provoked several political crises on both sides of the Mediterranean. While public opinion, internationally and in France, was slowly turning in favor of Algerian independence, the wealthy European settlers in Algeria dug in their heels. In May, students marched in Algiers and, for days, riotous mobs occupied government buildings. The same month, the French Army tried to seize power from civilian authorities. Faced with domestic disorder, as well as the full-fledged anticolonial war in progress in Algeria, President René Coty recalled General De Gaulle to power. The Algerian War had brought down the French Fourth Republic. But it would take this larger-than-life hero of World War II another four years to negotiate an end to French colonialism in Algeria.

Although they were French protectorates, Tunisia and Morocco had sympathy for the Algerian struggle at their borders. In Tunis, Djebar worked on the FLN political newspaper *El Moudjahid*, whose editor was the revolutionary West Indian writer and psychiatrist Frantz Fanon; visited refugee camps where she gathered details on the war; and finished a graduate degree in history with Louis Massignon, the highly acclaimed Islamic scholar. Her M.A. thesis dealt with a Muslim female mystic of the Middle Ages, Lla Aicha el Manoubia, the twelfth-century patron saint of the city. The thesis examined the ways in which ancient cultural practices survive and, often, subvert established religion. This interest would govern most of Djebar's subsequent work, shaping her determination to excavate and recover women's active participation in the collective history of North Africa. With *Loin de Médine* (1991, tr. *Far from Medina*, 1994), for example, as she focuses on the Prophet Mohammed's female entourage, she tackles women's essential contribution to the elaboration of the faith alongside the prophet himself, a memory long since occulted and silenced by successive generations of male theologians.[5] The end of 1959 found Djebar in Rabat, teaching North African history at the national university while continuing her work with refugees. Out of her time in Morocco would come a play, *Rouge l'Aube* (Red is dawn), a collection of poems, *Poèmes pour l'Algérie heureuse* (Poems for a happy Algeria), and this third novel.

That same year, 1959, the formerly disobedient student was reinstated to the Ecole Normale de Sèvres by General De Gaulle himself, on the grounds that she had too much talent as a writer to be deprived of her right to the finest education in the world.[6] One may assume that the cunning politician probably calculated that, with an independent Algeria in its future, France would need all the friends it could muster. Unlike Tunisia and Morocco, Algeria had been made a full-fledged part of the French national territory, a *département*, in 1848, as soon as the last resistance leader, Emir Abd-el-Kader, had been subdued.[7] The gifted if undisciplined student was therefore, at least technically, still a French citizen. She also fit the profile of a typically acculturated, educated, middle-class colonial, poised to reap the accolades of her intellectual masters and destined for a brilliant academic career. Or so it seemed. But this was a young woman who had been born Fatma-Zohra Imalhayêne, and had adopted the pen name Assia Djebar so as to bypass her culture's proscription against female writing. If her chosen first name evoked Asia, her last name was one of the ninety-nine virtues attributed to the Prophet that praying believers must invoke. Spelled and pronounced with one *b*, djebar meant "the merciful." With two *b*s, *djebbar*, it turned into "the intransigent."[8]

She had been born on June 30, 1936 in the ancient town of

Cherchell, a deep seaport settled by Phoenicians in the fourth century B.C.E. Hannibal's Carthaginians traders called it Iol; the Roman invaders of the first century C.E. called it Cesarea, in honor of their emperor (hence, the modern Arabic rendering of Cherchell). Under Jubal, a Numidian prince married to Cleopatra-Selene, daughter of the great Cleopatra, Cesarea became the flourishing capital of the Mauritanian half of Rome's territory in Africa, a territory stretching from Gibraltar to Libya. Although Islamicized and racially intermixed with their Arab conquerors, who had arrived in the eighth century C.E., the local people are prompt to evoke the Kahena, the Berber warrior queen who, at the end of the seventh century, had foiled Arab invaders for seven years and managed to push them back all the way into Libya. In later novels, *Fantasia* and *Vaste est la prison* (1995; *tr. So Vast the Prison*, 1999), Djebar would explore these personal roots.

This territory, known as the Maghreb, has always been a complex sociohistorical mix, at the North-South crossroads, commercially and ethnically, between Europe and sub-Saharan Africa; as well as the site of philosophical and religious exchanges between "Maghreb" (the land to the west) and "Mashrek" (the land to the east or the Middle East). The French conquerors, by offering citizenship and, often, land to Christian settlers from other nations around the Mediterranean, hoped to balance the demographic weight of the natives. By the middle of the twentieth century, Algeria contained a finely textured human variety that French conquest nevertheless stereotyped into two hostile camps: "the Europeans" and "the Arabs." Upward of one million strong, the former could be of French descent, or, often, Alsatian (refugees from the wars with Germany); they might also be Spanish, or Italian, or Maltese. One thing that distinguished them from the "Arabs" was that they generally met in public places where alcohol consumption was permitted. The "Arabs" numbered close to nine million, and claimed separate identities, whether Arab, or Kabyle, or Chawia, or M'zab, or Tuareg, or those of Turkish descent who stayed on after the French had triumphed over the Ottoman Empire.

Children of the New World deploys a careful choreography of these various groups on the central square of the little town, quite attentive to their mixed ethnic and class origins. Not to understand this complexity would reduce this intricate society to the binary opposition of the colonial vision, Europeans versus Arabs. In Djebar's third novel, her implied multiethnic vision is a clear sign that colonialism has failed. In her later works, this same pointed evocation of the commingled historical roots of present-day Algeria is used to refute the current "Arabization" policy of a regime that has refurbished the old nationalist slogan it once used against the French ("one religion, one language, one nation"), the better to oppress its own people. In much of Djebar's subsequent writing, the depth-sounding of this collective past is, as well, a loving homage rendered to her own parentage. Her nationalist father who, like all pious Muslims, had given his first-born female child the name of the Prophet's only daughter (Fatma or Fatima), was nonetheless a professed admirer of the French revolutionaries of 1789 who had proclaimed an end to all class-based privileges. Born into a very poor Berber family, he was a French-educated schoolteacher, who saw to it that his daughter would be neither veiled nor cloistered. The famous autobiographical opening scene to *Fantasia* of a little girl being led to her first day of school, "her hand in the father's hand," honors him for what she has since called "my escape from the harem."[9] In *Children*, the close relationship between Lila and the widowed father who confronts his entire clan over a daughter's education bears more than an accidental resemblance to Djebar's own circumstances. And her mother, who neither spoke nor read French during Djebar's childhood (she does now), was a fine musician who practiced classical Arabic, improvised poetry in the traditional Andalusian style, and saw to it that her daughter would attend a Qur'anic school. Djebar's maternal line belonged to a large, wealthy, and influential tribe of the Chenoua mountains around Cherchell, the Beni-Menacer, to whom Djebar would eventually devote her 1979 film *La Nouba des femmes du Mont Chenoua* (The celebration of the women of Mount

Chenoua). One ancestor, Mohammed ben Aîssa El Berkani, had served as a *khalifa* (aide) to the Emir Abd-el-Kader, rallying the hinterland against the French conquest throughout the 1840s. His nephew, the writer's own great-grandfather, led a subsequent rebellion in Kabylia and lost his life on August 2, 1871, beheaded on the battlefield in front of the women of his family. Djebar evokes this graphic death several times in her collections of poems.[10] The multilayered historical consciousness that, in *Children*, most of Djebar's characters possess comes directly from her own experience. If key incidents unfold at the town's political and spiritual center, this *place d'armes*, it is because the "Arabs" always remember what the "Europeans" promptly forgot: that the Emir's green banner was unfurled there in 1845, fanning the embers of what, in 1945, and again on November 1, 1954, would eventually burst into a successful war of liberation.

How, then, should readers approach *Children of the New World*, this document about a hopeful revolution—its romantic story line, its young protagonists so eager to embrace this new and wonderful world after a century and a half of colonial oppression that had denied and demeaned their own culture? As with the majority of Djebar's works, critics have preferred to look for the political, first. Useful as this urge may prove, it is often reductive.

As Assia Djebar returned home; moralizing attacks or paternalistic comments greeted her third novel. She was particularly criticized for her "bourgeois individualism," a quality considered suspect at this highly politicized time. Reviewing it for African readers in *L'Afrique et l'Asie* in 1962, journalist Patrick Catrice singled her out for being insufficiently engagé: "Thus, Assia Djebar, it would seem, is not nor does she want to be a committed writer."[11] Although Charles Bonn, a French-trained university professor who was teaching in Algeria at the time, was also severe, he acknowledged progress over her previous novels: "One must wait until *Children of the New World* (1962) to see Djebar's heroines seek their liberation in ways other than through an awkward self-centeredness, disconnected as they are from the real world, with a confused notion of the hopes and aspirations of numerous contemporary Algerian women."[12] Only one sharp reviewer understood how subversive such individualized writing could be, perhaps because he was a practicing novelist himself. Moroccan Abdelkébir Khatibi, while looking at all three novels, zeroed in neither on the party line demanded by Algiers, nor on the ethnographic documentary expected by Paris. Instead, as early as the first novel, he aligned Djebar's explicit political stance with a far more implicitly challenging private one, the evocation of female sensuality: "Has anyone truly understood that the discovery of her own body, for the central character of *La Soif* is just as important a revolution?"[13] In *Children*, as in the first two novels, this theme resurfaces in the intensely private difficulties of modern couples, such as Lila and Ali or Omar and Suzanne. Yet it is visible, as well, in the finely etched portrait of the stunningly beautiful Cherifa, a traditional woman unhappy enough physically to relish her own barrenness, refuse her husband's sexual attention (something which the Qur'an forbids), engineer her own repudiation; and, with Youssef, embark on a second marriage of true equality. So much for the plight of the oppressed Muslim woman.

Although they are made manifest through their erotic lives, these difficulties between men and women stem primarily from their inability to negotiate the phenomenological challenge of all human beings—that of embracing the other as completely as oneself. Here Djebar comes close to asserting that there exists a fundamentally nonnegotiable biological variable that renders men opaque to women and vice-versa. She has always grounded her writing primarily in the lived experience of the body, although she complicates this predicament with patient attention to modern sociopolitical conditions and her culture's traditions. Hers is a finely tuned position, one that those early critics—most of them either seduced or offended by scenes of female sensuality—were not willing to entertain.

This was not likely to endear Djebar to the new powers back in Algeria. At the first party congress on national culture, convened in

Algiers in 1963, Mostefa Lacheraf, who, like Djebar, was trained as a historian, dismissed those "bourgeois" novelists who, unable or unwilling to share the realities of a suffering people, dared to "cleverly conceal the new Algerian realities under a cheap poetic layer."[14] He repeated his barbed attacks at the end of the year during the cultural festival in Carthage, this time naming names—Assia Djebar and Malek Haddad. Haddad stopped writing; Djebar dug in her heels and carried on. She would produce a fourth novel by 1967, *Les Alouettes naïves* (The innocent larks). But the wildly exuberant hopes evoked in *Children* for a just society, this "new world" spawned by the success of the anticolonial war, had already faded. There would be no happy Algeria for a people "without memory," lulled by party apparatchiks and eager to forget their own past. Written upon her return home, a short story, "The Dead Speak," made this clear. It was included in *Women of Algiers in Their Apartment*, the 1980 collection where Djebar's not-so-veiled distaste for the ossified oligarchy then ruling Algeria comes to the fore.

Within a few years, the lines were drawn and a policy of full Arabization would attempt to unmoor the country from its Western ties. Artists were expendable. They must henceforth put themselves at the service of the socialist revolution or disappear. It was an eerie foreboding of the brutal eradication of artists and intellectuals in Algeria during the past fifteen years, in a civil war that shows little sign of waning and has remained, in the West, "mostly invisible."[15]

Much was made of the novel's biographical details by critics leery of a too-simple plot.[16] Was not this too, too patriotic tale intended by Djebar to atone for her spending the war in the safety of exile? Or, as the party men implied, was she trying to claim revolutionary credentials that could only be granted to the starving masses, the landless dispossessed, or the heroic fighters maimed in combat? Since the writer fit none of these stereotypes, hers was deemed a token book. Indeed, a fast read of *Children of the New World* might reveal only melodramatic binary fault lines between heroes and traitors, haves and have-nots, colonizers and colonized. Precipitating the tragedy to come, all of the novel's key actors, some of them conveniently related, cross paths in one single day. (Years later, Evelyne Accad still found such coincidences a bit too coincidental: "In fact, it may well be that adolescent rebellion and the search for identity are not the stuff of the great novels of tomorrow."[17])

The critical quarrel with Lacheraf festered. Not one to back down, Djebar responded in a 1968 essay for the Parisian journal *Europe*: "I did not trust, I still do not trust, a literature of ready-made testimonials."[18] She made it clear that she would follow no prescriptive line, whether dictated from Paris or Algiers. Many years later, this determination to refuse the colonial script remained unchanged. In accepting the Frankfurt Peace Prize in 2000, she said: "Faced with French critics that I would call traditionalists, who sought in formerly colonized writers only interpretive clues for a ready-made sociology, what attracted me? Leftover nationalism? Of course not: only language."[19]

"I DO NOT TRUST A LITERATURE OF READY-MADE TESTIMONIALS"

Much of *Children*, in obvious dialogue with real life, cuts close to the autobiographical bone. It was triggered by the story of an elderly neighbor lady killed by shrapnel inside her inner courtyard, as reported to Djebar by her own mother-in-law, a Blida native. This clever symbol of a war's senseless cruelty, which could reach everywhere and everyone, even the most feeble and the most innocent in the most secure of enclosures, makes for a stunning opening to the novel. It was, we now know, something that had actually occurred.

In her first two novels, Djebar had depicted the coming-of-age of romantic young women eager to abandon traditional practices, something that their exposure to French education encouraged.

Through a tightly Aristotelian structure (unity of time, place, and plot), the third novel marks an evolution, an ambitious expansion of her writing skills, and engages a much larger social canvas. *Children* moves our attention away from the rebellious singular of the first two novels to the collective plural—in and out of the occupied town, in and out of the embattled mountain, in and out of French jails. Although we witness scenes of pain, humiliation, betrayal, torture, and death, there is no single hero here—only the suffering of a people. The struggle is framed by two contrapuntal scenes of great beauty in which a filmmaker's eye is already at work. Indeed, Djebar's 1979 film *La Nouba des femmes du Mont Chenoua* reproduces such scenes and follows the dialectical movement we are given in the novel's opening, between the cloistered space of women praying inside traditional houses and the expanding horizon of their menfolk fighting in the mountains. If the beginning gives us the absurd death of a feeble-minded old woman on her doorstep, the ending moves us upward, physically and spiritually, with the arrival of guerilla fighters on a reclaimed mountaintop that stands, potentially, for an entire country: free at last.

The novel's structure juxtaposes the public square, territory of the colonizer, with the traditional courtyard, inner sanctum of the colonized. Unlike the post-1980 works that, in true postmodern fashion, eschew classical linearity of plot, scramble narrative continuity, and fragment or explode psychological consistency, *Children* is efficiently and cleanly built in nine chapters, each with a character around whom the other eight revolve, each character differently besieged by the personal burdens brought on by the war. The plot is tightly wound up around this spatial and symbolic center, taking place over twenty-four intense and ultimately tragic hours. Architecturally and sociologically, the same oppositional structure prevails: old Arab quarter versus European town; illiterate urban proletariat versus committed bourgeois intellectuals; traditional Qur'anic schools versus secular French high schools; and, perhaps, just versus unjust causes.

Children explores the well-known gendered thematics for which Djebar is famous, the escape "out of the harem." In the novel's well-honed use of spatial symbolism, the author stretches her writerly wings and plunges her characters into a specific historical situation where nothing is as it appears. Themes are systematically intertwined, just as the paths—physical and spiritual—of these men and women are. The balanced movements are made clear by the alternating chapters; the first four, dedicated to the women of the town (Cherifa, Lila, Salima, Touma) and the last three, to the men whose lives are forever changed by encountering them (Khaled, Bob, Ali).

These oscillations are articulated around chapter five, which functions as axis and hinge; it is devoted to Hakim, the native policeman, flanked by Touma and Hassiba . Touma, the young stool pigeon who will precipitate Saidi's death and Youssef's run for the hills, stands as the political, social, and psychological mirror opposite to Hassiba, the young urban partisan on her way to the mountain. Their positioning at the center of the story on either side of Hakim, forms a figure of unresolved and unresolvable contradictions. This growing sense of contradiction suggest to the reader that taking sides is not as simple, the distinction between good and evil, not as pure as we may have thought. For the year is 1956, the crucial internecine period among the various revolutionary factions, when brothers murdered brothers and women fighters were made unwelcome on the battlefield. In this careful balancing act between the sexes and the generations, the past and the present, hopes and impediments, *Children of the New World* finds its mark and its place within Djebar's *oeuvre*. It is simultaneously a joyous celebration of a better society in the making and a foreboding of the eventual difficulties of achieving social justice for all. A careful historical reading reveals the novel's attention to the sociopolitical underpinnings of colonization, the wretched condition of the urban poor, the good conscience of the wealthy settler who believes himself to be a decent boss. This subtext runs from the first Franco-Algerian conflict in 1845 through the failed uprising of 1945, all the way to the second Franco-Algerian War that starts on 1 November 1954, All Saints' Day. This is exactly two days, we are told, after Ali and Lila marry; a honeymoon steeped in blood (with overtones of one of Djebar's favorite poets, the murdered patriot Federico García Lorca).

Had we world enough and time here, we might view this novel

from yet another angle, in terms of its intertextual relationship with Djebar's entire corpus. The narrative stands in dialogue not only with the works that preceded it but, as well, with those that have come afterwards. We can, for instance, note its clear dialectical connection to *L'Amour, Fantasia* (*Fantasia: An Algerian Calvalcade*), the novel that recasts the first French conquest of the 1830s and, using the very documents of the French campaigns, rewrites colonial history against the grain. We can also see its relationship to *Vaste est la prison* (*So Vast a Prison*) (1995), a novel that moves through several successive conquerors of the Maghrebian past, in huge time frames (the several centuries of resisting conquest) as well as huge spatial frames (a sprawling narrative that eventually claims the entire continent). In this intertextual mise-en-abyme we might discover that Djebar's entire body of work is colored by the ethical position of *Children of the New World*: the conviction that this writer is answerable to history.

Crisscrossed by every character in the novel, the *place d'armes* is the nerve center of a psychological and political tragedy. There, in a painfully twisted display of national and sexual pride, at exactly 7:00 p.m., when the shuttle train arrives from Algiers, brother will murder sister on this sacrificial spot. The painful paradox is that Tawfik, to prove his loyalty to the new revolutionary values that the FLN had touted as socialist and secular, behaves exactly as if he were stuck in the most obsolete, primitive, and repressive of patriarchies. This public spot, so aptly named, is also a *lieu de mémoire*, an occulted memorial site. On Victory Day 1945, returning Algerian veterans were marching in several cities to celebrate the end of a war not of their making but one in which, as colonial subjects, they had shed their blood, when things turned ugly. Reprisals on both sides lasted a long week, with several hundred Europeans and many thousand Algerians dead. The nationalist party was banned, five thousand of its members arrested. Canceled were the promised elections that might have given them all a chance. Instead, marchers (young Kateb Yacine was one in Sétif) were thrown in jail and repression maintained for another nine years. It was the first salvo of the war that would flare up for good on All Saints Day in 1954.

In this public square, where the nineteenth-century colonial invaders used to conduct army drills (hence, its French name), they now parade on Bastille Day. Its one sickly palm tree, all that is left of a once fertile plain in which nomads freely roamed, stands in silent vigil next to the corrugated kiosque, an ugly, frilly example of colonial architecture. There, settlers take their ease in the open terraces of its cafés, oblivious to the wretched misery and near starvation all around, in the alcohol-free "Moorish" establishment where a small cup of coffee must last a hungry man all day. If naming is appropriating, who owns this plaza? What was it called when, centuries earlier, a holy man settled his tribe there? The repeated dirge of the Beni Mihoubs, driven out of their burnt-out mountaintop by yesterday's battle, reactivates the mnemonic trace as, watching them pass, an entire town falls silent. Algerian men, their women hidden from view, must proceed cautiously.

Embedded within the highly evocative space of the *place d'armes*, the public square, and in dialogical relationship to it, is a smaller, private square—the internal courtyard of the traditional house in the old quarter. And implicitly enfolding them all is the larger space of the encircling mountains under fire, where a child, roaming free, may eventually claim her revolutionary birthright. With true poetic justice, the *place d'armes* on which the Emir's green standard unfurled has been renamed *place du 1er novembre*, and his banner is now the official flag of modern Algeria.

To understand such spatial poetics, one needs to grasp their anthropological dimensions; to know that, while the streets belong to the men, the traditional house is a female space. In a gallery of rooms symmetrically spaced around a roofless courtyard, with a fountain or a well at the center, women share a common area for cooking, washing, doing laundry and, often, a room for private bathing. They move freely about without the impediment of a veil or a robe. Returning men must announce their approach to give their female neighbors time to move back behind their curtains. In *Les Impatients*, her second novel, Djebar underlines the instinctive courtliness of the heroine's uncle who, although blind, continues to clear his throat before entering his home. In contrast, *Children* shows us Hakim's precipitate return at an odd hour to question his wife. This breach in etiquette, as much as his striking Amna, conveys his disturbed state of mind. When the national good is uncoupled from the social, as it was during the final days of the Algerian revolution, the struggle for ethical justice and political equality flounders. Djebar has often surmised, in her public lectures, that women suffer more than men, since the culture under attack tends to go back to the comfort of age-old customs—a mental circling of the wagons, as it were, apparent in the musings of the humble family man who, rudely shoved about by trigger-happy soldiers, is nevertheless "inexplicably set free."

> "Yes, it's almost easy to forget," a man thinks when he comes home at night and looks at his wife whom the other one, the omnipotent master outside, will never know. They call her "sequestered" but, while he speaks without addressing her directly, as tradition prescribes, the husband thinks of her as "freed." And that, he decides, is why she is his wife and not merely a body he embraces in the dark [. . .] The husband beside her turns over, not forgetting the *chahâda*, the prayer that helps him face sleep, his heart empty, that peaceful emptiness that faith brings, pure and simple as light. [. . .] Here he is, inexplicably set free. Alone. (10-11)

Within what looks like an Orientalized vignette, ethnographically complete with the baby's cradle suspended beneath the high copper bed, Djebar has just given us an invisible political lesson: this is a fully self-sufficient society. There is nothing "exotic" about its practices, but the colonizer does not have the code. For those who do, clear signals move us through the tight sequence of a single day whose careful time-frame indicates a writer in full control of her material, twenty-four dramatic hours, punctuated by the twice-daily arrival of the shuttle train from Algiers at the edge of the town square: Hassiba alights at 1:00 p.m. and Touma is shot at 7:00 p.m. Saidi, arrested in the morning, will die in the afternoon. A frantic Cherifa locates her husband as Yahia, the apprentice, is about to close shop for the midday prayer. Youssef gives himself two hours to warn others before taking to the hills with Hassiba at exactly 3:00 p.m.. Having set fire to settler Ferrand's storerooms right before the 8:00 p.m. curfew, Bachir bumps into Lila, whom Khaled is seeing home. He will die at dawn. As jailed Salima figures it out, her interrogation at an end, the date is precisely May 24, 1956.

In this war novel, female protagonists are given equal time with their male comrades and, as in the real war, are made to run equal risks. The war is heating up and it is clear it will be a long one. With chivalrous Commander Jean soon to retire in France where he was born, the running of the political jail will fall to Blida-born Captain Martinez, ambitious son of poor Spanish settlers (like Camus), who will see to it that interrogations yield results. If male torture by water and electric burning of genitalia is clearly suggested in the death of Saidi, a contemporary reader in the 1960s would have needed no hint about female torture when encountering such characters as Salima, interrogated for ten solid days; and Lila, soon to be. French newspapers were full of reports on "the two Djamilas": Djamila Bouhired, arrested, tortured, and condemned to death at age twenty-two in 1957 (Fanon's *El Moudjahid* wrote about her); and in 1961, Djamila Boupacha, who, not yet twenty-one, was raped with a bottle. Such nauseating details came out during their trials. Both had transported bombs detonated in city cafés. Prominent intellectuals, such as Sartre, Beauvoir, Mauriac, Tillon, and Picasso kept their names in the public eye, so that their lives were eventually spared. Until then, only the North Vietnamese, proclaiming the complete equality of men and women, had encouraged and documented full female participation in war.

This is May 1956. All through spring 1956 various factions, of which the FLN was only the most visible, battled for political control of the revolution with a series of meetings in La Soummam valley. The FLN emerged victorious and free to implement a much tougher line, both ideologically and on the battlefield: no cease-fire; no negotiations. After La Soummam 1956, the FLN line became the official version of history. In the novel, these divisions at the top are implied in the finely shaded positions of some key characters; for example, the prescient disengagement of Omar, who, unlike his idealistic French wife, has become convinced that the struggle is riddled with greed and corruption; Ali, the upper-class medical student who had sacrificed woman and infant son with the same blind confusion as ghetto-bound Tawfik executing his sister; Youssef, the carpenter with a grim understanding acquired in jail; and Khaled, a walking colonial paradox, tribal foundling, and French-trained lawyer, who saves Youssef's head on this crucial 8 May 1945.

Embedded in the internecine fighting of La Soummam was the question of female autonomy—an issue that remains contentious in Algeria to this day. The belief that the leadership unreservedly embraced the participation of women guerilla fighters has become part of modern lore. But in reality, this was more wishful thinking than fact, for women's actual numbers were always small, and their reinsertion into public life next to impossible. The FLN soon quietly proceeded to withdraw women from the battlefield, where it deemed them "disruptive." So much for sound revolutionary principles trumping patriarchal customs. Djebar, who has publicly admitted having had first-hand knowledge of these tormented moments, simply moves a joyfully expectant Hassiba up into the mountains, without elaborating further.[20] Later referring to these "fire-carriers" ("les porteuses de feu") in *Women of Algiers*, she would pay them full homage; and, true to her training as a historian, connect them back to the long line of women who, throughout the nineteenth century, had resisted the first French conquest and paid with their lives. Breaking her self-imposed silence with the collection of short stories in 1980, she would not mince words in condemning the fast-accelerating cultural regression that followed independence, something that a corrupt regime did nothing to prevent. In 2002, with what was her fifteenth work, *La Femme sans sépulture* (The woman without a grave), she recreates the life of Yasmina Oudaî, code name Zouleikha, who went underground and was eventually captured on Chenoua mountain in 1956. Her body was never found, and she was left without a proper burial site, an unbearable spiritual wound for any Muslim.[21]

Children of the New World offers a varied gallery of female portraits that manage to meet every expectation of Western feminism and, simultaneously, to destabilize them all. Djebar introduces readers to the self-sufficient, French-born lawyer-wife (Suzanne), the self-indulgent, self-centered philosophy student (Lila), the abused cloistered wife with child at the breast (Amna), and the superstitious illiterate mother, suffering and scared (Tawfik's mother). When Marnia Larzeg, an Algerian sociologist teaching in the United States, complains that "Djebar's characters evolve out of time, out of space, oblivious to the constraints of the war," she must be reading too fast.[22] The novel offers these women to us in all the contradictions of a contingent history they do not control: they are, as are their men, works in progress, caught in an accelerating storm. To find this early novel wanting by measuring it according to the stunning achievement of the later works is merely to restate the obvious: that a young writer was learning her craft. Still, it offers fine surprises, such as the veiled woman's foray into a hostile town, which provides us with a particularly subtle reflection on the vexed question of female agency that Fanon had celebrated a bit too hastily in his essay "Algeria Unveiled." An outsider's piece, Fanon's essay suffers from its own voyeuristic dialectics on "the flesh of Algeria laid bare," and the conviction that, with full socialist equality, Algerian women would soon reclaim public spaces.[23] Instead, forty years later, they are still waiting. In both 1976 and in 1984, modifications imposed on the Algerian Family Code restricted women's rights further. After the 1991 victory at the polls of a majority of Islamic fundamentalist candidates, the government declared the elections invalid. By June 1992, the new president, Mohammed Boudiaf, a former FLN war hero recalled from exile, had been assassinated by Islamist sympathizers, plunging the country into a civil war from which it has yet to recover.

As always, Djebar resorts to lived experience to examine, very concretely, what the West sees as the symbol of female oppression, the veil, "the expression of the invisibility of women on the street, a male space *par excellence.*"[24] Which ideological space is claimed with Cherifa's foray? Is it a Fanonian gesture of autonomy for this woman, who discovers the very streets of her native town through which she has never walked? Will this send her timorously back to her cloistered existence? Although Djebar has already shown Cherifa as quite capable of asserting herself, this is hardly a celebration of unhampered female agency: rather, it is a double-bind. The veil that should have protected her against the colonizer's gaze and gained her the respect of her compatriots has, in fact, made her sexual prey for the loiterers on the square, who, in their prurience, "unveil" every inch of her. She is far from invisible and certainly not protected. The hostile response of her husband's apprentice is unnerving. Yahia, who, with obsessive religious conviction, throws her back into the streets, cruelly foreshadows the virulently misogynist aspects of the current civil war; the many, veiled as well as unveiled, who have had their throats cut for supposedly transgressing Islamic law. The incident is chillingly prescient. Blida was always a deeply religious town. In the twenty-first century, it has become a center for Islamic fundamentalism in Algeria. But before we feel too sorry for this traditional woman, Djebar also gives us, in Chérifa's afternoon conversation with Lila, a sense of their differences. The cloistered wife, in the quietly passionate way in which she expresses respect for her husband's decision to leave even though it brings her grief, offers self-centered Lila a lesson in courage as well as a demonstration of what happens inside the marriage of true equals.

In retrospect, *Children* may now seem to us overly optimistic in its faith that one pure-hearted revolution might breech the ancestral walls of the harem and free all the "children of the new world." Djebar has often commented on the exuberant feelings of those first few years in the newly independent republic, when everyone felt young and everything seemed possible, including achieving a full measure of female agency, and equal civil and political rights for all. But, in its finely textured writing, in its balanced symmetry, in its honest take on the difficulties of male-female relationship, and, above all, in the fine grain of its historical frame, wherein freedom comes at a great human cost, Djebar's third novel deserves to be read attentively.

This English translation of *Les Enfants du nouveau monde*, the first ever, is long overdue. Although the bulk of Djebar's vast corpus has been translated into well over two dozen languages, of all she wrote before 1980, only her first novel, *La Soif*, has ever appeared in English, as *The Mischief*. The Feminist Press now makes it possible for readers who cannot read her in the original French to assess her more accurately, thanks to Marjolijn de Jager's elegant translation.

As outsiders, Western and English-speaking readers may not always know what it is that we don't know because we don't have the code. This natural opacity presents the translator with a fine quandary: Grid and gloss too much, and the text loses its fluid grace. Gloss too little, and the story is made stranger, exoticized. The challenge is to contextualize as unobstrusively as possible. While bilingual readers may judge for themselves this version of *Les Enfants du nouveau monde*, Marjolijn de Jager's previous translation of a Djebar book, *Women of Algiers in Their Apartment*, was awarded the 1992 prize of the Association of American Translators.[25]

In such a society, whose innate civility and precise decorousness Djebar takes pains to underline, human beings address each other carefully, with full awareness of their anthropological situatedness. The dying old woman of the beginning is "Lla Aicha." Translating it literally, as "Lady Aicha," would favor the primacy of class and unwittingly evoke Eurocentric stratifications, whereas this honorific pays homage to her moral character, her advanced age, and her wisdom, mother of a humble carpenter though she may be. A good reader will eventually tease out the meaning of the honorific *Lla*. Likewise among men: trying to ingratiate himself with his neighbor, Hakim addresses him as "Si Slimane," a term of respect that is carefully not reciprocated. Many such linguistic clues can be found in the novel, but not all of them will communicate their meaning to a non-French reader. Locals talk of horrible war occurrences as "*les évènements*," the current events, in much the same way, perhaps, that the Northern Irish used to mention "the troubles" (and the definite article, in French, is always emphatic in intent: they are *these* current events). In today's Algeria, this obscenely off-the-mark euphemism, once employed to designate a colonial war, has been dusted off again for the current civil war. It is as if the brutal pitting of men against women, Algerians against Algerians, tribes against tribes, and ethnic clans against clans has not stopped since the French navy sailed into Algiers on July 5, 1830.

Djebar's punctuation itself is a challenge. Half-page-long single sentences fold and unfold in slow, long, sensual, and elegant stretches; one might say, arabesques. Then, a perfectly balanced paragraph suddenly turns into fragments that may be connected (or disconnected) by ellipses, or by sudden tense or pronoun shifts. The result is visually kinetic, almost three-dimensional. It feels as if the narrative voice were cracking, memory faltering and repeating itself; what Djebar called, in her first film, "imagination tracking down its tattered memory." Djebar is a published poet for whom sound rules meaning, for whom hidden rhythms, often alien to the French language she uses, are made to surge back within finely tuned symmetrical lines, something she has attributed to the mnemonic influence of her mother's Berber. She uses silences like a string of musical notes, perhaps even a "fugue," a term she employs in *Ces Voix qui m'assiègent* (Those voices that besiege me, 1999), the collection of essays that constitute her poetics.

"I AM NOT A SYMBOL. I AM A WRITER."

When Djebar returned home to teach history at the University of Algiers, flushed from her literary success in Paris, she discovered that her writings, when they were not politically attacked by men in power, were politely damned with faint praise. Favorable Algerian women critics, if there were any, kept silent. As she details in our interview on the 1992 U.S. edition of *Women of Algiers*, her slow political disenchantment resulted in ten years of self-imposed silence. To bypass censorship, she moved into theater and film, preparing sociological and ethno-musical broadcasts for national radio or television, and made frequent forays abroad for a breath of fresh air. In 1979, her first film, *La Nouba*, was awarded the International Critics' Prize at the Venice International Film Festival. Divorced, living in Paris as a Research Fellow to the Algerian Cultural Center there, she finished a second film, *La Zerda*, in 1982.

In 1996, she severed all connections with a government she could no longer serve, in revulsion for a civil war on which, at considerable risk to herself, she finally wrote openly and scathingly in *Algerian White* (*Le Blanc de l'Algérie* 1996). A collection of short stories, *Oran, langue morte* (Oran, dead language), followed in 1997. Djebar's resignation from the Islamic Cultural Center in Paris freed her for resident writer stretches in foreign universities: the University of California, Berkeley (1995); Trinity College, Cambridge (1996); and Louisiana State University, Baton Rouge (1997–2001), where she directed the Center for Francophone Studies. She is currently Distinguished Sterling Professor at New York University. In permanent, self-imposed exile, she now shares her time between Europe and the Americas. A member of the Royale Académie de Belgique since 1999, she was elected to the Académie Française in June 2005, the first Muslim so honored and the second African-born writer, after Senegal's Leopold Sedar Senghor. As the election results were being announced, French President Jacques Chirac, speaking on France 2, paid her tribute. Her own country and its president have yet to do so.

Assia Djebar is undisputably one of the major, if not *the* major contemporary woman writer from the Arab world. Her works are available around the world—except in her own birth country, where the long and ugly civil war has now claimed well over one hundred thousand victims. As fatigued apparatchiks maintain their ferocious grip on power, disaffected unemployed youths have turned to the promises of a radicalized religion that they believe will establish, with shari'a law, the social justice once promised by the revolution. Algeria is bleeding itself white, the brutally accurate pun of *Algerian White*. The Islamic color of mourning and of the shroud in which a believer must be put into the ground without a casket, is also the color of the traditional Algerian veil. In contemporary Algeria, social justice is still being sought at the expense of women. In *Algerian White*, Djebar offers what she calls "a liturgy," loving last rites rendered to lost friends and mentors. Among them are two men of Kabyle origins: Kateb Yacine, dead of leukemia in 1989, whose *Nedjma* (1954) remains the foundational text in the Algerian literary canon; and Tahar Djaout, journalist, poet, and novelist, murdered by religious fundamentalists in 1993. The fault line runs deep, from the beheaded friends mourned in real life to the beheading stories Djebar sets up in *Oran, langue morte*. Naming names, denouncing war butchers now feted as heroes, she bursts wide open an ugly secret that has festered for over forty years: that there was no single united front in the anticolonial war, no leaders ready to sacrifice for the higher good. Instead, rival factions practiced an internecine war of mutual elimination, often on ethnic grounds. Those who had deplored the writer's early lack of obvious political commitment can now rest easy. She has answered *Children's* final question as to what the new world and its new children may yet achieve, with powerful images that eviscerate the so-called mythically singular foundations of her country: one nation, one language, one religion.

Of the many prizes awarded her, two stand out as tributes to her personal and professional courage: the Neustadt International Prize for Literature (1996); and, in October 2000, the Frankfurt Peace Prize—which, in her acceptance speech, she dedicated to the memory of Kateb Yacine, himself *persona non grata* in his country, and to all assassinated intellectuals. She has registered her condemnation of a revolution that devoured its young many times in many public venues, as well as in the collection of her critical essays that constitute her poetics and deserve translation in their own right, *Ces Voix qui m'assiègent*: "They have soiled the word 'people'; they have used the term 'nation,' every which way; they have composed soliloquies around the word 'Algeria,' as though this real body did not possess innumerable eyes to look at them, at their pitiful make-believe."[26] A former president of the European Parliament of Writers and co-author of the petition to give persecuted writers and artists political asylum in the West, as well as a supporter of Salman Rushdie's right to write, Djebar is well aware that to write is to put one's life on the line.

This graceful and timely translation now offers us a new opportunity to assess Djebar as a writer of world stature, a human being fully engaged in the struggle for human rights, driven by the ethical and ontological claim she makes for writing: "anamnesis," the memorial duty of those whose nations are gripped by political amnesia. To a simplistic interview question recently posed to her by *Le Figaro* to celebrate yet one more prize, "What symbol do you represent?" she answers: "I am not a symbol. I am a writer."[27]

Clarisse Zimra
Southern Illinois University
Carbondale, Illinois
August 2005

NOTES

1. The most detailed history in English of the Algerian War is still Alistair Horne, *Savage War of Peace* (New York: Penguin, 1977). More recently, James Le Sueur, *Uncivil War* (Philadelphia: U. Pennsylvania, 2002) looks at French intellectuals' involvement. U.S. readers may wish to look at David Schalk, *War and the Ivory Tower: Algeria and Vietnam* (New York: Oxford, 1991).

2. For instance, Leslie Camhi, "An Algerian Writer Finds Her Lost Past Through Language," *New York Times*, 4 March 2000, praised "a complex, passionate and highly literary oeuvre . . . [that] explores the roots of Algeria's current crisis in language and history."

3. Djebar made this remark after I asked her, in preparing a special issue of *Yale French Studies* (1995), "Another Look, Another Woman: Retranslations of French Feminism," about her choice of a feminist press for her return to writing. After a ten-year silence she had given the 1980 collection of short stories *Femmes d'Alger dans leur appartement* to Editions des femmes. This issue of YFS contained the first English translation of "Le Blanc de l'Algérie" (Algerian white, pp. 138–48), the essay written to address the Strasbourg Parliament of Writers that would become the core of the book by that name. It was published in the Parliament's in-house bilingual organ, *Carrefour des littératures européennes* (Fall 1993), and translated by their in-house interpreter, Andrew Benson, who gave YFS permission to reproduce his translation. This was Djebar's first frontal attack on the political state of her country: the open war on intellectuals and the mounting ethnic conflicts.

4. Sylvie Marion, 22–24.

5. See her scathing comments in our interview, "When the Past Answers Our Present: Assia Djebar Talks About *Loin de Médine*," *Callaloo* 16.1 (1993): 116–31.

6. De Gaulle's decision is mentioned in Cyril Bensimon, "Une Algérienne à l'Académie française," *Le Monde*, 22 June 2005 (on-line edition).

7. Having rallied the tribes of the hinterlands in 1832, Emir Abd-el-Kader fought until 1845. Upon surrendering, he was exiled to Damascus in 1847, where he died. Naturalization as a French citizen was made available upon petitioning. However, one had to renounce one's right to Muslim customary laws, so few applied.

8. She gives a spirited explanation in "A Woman's Memory Spans Centuries," the interview that appears in the U.S. translation of *Women of Algiers in Their Apartments*, 159–211.

9. "My escape from the harem at the beginning of the 1950s" ("ma sortie sortie du harem au début des années cinquante"). In the same piece, in answer

to the question of language posed to a dozen prominent writers, she called French "my booty of war" ("du français comme du butin"). And she concludes, "to write in the alien language was tantamount to making love outside the walls of the ancestral faith" ("écrire en la langue étrangère devenait presque faire l'amour hors la foi ancestrale"). *Quinzaine Littéraire* 16-31 (March 1985), 25; also reprinted in Djebar, *Ces Voix qui m'assiègent: en marge de ma francophonie,* 69–71.

10. "Un pays sans mémoire" (A country without memory), in *Poèmes pour l'Algérie heureuse.*

11. "Donc, Assia Djebar, semble-t-il, n'est pas et ne veut pas être, un écrivain engagé." Catrice is quoted in Marie-Blanche Tahon, 39–50.

12. "Il faut attendre *Les Enfants du Nouveau Monde* (1962) pour voir les héroïnes de Djebar chercher leur libération ailleurs que dans un égotisme maladroit coupé du réel, dans une confusion des aspirations qui restent cependant celles de nombreuses Algériennes actuelles." Charles Bonn, 113.

13. "A-t-on vraiment compris que la découverte du corps pour le personnage de *La Soif* est aussi une révolution importante." Adbelkébir Khatibi, 62.

14. "Escamoter les nouvelles réalités algériennes sous une croûte poétique." Quoted in Déjeux, *Littérature maghrébine de langue française,* 248. Mostafa Lacheraf himself had impeccable revolutionary credentials, and represented the men in charge in Algeria. In October 1956, while over French air space, the plane in which he was traveling was forced down. Lacheraf and four other key FLN figures were to spend the rest of the war in jail. Among them was the man who would become the first president of an independent Algeria, Ahmed Ben Bella, who had served honorably in the French army during World War II, then escaped from a Blida jail in 1950 (at a time when Djebar herself was a student boarder in the high school that, her novel tells us, stood right across the street.) One wonders if Lacheraf's contempt might have proceeded equally from the urge to prove his own devotion to a revolution that he, too, had not spent on the battlefield.

15. In its editorial in a January 1995 special issue on Algeria, *The Middle East Report* described "This war [that] has been mostly invisible from the outside" (1). The first civilian blood was shed in the streets of Algiers in 1988, as tanks rolled in to contain rioting unemployed youths, and incredulous

patriots watched the people's army shooting down its own people (over one thousand presumed dead, many more unaccounted for). See also Hafid Gafaïti, 71–78.

16. Déjeux, who had led this charge in his first book, *Littérature maghrébine de langue française*, saw *Children* as a psycho-political return of the repressed, but eventually toned down his criticism ten years later in *Assia Djebar: Romancière algérienne, cinéaste arabe.*

17. Evelyne Accad, 801.

18. "Je me méfiais, je me méfie toujours d'une littérature à priori de témoignage." Djebar, *Le romancier dans la cité arabe*, 119.

19. "Face à une critique française, je dirais, traditionnelle, qui ne cherchait dans les textes des écrivains 'ex-colonisés' que des clefs pour interprétation sociologique immédiate, moi, qu'est-ce qui m'attirait ? Un nationalisme à retardement ? Non, bien sûr: seulement la langue." Djebar, Frankfurt Peace Prize speech.

20. During the question and answer sessions of the December 2003 colloquium, "Assia Djebar, nomade entre les murs" (nomad within walls), convened in Paris. About 10,949 women are estimated to have joined the struggle, of whom 2,200 were arrested and tried, and six condemned to death. The troubled question has been well documented by Danielle Amrane. English-language readers may refer to her translated essay, "Women and Politics in Algeria from the War of Independence to Our Day" in the 1999 special issue of *Research in African Literatures*, "Dissident Algeria," 1999 (62–77). This entire special issue is of interest, as is the special issue of the British journal *Parallax*, "Translating Algeria," April-June 1998. For present consequences, see Meredith Turshen, "Algerian Women in the Liberation Struggle and the Civil War: From Active Participants to Passive Victims," *Social Research* 69.3 (Fall 2002): 889–911.

21. Djebar's first film, *La Nouba des femmes du Mont Chenoua* (1979), is "dedicated posthumously to Zouleikha who coordinated the national resistance on the mountains and the town of Cherchell."

22. Marnia Lazreg, 220.

23. Franz Fanon, 42.

24. Fatima Mernissi, 97. It is worth noting that the Moroccan sociologist is writing here specifically for a Western readership.

25. See Marjolijn de Jager, 856–58.

26. "Ils ont sali le mot 'peuple; ils ont usé à tort et à travers du vocable de 'nation;' ils ont soliloqué avec le mot 'Algérie,' comme si cette réalité-là n'avait pas eu de multiples yeux pour les regarder dans leur pitoyable comédie." *Ces Voix qui m'assiègent,* 22.

27. "Je ne suis pas un symbole. Ma seule activité consiste à écire." Le Figaro, on-line edition, 22 June 2005.

WORKS CITED

Accad, Evelyne. "Assia Djébar's Contribution to Arab Women's Literature." *World Literature Today* (Autumn 1996), 801-11.

Amrane-Minne, Danielle Djamila. "Women and Politics in Algeria from the War of Independence to Our Day," *Research in African Literatures* 30.3. Special issue "Dissident Algeria," (Fall 1999), 62–77.

Bonn, Charles. *La littérature algérienne et ses lectures.* (Readings in Algerian literature). Sherbrooke: Naaman, 1972.

de Jager, Marjolijn. "Translating Assia Djebar's Femmes d'Alger: Listening for the Silence." *World Literature Today* (Autumn 1996), 856-58.

Déjeux, Jean. *Littérature maghrébine de langue française.* (Francophone north African literature). Sherbrooke: Naaman, 1972.

———. *Assia Djebar, écrivain algérien, cineaste arabe.* (Assia Djebar, Algerian writer, Arab filmmaker). Sherbrooke: Naaman, 1984.

Djebar, Assia. *La Soif.* Paris: Julliard, 1957. Trans. Frances Frenaye. *The Mischief.* New York: Simon & Schuster, 1958.

———. *Les Impatients* (The impatient ones). Paris: Julliard, 1958.

———. *Les Enfants du nouveau monde.* Paris: Julliard 1962. Trans. Marjolijn de Jager, *Children of the New World.* New York: Feminist Press at CUNY, 2005.

———. *Les Alouettes naïves* (The innocent larks). Paris: Julliard, 1967.

———. "Le romancier dans la cité arabe" (The novelist in the Arab city) *Europe* 474 (1968), 114-20.

———. *Poèmes pour l'Algérie heureuse* (Poems for a happy Algeria). Algiers: SNED, 1969.

————. *Rouge l'aube* (Red dawn). Algiers: SNED, 1969.

————. *La Nouba des femmes du Mont Chenoua* (*The Celebration of the women from Mt. Chenoua*) (film). 1979.

————. *La Zerda et les chants de l'oubli* (Zerda and other songs of forgetting) (film). 1982.

————. *Femmes d'Alger dans leur appartement*. Paris: des femmes, 1980. Trans. Marjolijn de Jager. *Women of Algiers in Their Apartment*. Charlottesville: U.P. Virginia, 1992.

————. *L'Amour, la fantasia*. London: Quartet 1989; trans. Dorothy Blair, *Fantasia: An Algerian Cavalcade*. London: Quartet Books, 1985.

————. *Ombre sultane*. Paris: Lattès, 1987. Trans. Dorothy Blair. *A Sister to Scheherazade*. London: Quartet Books, 1988.

————. *Loin de Médine: filles d'Ismaêl*. Paris: Albin Michel, 1991. Trans. *Far from Medina*. London: Quartet Books, 1994.

————. *Vaste est la prison*. Paris: Albin Michel, 1995. Trans. Betsy Wing. *So Vast the Prison*. New York: Seven Stories Press, 1999.

————. *Le Blanc de l'Algérie*. Paris: Albin Michel, 1996. Trans. Marjolijn de Jager and David Kelley. *Algerian White*. New York, Seven Stories Press, 2000.

————. *Oran, langue morte* (Oran, dead language). Arles: Actes Sud, 1997.

————. *Ces Voix qui m'assiègent: en marge de ma francophonie* (Those voices that besiege me). Paris: Albin Michel and Montreal: Presses de l'université, 1999.

————. *La femme sans sepulture* (The woman without a grave). Paris: Albin Michel, 2002.

————. Frankfurt Peace Prize speech "Le désir sauvage de ne pas oublier" (The savage desire not to forget), reproduced in *Le Monde*, 24 October 2002.

Fanon, Franz. "Algeria Unveiled." Chapter 1 of *A Dying Colonialism*. New York: Evergreen, 1967.

Gafaïti, Hafid. "Culture and Violence: The Algerian Intelligentsia Between Two Political Illegitimacies." *Parallax* 7 (1998), 71-78.

Horne, Alistair. *A Savage War of Peace: Algeria 1954–1962*. New York: Penguin, 1977

Kateb Yacine. *Nedma*. Paris: Seuil, 1956.

Khatibi, Adbelkébir. *Le Roman maghrébin*. (The North African novel). Paris: Maspéro, 1968.

Lazreg, Marnia. *The Eloquence of Silence: Algerian Women in Question*. London: Routledge, 1994.

Le Sueur, James. *Uncivil War: Intellectuals and Identity Politics During the*

Decolonization of Algeria. Philadelphia: U. Pennsylvania P., 2002.

Marion, Sylvie. "Assia Djebar: La nouvelle algérienne," *France Observateur*, 24 May 1964, 22-24.

Mernissi, Fatima. *Beyond the Veil*. Bloomington: Indiana U.P., 1987.

El Saadawi, Nawal. *Ferdaous*. Trans. *Woman at Point Zero*. London: Zed Books, 1997.

Schalk, David. *War and the Ivory Tower: Algeria and Vietnam*. New York: Oxford University Press, 1991.

Tahon, Marie-Blanche. "Women Novelists and Women in the Struggle for Algeria's National Liberation (1957-80)." *Research in African Literatures* (Summer 1992), 39-50.

Thursen, Meredith. "Algerian Women in the Liberation Struggle and the Civil War: From Active Participants to Passive Victims," *Social Research* 69.3 (Fall 2000), 889–11.

Zimra, Clarisse. "A Woman's Memory Spans Centuries." *Women of Algiers in Their Apartment*. Charlottesville: U.P. Virginia, 1992.

——. "When the Past Answers Our Present: Assia Djebar Talks About *Loin de Médine*. *Callaloo* 16. (1993), 116–31.